"Up and at 'em!" Butsko yelled.
"Follow me!"

In one mighty leap, Butsko was out of the hole, standing on the same ground as the human wave of Japanese soldiers who rampaged toward him and his men. He gripped his submachine gun tightly, clasped the butt against the right side of his waist, and pulled the trigger. The bullets ripped into the Japanese soldiers like rain into water...

Kill Crazy

by
John Mackie

A JOVE BOOK

Excepting basic historical events, places, and personages, this series of books is fictional, and anything that appears otherwise is coincidental and unintentional.

The principal characters are imaginary, although they might remind veterans of specific men whom they knew. The Twenty-third Infantry Regiment, in which the characters serve, is used fictitiously—it doesn't represent the real historical Twenty-third Infantry, which has distinguished itself in so many battles from the Civil War to Vietnam—but it could have been any American line regiment that fought and bled during World War II.

These novels are dedicated to the men who were there. May their deeds and gallantry never be forgotten.

KILL CRAZY

A Jove Book / published by arrangement with
the author

PRINTING HISTORY
Jove edition / January 1985

ISBN: 0-515-08080-2

Jove books are published by The Berkley Publishing Group,
200 Madison Avenue, New York, N.Y. 10016. The words
"A JOVE BOOK" and the "J" with sunburst are trademarks
belonging to Jove Publications, Inc.

PRINTED IN THE UNITED STATES OF AMERICA

ONE . . .

Butsko parted the leaves in front of him and peered at the Japanese encampment. It was two o'clock in the morning and a full moon provided sufficient illumination for his battle-trained eyes. The encampment was a field motor pool, with gas and oil stored in large tanks, and vehicles coming and going. Barbed wire surrounded the encampment, and camouflage netting hung overhead.

A smile came over Butsko's weather-beaten face. The patrol had been uneventful so far, but now he could do some damage. Within the encampment he saw tents where Japanese soldiers were sleeping. Two guards patrolled the perimeter of the barbed wire on the inside. The encampment was far behind the front lines, and the Japs thought they were safe. They didn't know the recon platoon was in the area.

Butsko turned to Corporal Sam Longtree, a full-blooded Apache Indian from Arizona, and angled his head in the direction from which they'd just come. Longtree nodded and

1

eased backward, turning around and moving close to the ground. Butsko followed in a similar crouch, his mind filled with a variety of plans for the destruction of the Jap motor pool. Out of all those plans, he'd have to select one and hope it was the best one.

Butsko and Longtree slipped through the jungle, leaves brushing their bodies. Somewhere in the distance a wild dog howled and random shots could be heard far away, but it was a quiet night on Bougainville—so far.

They came to a small clearing, and in the moonlight six soldiers were lying around. They stirred as Butsko and Longtree joined them.

"Wake up!" Butsko said in a hoarse whisper. "We got work to do!"

The GIs picked themselves up off the ground and crowded around Butsko and Longtree.

"What's out there?" asked Frankie La Barbara, his handsome face marred by a nose bent out of shape in hand-to-hand combat four weeks earlier.

"Shaddup," Butsko growled. "I'll tell ya when I tell ya."

Butsko tried to figure out who should do what. He knew the strengths and weaknesses of all of his men, and had to match each man to his job. He looked at them one by one. Longtree was silent and could creep up on you, cutting your throat before you knew he was there. Corporal Charles Bannon, a Texan, was smart, deadly, and a born leader. Private Nutsy Gafooley, the former hobo, was small, fast, and surprisingly strong despite his scrawny stature. Pfc. Homer Gladley, a farmboy from Kansas, wasn't very smart but was the biggest man in the platoon and the strongest man Butsko had ever known. Pfc. Shaw had been a professional heavyweight boxer before the war; he was a good all-around soldier. And Frankie La Barbara loved dirty work, once you got him going. The problem was getting him going.

Butsko jerked his thumb over his shoulder. "There's a Jap motor pool back there. We're gonna blow it up. It's surrounded by barbed wire and's got two guards. Where's the wire-cutters?"

"I got 'em," replied Bannon.

"Check to make sure."

"I toldja I got 'em, Sarge."

"An' I told you to make sure."

Bannon took his pack off his back and opened it up. It annoyed him when Butsko treated him like an idiot, but Butsko treated everybody like an idiot. Bannon pulled the wire cutters out of his pack and held them up. "See?"

Butsko grumbled and picked up a twig fron the ground. He drew a rectangle near his feet and jabbed the stick in the middle. "Here's where the gas and oil is, and there's Japs sacked out over here." He pointed to another area inside the rectangle. "The guards'll be the hard part. We gotta get them before they see us. Shaw you cut the wire and go in with Longtree. Longtree'll kill the first guard, and then, when the second one comes around, Longtree'll get him too. Then Longtree'll signal to the rest of us and we'll go in through the place where the barbed wire is cut. Any questions so far?"

Frankie raised his finger in the air.

Butsko frowned. "What now?"

"What're we doin' this for, Sarge? Why don't we just go back and give the coordinates to Major Cobb? Let the fuckin' flyboys take care of it. Why does it haveta be us?"

"Because I said so. Any other questions?"

Nobody said anything.

"Good, because I hate questions. Where was I? Oh, yeah. The guards are dead, and we're comin' through the barbed wire. Nutsy and me will link up with Shaw and Longtree and go after the gas tanks with hand grenades. Bannon, you take Frankie and Gladley and shoot up them tents. It's up to you to keep the Japs off us. Got it?"

"I got it, Sarge."

"Any questions? And if Frankie La Barbara asks another question, I'm gonna punch his fucking lights out."

Frankie's mouth was half open, when he realized the full import of what Butsko had said. He closed his mouth and shrugged. No one else said anything.

"I'm glad yez all understand," Butsko said. "Let's move it out. Longtree and Shaw go first, and the rest of us'll follow. Keep it quiet. Go."

Longtree and Shaw crouched low and moved into the jungle, carrying their Thompson submachine guns in their right hands. Butsko followed them, and the rest of the men fell in behind him.

3

The patrol moved silently through the jungle, dodging trees, stepping over exposed roots. The men wore soft fatigue caps, similar to baseball caps, instead of their steel helmets, and their faces were camouflaged with black face cream. Longtree was in front and he was the first to see the motor pool. Dropping to one knee, he held out his hand behind him.

The rest of the patrol stopped and got down on their bellies. Longtree and Shaw looked through the foliage at the motor pool. They saw one guard marching inside the barbed wire, his Arisaka rifle slung over his shoulder. The other guard was out of sight; they figured he was on the far side of the motor pool. They saw the tanks of gas and oil, plus stacks of metal barrels that presumably held more petroleum products. The whole mess would go sky high once they got in there, but first they had to get in there.

A truck was parked near the gas tanks, and a Jap stood with a nozzle in his hand, filling the truck's tank. No one else was about. The guard turned the corner and headed toward the rear of the motor pool, and Longtree and Shaw watched him disappear into the night. A minute later the other guard appeared, walking toward them.

Shaw wiped his nose with the back of his hand. "We won't have much time between the first guard and the second guard."

"It don't take long to slit a throat," Longtree replied. "I'll go in as soon as this guy is out of sight. Get ready with the cutters."

Shaw took the cutters out of his shirt pocket and squeezed them. His face was lopsided due to hasty work by Army plastic surgeons, for he'd been shot in the face on New Georgia, and been awarded a Purple Heart. Everybody on the patrol had been wounded somewhere along the line. Bannon had a steel plate in his head.

The coast was clear, but it wouldn't stay clear for long.

"Let's go," Longtree said.

They moved swiftly through the jungle, making more noise than usual, but no Japs were close enough to hear it. The jungle had been cleared for twenty yards in front of the barbed wire, and they dropped down on their bellies, crawling furiously toward the wire.

Longtree got there first, and Shaw was moments behind

4

him. Shaw reached forward with the wire cutters and snipped one strand. Reaching up, he clipped another strand. The wire snapped apart and Longtree burst through the opening, running with his head low toward a pile of metal barrels. Longtree looked right, left, and forward, hoping no Japs were about, because he didn't want to get trapped inside the motor pool. Shaw followed Longtree, and they dived behind the metal barrels.

Longtree peeked around the barrels and saw the next Jap sentry march into sight. He and Shaw had made it just in time. He pulled his Ka-bar knife from its sheath.

"I'll get him," Longtree said.

Shaw nodded. Longtree crouched with the sharpened blade pointed straight up in the air, glinting in the moonlight. This was the part of war he liked best, when it was one to one and close, so you could see who your opponent was. The Japanese soldier marched closer; he was skinny and tall. His back had a crook in it, and he wore a Fu Manchu mustache. *He looks like a Jap sad sack,* Longtree thought. *Pretty soon he's gonna be a dead sack.*

Longtree licked his thin lips as he waited for the Jap guard to come abreast of him. The Jap guard took a few more steps, and then his back was to Longtree. Longtree sprang up like a puma from the American Southwest and dashed toward the Japanese guard, who heard the sound and spun around. He opened his mouth to scream, but Longtree's hand clamped over his lips, and a split second later Longtree's Ka-bar knife went into the Jap's belly to the hilt. Longtree pulled the Ka-bar out, drew back his arm, and slashed the Jap's throat as the Jap was on the way down. The Jap's blood sprayed out onto Longtree's face and uniform, and he collapsed at Longtree's feet. Longtree grabbed him by the collar and dragged him behind the metal barrels, dropping him beside Shaw. Looking back to the scene of the killing, Longtree hoped the next guard wouldn't see the cut wire and blood on the ground until it was too late.

Longtree and Shaw waited for the next guard as the dead Japanese soldier's lifeblood leaked onto the ground beside them. The Japanese soldier's eyes were wide open and stark with terror. His mouth sagged and his teeth were stained with blood. Shaw gazed at him with fascination, because he'd seldom seen

5

an enemy soldier at such close range.

The Japanese soldier had a fishy smell and made Longtree nauseous.

"Here comes the other one," Longtree whispered.

Shaw peeked around the barrels and saw the next guard marching toward a corner of the encampment. This one was short and fat, with his cap on the back of his head and the cap's bill pointing upward. His rifle was slung over his shoulder and he made a right-face at the corner, heading toward Shaw and Longtree. The Japanese soldier stumbled along as if half asleep, his eyes half shut and the corners of his mouth turned down. Shaw recalled being sleepy while pulling guard duty and now realized how dangerous it could be.

Longtree was poised in his attack crouch, holding his Kabar knife blade point up in his fist. The Japanese soldier trudged closer, as if walking in his sleep. Longtree prepared to leap at him, tensing on the balls of his feet, when suddenly the Japanese soldier stopped cold. The Japanese soldier wrinkled his forehead and extended his head forward, trying to get a better look at what lay ahead.

"Uh-oh," said Shaw.

The Japanese soldier unslung his rifle and advanced carefully, looking down at the ground. Shaw and Longtree realized he'd seen something. He hadn't been as sleepy as he'd appeared.

"What now?" Shaw asked in a whisper.

"I have to kill him," Longtree replied, and then leaped forward.

The Japanese soldier heard him charging and spun around. He hesitated a moment, not believing his eyes, and then opened his mouth wide, screaming an alarm. His voice pierced the stillness, and then he raised his rifle to protect himself from Longtree's knife.

A burst of submachine-gun fire shattered the night, and the Japanese soldier closed his eyes and dropped to the ground. He fell at Longtree's feet, and Longtree looked up to see Butsko poised at the edge of the jungle, his submachine gun aimed toward the dead Jap.

"*Let's go!*" Butsko shouted.

Butsko jumped to his feet and charged like an angry bull toward the opening in the barbed wire. The other men followed him, holding their submachine guns high. Butsko drew close to the barbed wire, lowered his head, and dived through, but he was a big, bulky man and there wasn't enough space. A snag of barbed wire drew a red line on his massive left bicep, and he jumped to his feet inside the compound, looking around.

Japanese soldiers burst out of their tents, carrying their rifles. They were half naked and bewildered, trying to see what was going on.

"*Follow me!*" Butsko yelled, heading toward Longtree and Shaw. "*Let's go!*"

Nutsy Gafooley followed Butsko, a hand grenade in each hand. Nutsy had loosened the pins while in the bushes, waiting for the order to move out. Now all he had to do was yank them out with his teeth and let them fly.

Meanwhile, Bannon was leading Frankie La Barbara and Homer Gladley toward the tents. They held their submachine guns tightly in their hands and sprayed out big, fat .45-caliber bullets as they sped over the ground. Their first volley hit the Japs before the Japs knew what was happening, and eight of them dropped to the ground, dead or wounded.

The rest of the Japs hit the dirt, looking for cover. They didn't know how many enemy soldiers were attacking or what was going on. A Japanese officer shouted orders to attack, but the Japanese soldiers couldn't figure out *what* to attack. Bannon, Frankie La Barbara, and Homer Gladley each dropped to their stomachs and continued firing at the large group of Japanese soldiers in front of them. One Jap raised his head to see what was happening. Frankie La Barbara noticed him and swung his submachine gun around, leveling a stream of bullets at the Japanese soldier's head; it shattered, sending blood and brains flying all over the landscape.

Another Jap rose up to throw a hand grenade, and Bannon caught him in the chest, ripping apart his ribs and lungs with those vicious .45-caliber bullets. The Jap soldier collapsed backward, dropping his hand grenade, which he'd already armed.

The grenade exploded with a thunderous roar, and bits of shrapnel flew in all directions, tearing apart Japanese bodies and tossing them into the air. Bannon, Frankie La Barbara, and Homer Gladley continued to fire their submachine guns, pinning the Japanese soldiers down, hoping Butsko and the others would blow up the gas tanks before the Japanese soldiers could figure out that they were being invaded by only six men.

Butsko, Longtree, Shaw, and Nutsy Gafooley ran toward the tanks of gas and oil. Butsko and Longtree held their submachines, prepared to shoot down anyone who got in their way, while Nutsy and Shaw held their grenades ready. They passed trucks and a light tank whose engine was exposed because it was halfway through a repair job. Two Japanese soldiers appeared out of the night and ran toward them, carrying rifles, and Butsko machine-gunned them to smithereens. They fell backward, spurting blood from their mangled bodies, and Longtree gave them another burst to make sure.

Ahead were the gas and oil tanks. The four GIs ran toward them. Butsko's eyes darted around, looking for Japs. He didn't see any but that didn't mean there weren't any around. The Japanese soldier manning the pumps had been sleeping behind some barrels full of gas. He peered around the barrels and saw the four GIs headed his way, but in the dimness the four GIs didn't see him. The Japanese soldier picked up his rifle and aimed it around the barrels.

Butsko saw him and opened fire. The bullets hit the Japanese soldier and tore off the side of his head, and some of the bullets struck the metal barrels full of gasoline, striking sparks off the metal and making holes. In a sudden *swwooooossssshhhhhh* the barrels became covered with flames.

"Get Down!" Butsko yelled.

Brrrrooooooommmmm! The barrels full of gasoline exploded sending metal and sheets of flame flying in all directions. Butsko ducked his head as night became day in the motor pool. He looked around and saw a blazing inferno surrounding him, but the gas tanks in the center of the clearing were still untouched.

"Get them tanks!"

Nutsy and Shaw threw their hand grenades at the tanks. The dark metal shapes flew through the air. One landed on top of a tank, and the other on the ground nearby. Butsko squinched his eyes shut and poked his fingers into his ears.

Barrrrooooooommmmmmm! The ground trembled and flaming gasoline exploded in all directions.

"Retreat!" Butsko hollered.

He jumped up and ran back toward the opening in the barbed wire, the flames behind him casting weird quivering shadows everywhere. Nutsy, Longtree, and Shaw followed him. To his left he could see Bannon, Frankie La Barbara, and Homer Gladley backing away from the tents, their submachine guns blazing.

"Retreat!" Butsko yelled. *"Get out of here!"*

Butsko approached the barbed wire. He spun around and dove through the hole, cutting open his left hip this time. Nutsy followed him, scratching nothing, and then came Shaw, Bannon, and Frankie La Barbara.

Homer Gladley bent to crawl through the hole, and just then a Japanese soldier fired a wild shot, but it was a lucky one. Homer Gladley felt it slap into his back, and the sudden pain straightened him up. He fell forward on the strands of barbed wire, his arms outstretched. One barb ripped open his nose, another his chest, a third his right wrist, and a fourth his left thigh. He hung on the wire like Christ on the cross, blood oozing out of his back and the cuts made by the barbed wire.

Frankie La Barbara heard Homer cry out when the first bullet hit, and turned to see him suspended on the barbed wire. Frankie's first impulse was to save his own skin, and to hell with Homer Gladley, but his second, deeper impulse was that he had to save one of his buddies.

"Bannon!" Frankie called out.

Bannon turned around and saw Homer Gladley on the wire, and then a jolt went through Homer as another bullet whacked him. Frankie La Barbara lunged through the barbed wire and Bannon followed him through. They stood as Japanese bullets flew around them like angry bees, and they tore Homer Gladley off the barbed wire, leaving one quarter of Homer's nose still on a barb. Homer collapsed onto the ground like a sack of potatoes, and Frankie La Barbara, assisted by Bannon, pulled Homer through the hole in the barbed wire, cutting him further in the process.

The Japanese shooting diminished as officers ordered their men to put out the fires, but a few of them had the retreating GIs in their sights and thought they'd pull their triggers a few more times. Bullets whizzed past the GIs, and then Frankie felt as if someone had slammed him in the back of his left thigh with a sledgehammer. The force of the bullet spun him

9

around and he fell on his face in the jungle muck.

Butsko reached the safety of the jungle and turned around to see what was going on. Longtree, Shaw, and Nutsy were almost in the jungle, but the other three still were out there, and two were hurt. Without a moment's hesitation Butsko charged out of the jungle.

"Come with me!"

He ran toward the three who had faltered in the clear-cut, wide-open area between the barbed wire and the jungle. Longtree, Shaw, and Nutsy turned around and followed him. They saw Bannon struggling with Homer Gladley, and Frankie La Barbara trying to stand. Butsko scooped up Homer Gladley, adjusted him on his shoulder, and carried him toward the jungle. Longtree and Shaw grabbed Frankie by each of his arms and dragged him behind Butsko as Frankie cursed and bellowed in pain. Bannon turned around and dropped to one knee, hugging the butt of his submachine gun to his waist and opening fire to cover the others.

Click!

He was out of ammo. Pressing the button on the submachine gun, he pulled out the empty clip and tossed it to the side. He opened the ammo pouch on his belt, pulled out a fresh clip, jammed it into the slot, and pulled the trigger. Bullets and sparks flew out of the barrel of the gun as Bannon swung it from side to side, spraying bullets into the motor-pool compound.

"Let's go, Bannon!"

Bannon turned and ran toward Butsko, and a stray Japanese bullet zinged passed his face so closely that he could feel its heat. He plunged into the jungle and saw Butsko kneeling beside Homer Gladley, who lay facedown on the ground. Butsko took his pulse while Nutsy Gafooley ripped open his shirt, exposing an ugly entrance wound.

"Bullet's still in him," Nutsy said.

Shaw and Longtree lay at the edge of the clearing, ready to shoot any Japs who came after them. Bannon dropped down to the right of Longtree and raised his submachine gun. Frankie La Barbara lay a few feet from Homer Gladley, grasping his bloody leg with both his hands and gritting his teeth.

Butsko let go of Homer Gladley's wrist. "He's alive, but it don't look good."

Nutsy looked up at him. "You want me to treat the wound here, or should we do it deeper in the woods?"

"Do it now, but hurry the fuck up!"

Nutsy opened his pack and took out the articles he needed. He wasn't a trained combat medic, but he could sprinkle sulfa powder and blood coagulant on wounds and tie a bandage.

"What about me?" said Frankie La Barbara through clenched teeth.

"I'll take care of you," Butsko muttered, kneeling beside Frankie and waiting for Nutsy to finish.

Frankie, trembling with rage, looked at Butsko. "This happened because of you!"

"Shaddup!"

"You always volunteer us to do shit that we don't have to do!"

"Shaddup or I'll punch you right in the fucking mouth!"

Frankie La Barbara raised his chin. "Go ahead—I dare you!"

Butsko drew back his fist and punched Frankie right in the fucking mouth, and Frankie went slack on the jungle floor, out cold.

Nutsy worked swiftly, taping a big bandage over the hole in Homer Gladley's back, which had stopped bleeding. Butsko poured coagulant powder and sulfa into the holes in Frankie's leg, because the Japanese bullet had made entrance and exit wounds. Longtree saw figures moving in the smoke and flames inside the Japanese encampment.

"Somebody's coming!" he said.

"Let's get out of here," Butsko replied. "I'll carry Homer. Shaw, you carry Frankie. The rest of you, cover us."

Butsko heaved Homer Gladley onto his shoulder, and Shaw did the same with Frankie La Barbara, who was waking up.

"What happened?" he asked as Shaw carried him into the jungle.

Behind them, Bannon and Longtree and Nutsy poured lead into the Japanese encampment, and the figures dropped down out of sight. Bannon and Longtree retreated several steps, still firing their submachine guns, then turned and followed the others into the thick moonlit jungle, which provided cover and gave them shelter.

11

TWO . . .

The sounds of the explosions reverberated through the jungle, and they awakened Lieutenant General Harukichi Hyakutake, commander in chief of all Japanese forces on Bougainville. A short thin man of fifty-five, with large ears, he sat up on his cot and called for his orderly.

"Yes, sir?" said his orderly, Lieutenant Oyagi, poking his head into General Hyakutake's tent.

"What were those explosions all about?"

"I don't know, sir."

"Find out and report back to me."

"Yes, sir."

Lieutenant Oyagi withdrew his head. General Hyakutake swung his legs around and planted his feet on the tatami mat underneath his cot. He reached to the small table beside the cot, found matches, scratched one to flame, and lit the kerosene lamp. The inside of the tent became illuminated in the yellow glow of the lamp. General Hyakutake reached for his package of cigarettes, extracted one, placed it in his mouth, and brought the flame of the lamp to its end, puffing smoke out of his mouth.

He looked at the end and was satisfied that it was lit well, then took a deep drag. He checked his watch. It was almost three o'clock in the morning. Those explosions hadn't sounded too far away. He'd come from his headquarters on Erventa Island to this part of Bougainville to find out for himself what the situation at the front was like, but he hadn't realized that the fighting was this close. Maybe it was time to get back to Erventa.

"I'm back, sir!" Lieutent Oyagi shouted outside the tent.

"Come in."

Lieutenant Oyagi pushed aside the tent flap and stepped inside, standing at attention. "A gasoline dump approximately three miles southeast of here has been blown up by American sappers, sir!"

"Were the Americans caught?"

"I don't know, sir."

"Why don't you know?"

Lieutenant Oyagi was so intimidated, he couldn't say anything. He shivered and swallowed hard, wishing he were someplace else.

"Get Colonel Akai for me on the telephone!"

"Yes, sir."

Lieutenant Oyagi lurched toward the telephone on General Hyakutake's desk and picked up the receiver. The operator came on and Lieutenant Oyagi asked him to connect General Hyakutake with Colonel Akai.

"Colonel Akai speaking."

"General Hyakutake would like to speak with you, sir. Hold on a moment."

Lieutenant Oyagi held up the telephone receiver, and General Hyakutake plucked it out of his hand and sat down behind his desk.

"Have any of those American sappers been taken prisoner?" General Hyakutake asked.

"Not that I know of, sir."

"Why don't you know?"

"There's chaos at Gasoline Dump Number Six, sir. They're devoting all their efforts to putting out the fire. They're not

13

even sure of what's happened. The attack was very sudden."

"Security must have been poor. Have the officer in charge punished."

"He's dead, sir."

"Dead?"

"Yes, sir. Shot dead."

"Do we know how many sappers there were?"

"No, sir, but there must have been a substantial number to have done the damage they did."

"They may be headed this way. Double the guard. And send out a patrol to track them down. We don't want American sappers running around loose this far behind our lines."

"Yes, sir."

"I'll return to my base first thing in the morning. Make arrangements."

"Yes, sir."

"That is all."

General Hyakutake placed the telephone receiver on its cradle. Wearing only his undershorts, which resembled a jock-strap, he reached for his pants, hanging from a peg on the tent pole, and put them on. Lieutenant Oyagi watched, thinking that General Hyakutake looked like a gnomish little school-teacher without his uniform.

"What're you looking at?" General Hyakutake snapped.

"I'm waiting for further orders, sir."

"Coordinate our return to headquarters with Colonel Akai's staff! You're dismissed!"

Lieutenant Oyagi saluted and fled from the tent. General Hyakutake sat behind his desk and puffed another cigarette. Tomorrow he had to report to his commanding officer, General Hitoshi Imamura, and tell him of the situation on Bougainville, which wasn't good. General Hyakutake's big offensive, launched a week earlier, had been stopped cold, and now his army was on the retreat. He didn't have enough men and matériel for another offensive, but he intended to conduct a fighting with-drawal, making the Americans pay for every inch of ground they took. If he could convince General Imamura to send him reinforcements, he'd attack again and perhaps do better this time.

General Hyakutake stubbed out his cigarette in the ashtray on his desk and sighed, because he felt tired and discouraged.

The Americans had defeated him on Guadalcanal, and now they were beating him on Bougainville. If the Americans forced him to evacuate Bougainville, it would mean the end of his career. He'd spend the rest of his life behind a desk in Tokyo, and younger officers would be contemptuous of him.

I'll commit hara-kiri before I let that happen, he said to himself, *but before I commit hara-kiri, I must somehow obtain reinforcements from General Imamura so I can inflict a terrible defeat on the Americans here on Bougainville.*

"He's alive," Nutsy Gafooley said, his ear on Homer Gladley's chest.

"I told you he was," Butsko replied, sitting on a log nearby, trying to read his map by the light of the moon. "You can't kill an elephant like Homer Gladley with two measly bullets. He's a tough son of a bitch. I wish you all were as tough as he is."

Frankie La Barbara spat at the ground. "So's you could make us take on more cruddy jobs?"

"Shaddup, fuckhead."

"I won't shaddup! Why should I shaddup? Everybody else is afraid to speak up, but not Frankie La Barbara! I'm sick of this shit! Homer's damn near dead, I'll probably never walk again, and you'll get another medal! Big fucking deal!"

"If you don't shut up, I'm gonna kick you right in the fucking head!"

"I dare you!"

Butsko took a deep breath and sighed. "You asked for it."

He stood, walked toward Frankie La Barbara, and drew his leg back. Frankie waited, because he wanted to tackle Butsko, bring him down, and punch him out. Butsko shot his leg forward, and Frankie grabbed it in both his arms, twisting to the side. Butsko lost his balance and fell on his ass. Frankie tried to leap on him, but he didn't have the strength to move quickly, having lost too much blood. Butsko twisted out of the way, got to his feet, dodged another of Frankie's lunges, and kicked him in the mouth. Frankie collapsed onto his face, out cold once more.

"C'mon, Sarge," Bannon said. "Leave him alone."

"I'll leave him alone when he learns to keep his big mouth shut."

15

"He'll never do that."

"Then I'll never stop kicking the shit out of him. Maybe one day I'll kick the shit out of him so much he'll die, and then I'll throw a party."

"You don't mean that, Sarge."

"Oh, yes I do."

Butsko sat down again and studied his map. He was trying to figure out the best way to get back to his lines. They were a long way off and he wasn't sure he and his men could make it back by daylight.

Nutsy Gafooley rolled Frankie La Barbara onto his back and felt his face. "I think you broke his nose again, Sarge."

"He deserved it."

"You shouldn't beat up on him when he's wounded like this."

"I'll beat up on him when he's better, too, and I'll keep beating up on him until he starts keeping his mouth shut."

Butsko placed his forefinger at the point on the map where he reckoned their position to be. He drew a line on the overlay with his pencil, connecting their position to the nearest point on the American front lines, then laid his compass on the line so he could get the azimuth.

"About 132 degrees," he said. "Okay, let's saddle up. I'll carry Homer; which one of you heroes wants to carry big-mouth?"

"I'll do it," Bannon said, "but he'd be able to limp along if you didn't kick him in the mouth."

"But is like *if* and *maybe*. Shove 'em all up your ass. Let's move it out. I don't wanna spend all night shooting the shit with birdbrains, nitwits, and scumbags."

Butsko picked up Homer Gladley and lowered him onto his shoulder, and Bannon couldn't help admiring that, because Homer Gladley weighed 250 pounds. Frankie La Barbara weighed 185 pounds, and Longtree had to help Bannon lift Frankie La Barbara up. Bannon positioned Frankie La Barbara on his shoulder and staggered behind Butsko, whose gait was steady under Homer Gladley's weight.

The others fell in behind them as they made their way back to their front lines.

• • •

"Wake up, sir."

Captain Mitsuru Shimoyama opened his eyes. He was lying in a ditch half full of water, and Sergeant Kikusaki was standing over him.

"What is it?" Captain Shimoyama asked.

"Colonel Akai wants to speak with you on the radio."

"You have the radio with you?"

"It's in the radio tent."

Captain Shimoyama sat up in his hole and debated whether to have Sergeant Kikusaki bring the radio to him, but decided he'd look silly speaking to Colonol Akai while sitting in a puddle of water, and he might even get electrocuted from the batteries.

Sergeant Kikusaki grinned maliciously, because he and Captain Shimoyama didn't like each other and both knew it. "I think you should hurry, sir. The call sounded urgent."

Captain Shimoyama looked up at Sergeant Kikusaki. "You don't tell me to hurry, Sergeant. I tell you to hurry. Is that clear?"

"Yes, sir."

Captain Shimoyama didn't like the surly tone of Sergeant Kikusaki's voice, but he couldn't do anything about it. Not yet, at least. But someday Sergeant Kikusaki would really step out of line, and Captain Shimoyama would nail his ass to a wall.

Captain Shimoyama climbed out of the ditch and walked toward the communications tent, a serious expression on his face. He had the air of an intellectual about him, which he was. He'd been a staff officer in General Hyakutake's headquarters before the failure of the big offensive, and his ambition had been to attain high rank as a staff officer, but there'd been a shortage of officers at the front, because so many had been killed in the big offensive, and Captain Shimoyama had been given command of a line infantry company. It was the last assignment in the world that he wanted, because he considered himself too smart to be a line infantry officer. Clever men like him were needed to tell line infantry officers what to do, but the big offensive, which Captain Shimoyama helped plan, had failed, and Captain Shimoyama still wondered what had gone wrong.

17

Captain Shimoyama entered his communications tent. Corporal Teramoto sat at the radio and jumped to attention.

"Get me Colonel Akai."

"Yes, sir."

Captain Shimoyama leaned against the bench on which the radio sat and crossed his arms. He hoped and prayed that Colonel Akai would tell him that his talents were needed at General Hyakutake's headquarters and that he'd been missed.

Corporal Teramoto handed the headset to Captain Shimoyama, who put it on. "This is Captain Shimoyama," he said into the mouthpiece.

A voice on the other end replied: "The colonel will be with you in a few moments, sir."

Captain Shimoyama shifted his ass on the bench and waited. He didn't light a cigarette because he didn't smoke. He thought nicotine was bad for the brain, and he wanted his brain to be quick and keen, although it hadn't been so quick and keen lately, because he hadn't been able to get much sleep in holes in the ground that filled with water after they were dug.

"Captain Shimoyama?" asked Colonel Akai.

"Yes, sir."

"Took you long enough to call back."

"I just received the message, sir."

"You should always be near your radio."

"I was near my radio."

"Then it shouldn't have taken you so long to call back. Where is your company right now?"

"At the same position I reported earlier in the evening."

"I have an important mission for you. Do you have your map with you?"

"Yes, sir."

"Spread it out in front of you."

"Yes, sir." Captain Shimoyama took his map out of his shirt and unfolded it on the bench. "I've done as you've ordered, sir."

"Do you see the location of Gasoline Dump Number Six?"

"Yes, sir."

"Do you know what happened at Gasoline Dump Number Six tonight?"

"No, sir."

18

"It was blown up by enemy sappers. You didn't hear the explosions?"

"No, sir."

"Why not?"

Captain Shimoyama became flustered. "I don't know, sir. I guess I was asleep."

"They were very close to you. You should have been notified. In well-run companies, commanders are notified immediately of all untoward events. I think you'd better straighten a few things out there."

"Yes, sir," Captain Shimoyama replied, gritting his teeth. Sergeant Kikusaki should have awakened him, but he hadn't, and now Captain Shimoyama looked bad. "I'll make sure this doesn't happen again, sir."

"You'd better. Now, let's move on to the matter at hand. American sappers, as I said, have blown up Gasoline Dump Number Six, and I assume they're headed back toward their lines. Your company is bivouacked directly between Gasoline Dump Number Six and the American lines. Therefore we expect the American sappers to pass through your general area any time now. Fan out your company into a long skirmish line and intercept them. Take prisoners if you can, but if you can't, don't worry about it. Just make sure you intercept and stop them."

"How many Americans are there, sir?"

"We don't know for sure, but judging from the damage they've done, we estimate from forty to sixty men. How many are in your company?"

"One hundred and sixty fit for duty, sir."

"Good. You'll have a numerical advantage, plus the advantage of surprise. By the way, General Hyakutake is here, and the orders to stop those sappers have come directly from him. It will not be good if you fail in this mission. Is that clear?"

"Yes, sir."

"Over and out."

Captain Shimoyama handed the headset to Corporal Teramoto and stormed out of the communications tent. He marched toward the hole occupied by Sergeant Kikusaki and found him sitting in it with two of his cronies.

"Sergeant Kikusaki!" Captain Shimoyama shouted.

19

Sergeant Kikusaki looked up with an amused expression. "Yes, sir?"

"Stand at attention when I talk with you!"

Casually, Sergeant Kikusaki drew himself to his full height and stood at attention, a faint smile playing on his face. Captain Shimoyama was so angry, he wanted to pull out his Nambu pistol and shoot Sergeant Kikusaki in the head.

"I wish to speak with Sergeant Kikusaki alone! The rest of you, find something to do!"

The two other soldiers climbed out of the ditch and walked away. Captain Shimoyama jumped into the ditch and stood so that his face was only inches away from Sergeant Kikusaki's face.

"Sergeant!" he shouted, spittle from his tongue flying into Sergeant Kikusaki's face, making Sergeant Kikusaki wince. "Did you hear explosions in this vicinity within the past hour!"

"Yes, sir!"

"Why was I not notified of them?"

"I assumed you heard them, just as I heard them, sir!"

This stopped Captain Shimoyama cold and undermined his confidence, because he realized that front-line combat soldiers like Sergeant Kikusaki had their ears tuned for sudden unusual sounds, but that he, who was accustomed to life far behind the lines, did not possess those sensibilities yet.

"Sergeant Kikusaki, I do not want you to assume anything of the sort in the future! Your job is not to make assumptions but to follow orders! In the future I expect to be informed of all unusual events! Is that clear?"

"Yes, sir."

"Those explosions were caused by American sappers who have blown up Gasoline Dump Number Six. They are said to be headed this way, and I have just received orders to intercept them. Awaken the company and have them stand in formation in front of my headquarters. Hurry!"

With a condescending expression on his face, Sergeant Kikusaki climbed out of the hole and marched away. Captain Shimoyama watched him go, hating his guts.

THREE . . .

The sun was a sliver of light on the horizon. The patrol from the recon platoon sat in the depths of the jungle, eating C rations. Butsko studied his map, measuring distances.

"Only a couple more miles to go," he said, "but there's Japs scattered all around this area between us and our lines, so we'll have to be extra careful from now on."

Frankie La Barbara couldn't eat because several of his teeth were loose, and one was hanging by a thread. He also had a split lip, and the wound in his leg hurt like hell, plunging him into a rotten mood.

"We coulda been home already," he said, "if we hadn't took time out to blow up that Jap motor pool. The flyboys could be bombing it right now, but somebody around here—I'm not mentioning any names—likes to play hero, so we're not home."

Butsko took a pack of Luckies out of his shirt pocket and lit one with his trusty Zippo. "It's okay to smoke now. Sun's up."

Frankie lit a Chesterfield but had trouble drawing smoke, because his lips were mangled. "I'm sick of risking my ass so's a certain somebody can make points with the colonel."

Bannon smoked a Chesterfield too. "Shut up, Frankie."

"I won't shut up. I'm sick of everybody telling me to shut up. It's too bad I'm the only one who's got the guts to say the truth around here. Homer'll probably die and I'll be crippled for life because a certain big ugly sergeant likes to play fiddle-fuck with everybody's life."

Nutsy Gafooley examined Homer Gladley's wound. "Homer won't die and you won't be crippled for life. You've only got a little flesh wound and you make it sound as if your whole leg's been blown away."

Frankie spat blood onto the ground. "That's easy for you to say, because you're not the one wearing a bullet hole."

"Knock it off!" Butsko said.

Frankie opened his mouth to talk back but decided he'd better not. He didn't feel like getting kicked in the teeth again. *When I get better, I'll kill that son of a bitch,* he said to himself.

Butsko blew smoke out the side of his mouth as he sat on a log, his map spread out on the ground between his enormous combat boots. "A certain somebody on this patrol is a stupid fuck and all he ever thinks about is himself," Butsko said. "Sometimes he forgets we're in a war and that the purpose of this war is to kill as many Japs as we can and destroy the stuff they use to kill us with. The motor pool we blew up last night was camouflaged and couldn't have been spotted from the air. It was too small to pinpoint from rough coordinates. We could have walked away from it, but that gas would have been used to fuel tanks and trucks full of Japanese soldiers who might have killed hundreds of GIs, and maybe even us. Sure, it was a risk, but everything in war is a risk. Sure, we have two men wounded, but that's better than hundreds of casualties. You guys should know all this by now, but since you don't, I'm explaining it this one last time. And when we get back, I'm having that fucking wop from New York transferred out of the recon platoon forever!"

Frankie bristled and his busted lips quivered with rage. "Who're you calling a wop!"

Butsko calmly picked up his submachine gun and aimed it

22

at Frankie, flicking off the safety. "One more peep out of you and I'm going to kill you."

"You wouldn't dare!"

Butsko raised the sights to his eyes and took aim. Frankie held up his hand. "Wait a minute!"

"Your life doesn't mean a fuck-all to me," Butsko said. "I don't like you and I never have liked you. I could kill you and leave you here and say you were shot by Japs, and nobody would ask any questions. If that's what you want, go ahead and mouth off."

Frankie knew Butsko was speaking the truth. The other guys on the patrol would never contradict what Butsko had said, because they were all afraid of him. *I'm the only one with any guts around here,* he thought.

"You win," he said to Butsko, "and I'm gonna hold you to your word. When we get back, I want that transfer."

"You got it," Butsko said.

Captain Shimoyama walked through the jungle, inspecting his company's position. He slapped a long, thin stick against his leg as he swiveled his head around, examining holes in the ground, snipers high in the trees, and machine-gun nests set up behind rock formations. His men were making use of natural concealment, because they didn't want to make noise digging. As a result, their positions weren't as well protected as fixed fortifications.

Sergeant Kikusaki walked behind Captain Shimoyama, wanting to kick him in the ass. He thought Captain Shimoyama was a sissy and a weakling, quite a different commanding officer from Captain Abiru, who had been shot while leading a banzai charge during the big offensive.

Captain Shimoyama looked at his watch. It was six o'clock in the morning. The sun had risen above the horizon and shone blood red in a clear blue sky. Birds flitted from branch to branch above, and monkeys chattered. Sometimes he wondered what the monkeys thought about the war going on underneath their noses.

His men were spread out in a skirmish line over one thousand yards long. He hoped that would be a big enough net for the interception of the Americans. He had given orders to open

23

fire at the first sight of the Americans and that prisoners should be taken if possible.

Captain Shimoyama reached the right flank of his position and turned back, slapping the stick against his leg. *The Americans may not come this way,* he thought, *but if they do, I'll get them.*

Butsko's body was soaked with sweat that plastered his uniform against his skin. He carried Homer Gladley on his back, and it was slow going. Behind him, Bannon and Shaw helped Frankie La Barbara limp along. Longtree was in front of the column, and Nutsy Gafooley brought up the rear.

Butsko knew that the area they were passing through was infested with Japs who'd retreated from the high ground around Empress Augusta Bay after their big offensive failed. It hadn't been too difficult slipping through them last night, but it would be a different story in broad daylight with two wounded men.

Butsko heard a groan escape from Frankie La Barbara's lips. He turned around angrily to chew Frankie out and saw that Frankie's eyes were closed, his skin was pale, and his mouth was hanging open. His legs hung limply to the ground.

"What's the matter with him?" Butsko asked.

"I dunno," Bannon said. "He just went slack."

Shaw craned his head and looked at Frankie's face. "He's passed out."

Butsko frowned. "Just what I need. Nutsy, take a look at him. Maybe his wound's infected. The rest of you, take a break."

Bannon and Shaw laid Frankie on the ground and Nutsy knelt beside him, taking his pulse, noting that Frankie's skin was hot. Nutsy pressed his hand against Frankie's forehead. It felt like the exterior of an oven.

"He's got a bad fever," Nutsy said.

"Maybe he's getting another attack of malaria," Bannon replied.

"That's probably it," Nutsy told him. "I don't have any medicine to treat malaria."

Butsko unslung his submachine gun. "Maybe I should just shoot the son of a bitch."

"C'mon, Sarge," Bannon said. "This ain't no time for jokes."

"Who's joking?" Butsko slung his submachine gun over his

24

shoulder, took out his map, and unfolded it. "We've got another two or three miles to go, and they ain't gonna be easy."

"Maybe we should stay where we are and wait for night," Bannon suggested.

"That ain't a bad idea," Butsko replied.

"Ain't a good idea either," Nutsy said. "We got two wounded men who need medical attention fast."

"That's your job," Butsko said.

"I ain't no doctor. I ain't even a medic."

"It comes down to this," Butsko said. "We risk all our asses if we move now, and we risk only two asses if we wait till tonight."

"Homer's got a bullet in his back someplace," Nutsy said. "Who knows what kinda damage it's done."

Butsko hunched over and dropped to his knees on the other side of Homer Gladley. "He ain't bleeding from the mouth, so it missed his lungs and throat. His heart is still strong, so that's okay. I think he can last the night."

"I don't think we should take the chance."

Butsko looked at Nutsy Gafooley and furrowed his brow. He couldn't understand how somebody as small and puny as Nutsy could stand up to him like that. "I tell you what," he said. "We'll take a vote. Who wants to go now? Raise your hands."

Everyone raised his hand except Butsko.

"You guys are even dumber than I thought," he said. "Okay, if that's the way you want it, that's the way it's gonna be. Let's move it out. If you guys get me killed, I'm gonna make you sorry."

Nutsy was confused. "If you're dead, how could you make us sorry?"

"I'll figure out a way. Saddle up and let's get going."

Butsko stood and slung his Thompson submachine gun crosswise on his back. Then he bent over and picked up Homer Gladley. Bannon and Shaw dragged Frankie to his feet and draped his arms around their shoulders. The patrol, with Long-tree on the point, moved toward the American lines.

It was an hour later and Longtree prowled forward in a crouch, swiveling his body from side to side, looking in all directions for traces of Japs. He knew he was in Jap territory, and Japs had to be around someplace. He was the eyes and ears of the patrol and had to spot Japs before Japs spotted him.

Longtree had sharp eyes, but they weren't superhuman. He could spot movement and discern things that weren't where they were supposed to be, but he couldn't see a motionless Japanese soldier covered with camouflage, hiding behind a mass of branches and leaves. Such a Japanese soldier was fifty yards in front of Longtree and saw Longtree coming. The Japanese soldier flicked the safety off his Arisaka rifle and took aim at Longtree.

Longtree heard the faint *snick* sound of the safety and dropped to his stomach on the jungle floor.

Blam! The bullet zipped over Longtree's head a split second after he got underneath it. Behind him the patrol from the recon platoon hit the dirt. The jungle was silent for a second, then Japanese voices could be heard blabbering away.

Butsko felt a sinking sensation in his stomach. It sounded like many Japs were out there, and they were too close for him to give voice commands. He raised his hand and moved it in circles around his head, the Army signal for *Assemble on me*. Longtree crawled back, and the others gathered around.

Butsko tried to smile, but he didn't have his heart in it and the smile looked gruesome. "Looks like we're in the soup again," he said. "We'll have to work around them. Be quiet and don't get trigger-happy. We don't want a fight because we don't have much ammo left. Everybody ready?"

"Banzai!"

Butsko looked up and saw a dozen Japanese soldiers charging through the jungle, heading toward the spot where Longtree had been, which was only ten yards ahead of the others. Butsko didn't give any orders because there was only one thing they could do: fight for their lives.

The Japanese soldiers rampaged forward. One carried a samurai sword that flashed in the morning sunlight, and the others brandished Arisaka rifles with fixed bayonets. The GIs put themselves between the Japs and their two wounded comrades, then spread out into a skirmish line, raised their submachine guns, and waited for the Japs to get closer.

The Japs burst through the jungle, screaming at the tops of their lungs, looking for the American soldiers. They ap-

26

proached the spot where Longtree had been, passed over it, and continued their charge.

The GIs opened fire with their submachine guns and cut the Japanese soldiers down. The submachine guns sounded like thunder throughout the jungle, and a cloud of blue gun smoke rose into the air above them. The firing stopped as suddenly as it had started, and everybody's ears rang in the silence. The jungle ahead was littered with dead Japs.

"Longtree and Bannon, go strip them and make it fast!" Butsko said. "Get their uniforms too!"

Longtree and Bannon crawled forward. Butsko, Shaw, and Nutsy Gafooley covered them with their submachine guns in case the Japs attacked again.

"What's going on out there?" Captain Shimoyama screamed.

Corporal Teramoto knelt in front of the field radio. "I'm trying to reach the Second Platoon, sir."

"Try harder!"

Corporal Teramoto spoke into the headset. Captain Shimoyama lay on the ground beside him, and Sergeant Kikusaki sat with his back against the trunk of a tree.

"You shouldn't have told them to fire at the first sight of the Americans," Sergeant Kikusaki said. "You should have told the men to wait until the Americans were closer. Now the Americans will probably get away."

"They will not get away!" Captain Shimoyama said through teeth clenched in anger. "If you thought my previous order was wrong, why didn't you tell me?"

"I didn't think it was my place to lecture the famous captain from Seventeenth Army Headquarters on field tactics."

Captain Shimoyama thought he'd blow a fuse, but he made himself calm down.

"Sir," said Corporal Teramoto, "I have Corporal Shima-bukuro."

Corporal Teramoto held out the headset, and Captain Shimoyama spoke into it. "What's going on out there?"

"One squad charged the Americans, and the Americans opened fire with automatic weapons. We believe the squad was annihilated."

"You *believe?* Don't you *know?*"

27

"We're checking right now. Any further instructions?"

"Hold the line. Report the disposition of that squad as soon as possible."

"Yes, sir."

Captain Shimoyama handed the headset back to Corporal Teramoto, then looked at Sergeant Kikusaki. "The Americans have automatic weapons and therefore must be a unit of substantial size. Direct the company to move out and encircle them."

"May I say something, sir?"

"Go ahead."

"The American unit may not be of substantial size at all. It could be a small unit armed with submachine guns. American patrols are sometimes armed with submachine guns. I think you should rush them en masse and overwhelm them."

"Are you crazy? If you're wrong, half of them will be slaughtered. Too many Japanese soldiers have been killed already in this war as the result of outmoded strategies such as the one you now suggest. Follow my orders, and hurry!"

Japanese rifles, ammunition, and the samurai sword lay on the grass beside Longtree and Bannon, who were stripping off the Japanese soldiers' uniforms as Butsko had ordered. Both could guess what Butsko had in mind. They'd disguise themselves as Japanese soldiers and try to slip through their lines.

"I hear something," Longtree said.

Bannon perked up his ears and heard nothing, but he trusted Longtree's ears. Both hunkered down behind the bodies of the dead Japanese soldiers. In front of them, five Japanese soldiers appeared, advancing cautiously. They seemed unsure of themselves, because they knew American soldiers were in the vicinity. One of them spotted their dead comrades and pointed.

"Now!" said Bannon.

He and Longtree raised their submachine guns and pulled the triggers before the Japs knew what was happening. The submachine guns barked viciously, and the bodies of the Japanese soldiers became peppered with .45-caliber holes. They spun through the air, spurting blood in all directions, and collapsed on the ground.

"Let's get out of here!" Bannon said.

28

Gathering up the Japanese weapons and uniforms, Bannon and Longtree dashed back toward Butsko and the others.

"What was that?" Captain Shimoyama shouted.

He'd just heard the firing of Bannon's and Longtree's submachine guns and wondered why the Americans were firing and his men weren't. He pondered moving to that sector of his line and taking command of it himself, but then who'd command the company?

"Corporal Shimabukuro is on the radio, sir."

Corporal Teramoto handed over the headset, and Captain Shimoyama put it on. "What's going on out there?"

"I sent out five men to find out what happened to the two squads and they haven't returned either," Corporal Shimabukuro said.

"I see." Captain Shimoyama tried to think of something significant to do, but nothing came to mind. "Don't send out any more men, because we don't want to lose them too. Stay put and await further orders."

Captain Shimoyama gave back the headset and tried to think. His eyes fell on Sergeant Kikusaki, who was smiling sarcastically.

"What's so funny?" Captain Shimoyama demanded.

"Nothing, sir."

"What are you smiling at?"

"Nothing, sir."

Captain Shimoyama scowled. Front-line command was proving to be loathesome from every conceivable point of view. Captain Shimoyama felt himself losing his temper. "Well, Sergeant Kikusaki, if you're so smart, what would *you* do right now?"

Sergeant Kikusaki scratched his tiny nose and said casually, "I already told you what I'd do. I'd order an all-out charge against those Americans and wipe them out. There can't be many of them. A large unit could not have penetrated this deeply into our lines."

Sergeant Kikusaki's condescending manner irritated Captain Shimoyama. "Very well," he said, "if that's what you think, you may order the charge and lead it yourself. Report the results to me here when you're finished."

Sergeant Kikusaki drew himself to attention and threw a snappy salute. "Yes, sir!" He did a smart about-face and marched away.

Captain Shimoyama collapsed onto the ground. *What have I done?* he asked himself. *If he's successful, I'll lose face. No one in the company will have respect for me anymore. I'll become a laughing stock.* Captain Shimoyama didn't smoke cigarettes, but he felt like starting. He found himself hoping that Sergeant Kikusaki's banzai charge would fail miserably and that Sergeant Kikusaki would be killed in action.

"Everybody ready?" Butsko asked.

The others grunted in assent or nodded. Bannon, Longtree, and Nutsy Gafooley wore Japanese uniforms, but only Nutsy fit into his. Bannon's and Longtree's were too tight, with the sleeves and pants too short, while Butsko and Shaw couldn't fit into Japanese uniforms at all, because Butsko and Shaw were enormous men.

Butsko took out his compass and figured out which way to go. He pointed to the left, because he wanted to sneak around the Japanese positions in front of him. "This way! Longtree take the point, and keep your fucking eyes open!"

Butsko lifted Homer Gladley onto his shoulders. Bannon and Shaw carried Frankie La Barbara, who was unconscious and drooling onto the front of his uniform. Longtree led the way and disappeared into the thick, leafy jungle.

The Japanese soldiers stood in a long skirmish line, shifting nervously from foot to foot, checking their rifles and bayonets, trying to work themselves into the mood for a wild banzai charge.

Sergeant Kikusaki paced back and forth, checking them over, making sure everything was right. He wanted desperately to wipe out the Americans in front of him, because that would humiliate Captain Shimoyama, whom he despised. He'd picked thirty of his best men and figured that was all he'd need. They'd roll over the Americans and kill them all!

"Are we ready?" Sergeant Kikusaki asked.

His men nodded, holding their rifles and bayonets tightly, their eyes glazed with excitement.

Sergeant Kikusaki drew his samurai sword and turned around,

facing the last known position of the Americans. He waved his samurai sword in the air and screamed: *"Banzai!"* then jumped into the air and hurled himself toward the American lines, running as fast as he could.

"Banzai!" replied his men, following him through the jungle, which resounded with the echoes of their voices. Monkeys looked down at them curiously, and birds shrieked, scattering in all directions. *"Banzai!"* the Japanese soldiers cried. *"Banzai!"* bellowed Sergeant Kikusaki.

They charged through the thick foliage, shaking their weapons, eager to kill Americans before the Americans opened fire with their submachine guns. The Japanese soldiers tried not to think of those submachine guns as they sped through the jungle. They preferred to think positively of stabbing American soldiers with their bayonets or shooting them with their rifles.

They reached the spot where their five comrades had been gunned down and jumped over the bodies because once a banzai charge was under way, it didn't stop unless it ran into a brick wall.

"Yaaaahhhhhhh!" screamed Sergeant Kikusaki. *"Kill them all!"*

He saw the scattered, bullet-torn corpses of the two squads that had been massacred by submachine-gun fire, but was so excited he didn't notice that some of the bodies had been stripped of their uniforms and that their rifles and ammunitions were missing.

"Follow me!" he yelled, slashing his samurai sword through the air.

"Banzai!" replied his men, rushing through the jungle.

Leaves and branches scratched their faces and arms, but they kept on going. Some tripped over exposed tree roots and fell on their asses, but they leaped to their feet and continued the charge. Sergeant Kikusaki and his men rampaged through the jungle, expecting to hear the rattle of automatic-weapons fire.

"Banzai!" they screamed. *"Banzai!"*

They ran past the area where Butsko and his men had rested, but didn't notice the flattened grass and other signs of recent activity. Their breath came in short gulps. They expected the fight to begin at any moment.

They pushed through the jungle, although some were getting

31

tired and couldn't yell so loud anymore. Leading them, Sergeant Kikusaki wasn't sure of what was happening. *Where are the Americans?* he wondered as he hurdled a log. *How far have we come?* he asked himself as he dodged around a tree.

He wanted to sit down and take a rest, but how could he do that when he was leading an all-out banzai charge? The only thing to do was keep going, and he kept going. His tongue hanging out of his mouth, he trotted through the jungle because he could no longer run. His feet felt like lead and so did his samurai sword. Thorns ripped open his shirt, and then he tripped over a rock and fell on his stomach.

His men didn't know what to do. They didn't want to disgrace him by acknowledging that he'd lost his footing, so they made believe it hadn't happened and ran past him, shouting *"Banzai!"* weakly, staggering through bushes and gulping down air. They were beginning to think that maybe the Americans had flown the coop.

Sergeant Kikusaki raised himself to his knees, his chest heaving. "That's enough!" he croaked through his parched throat. *"Halt! Come back!"*

His men stopped, looked at each other in dismay, and dragged their feet back to where their sergeant was. Their great banzai attack had been a bust.

The recon platoon had hit the dirt and set up a defense perimeter when they heard the commencement of the charge. It soon became clear to them that the Japanese soldiers were charging the place where they had been, not where they were now.

"Listen to them," Butsko said, a sneer on his face. "Japs are the biggest assholes in the world. They only know how to do two things: charge like maniacs, and sneak up on a GI at night and slit his throat. If I had two .30-caliber machine guns and ten more men with rifles, I could wipe them all out. Let's get going. Saddle up and move out!"

32

FOUR . . .

Sergeant Kikusaki approached Captain Shimoyama, his face flecked with anxiety. It would be painful for him to confess that the charge had failed miserably. Captain Shimoyama could deduce from one quick glance at Sergeant Kikusaki that something had gone wrong, and his spirits improved instantly. He crossed his arms over his chest and his eyes glittered with pleasure.

"Well?" he asked. "What happened?"

Sergeant Kikusaki gazed at the ground. "Nothing happened, sir."

"*Nothing* happened. But surely *something* happened, Sergeant. Did the charge take place?"

"Yes, sir, but the Americans weren't there."

"Weren't there? Then, where are they?"

"I don't know, sir."

Captain Shimoyama smiled for the first time in days. "But

how can that be? You're supposed to be so experienced in these matters, Sergeant, whereas I am a mere staff officer—a rank amateur, as it were—yet, I think *I* know where they are. They are probably trying to circle one of our flanks in an effort to return to their lines. Please notify our flank units to be on the lookout for them. And, Sergeant, please don't walk around here with such a sorrowful expression on your face. I don't want you to demoralize my troops."

With a chuckle Captain Shimoyama turned away. Sergeant Kikusaki made his way to the field radio, murder in his heart.

Longtree was on the point again, dressed in a Japanese uniform that was several sizes too small for him. He couldn't even button the shirt, and it hung loose over his bronzed skin. The seat of the pants were torn because he'd bent over and ripped it out. Japanese blood was on the shirt and it spooked Longtree. He thought the soul of the dead Jap was hanging around him, and he had enough to worry about.

"DARE SOKO!" said a voice in front of him.

Longtree dived toward the ground. A Japanese soldier was out there talking to him, thinking he was Japanese because of the uniform. Behind Longreee, the others hit the dirt too.

"DARKE SOKO!" the voice said again.

Longtree looked behind him for instructions. Butsko pulled a hand grenade from his lapel and held it in the air. Longtree understood what Butsko wanted. He withdrew a hand grenade from his belt and pulled the pin.

"DARE SOKO!" the voice called out with greater urgency.

Longtree aimed at the direction of the voice and threw the grenade. It sailed through the air and landed with a thud. Longtree heard scrambling in the underbrush as the Japanese soldier tried to get away.

Barrroooooommmmmm! The grenade exploded in a reddish-orange blast, and the concussion pounded Longtree's ears. He sprang up and charged the spot where the Japanese soldier had been, and found him splattered all over the area. Running feet approached from Longtree's rear and he spun around. It was Butsko and the others, coming up fast.

"Keep moving!" Butsko said. *"Go!"*

The unconscious Homer Gladley bounced up and down on Butsko's shoulders as Butsko ran in the direction of the Amer-

34

ican positions, while the rest of his patrol followed him. Butsko suspected that the Japs had only a thin skirmish line in the vicinity, and if he could break through it, he'd be home free.

Longtree sprinted in front of Butsko so he could take the point again, and Shaw and Bannon dragged Frankie La Barbara. Nutsy Gafooley brought up the rear, carrying his M-1 rifle with telescopic sight attached. The GIs heard Japanese voices to their right and left, and knew that every Jap in the area would converge on the sound of the grenade blast. The GIs ran as fast as they could to get as far away as possible.

Captain Shimoyama jumped six inches off the ground when he heard the grenade explode on his right flank. *"What's that?"* he screamed. He turned around and faced his right flank, thinking furiously. The explosion meant there was fighting going on there, although he didn't hear any shots. What was the cause of the explosion?

"Sergeant Kikusaki!"

"Yes, sir!"

"Find out what that explosion was all about!"

"It sounded like a hand grenade, sir!"

"I'm not interested in your opinions! Find out for sure!"

Sergeant Kikusaki snatched the radio headset out of Corporal Teramoto's hands. Captain Shimoyama rubbed his fingers over his stubbled chin. *The explosion must mean that the Americans are trying to break through my right flank,* he thought. *If I shift my line in that direction, perhaps I can stop them!*

Captain Shimoyama's eyes narrowed, and he felt a deep sense of satisfaction. He thought that his mind was functioning clearly and rationally and that he could outsmart the Americans. It occurred to him that small-unit tactics were basically not very different from the large-scale operations he'd planned at General Hyakutake's headquarters, except that now he could do whatever he wanted, without having to compromise on a decision with other people and then get the decision approved by old fuddy-duddy officers who were afraid of their own shadows.

"Sir," said Sergeant Kikusaki, "one of our men has been blown to bits, apparently by an American hand grenade, as I suggested a few minutes earlier! A great many footprints of American boots have been found in the area! Evidently the

35

Americans have broken through our right flank!"

"Exactly as I suspected," Captain Shimoyama said coolly. "Nothing to worry about. Shift platoons A, B, and C behind our right flank so that we can block the retreat of the Americans. Do you think you can handle that, Sergeant Kikusaki, without any more mistakes?"

"Yes, sir."

"Good. Carry out your orders."

The patrol from the recon platoon was taking a break after their headlong dash through the jungle. They sat around, hidden by the dense foliage, and smoked cigarettes. Nutsy Gafooley examined Homer Gladley's wound and saw that it wasn't bleeding and wasn't turning green. Homer's pulse was steady and strong. Homer would pull through if he could get to a doctor within the next several hours.

Nutsy moved to the prostrate Frankie La Barbara, peeled off the bandage on Frankie's leg, and looked at the wound. It didn't look very serious. Frankie's problem was the malaria. Frankie's face was pale and his forehead was hot. Occasionally he moaned softly. Nutsy wasn't afraid to be near Frankie, because malaria was contagious only through the bloodstream—from the bites of infected mosquitoes, infected hypodermic needles, or blood transfusions from those who had malaria already. Once you caught malaria, you could get recurrent attacks for the rest of your life.

Butsko puffed his cigarette and watched Nutsy pour water from his canteen onto his handkerchief and press the handkerchief against Frankie's forehead. Butsko tried to figure out his next move. He thought that if he were a Jap, he'd try to deploy his men between the American patrol and the American lines, and if the Japs were doing that, Butsko's best response would be to outmaneuver the Japs. This meant that he'd have to move either to his right or left. But which direction should he choose? Butsko had no way of knowing where he was in relation to the Japs.

It was six of one and a half a dozen of the other. He might as well leave it to Lady Luck. "Hey, Nutsy!"

Nutsy was applying a fresh bandage to Frankie La Barbara's wound. "Whataya want?"

"See if Frankie's got his dice on him!"

An expression of bewilderment came over Nutsy's face. "Hey, Sarge, this ain't no time for a crap game!"

"Your fucking head is a crap game. Gimme the dice."

Nutsy reached into the left pocket of Frankie's shirt and pulled out Frankie's white dice with black dots. Nutsy tossed them to Butsko. "Here ya go, Sarge."

Butsko caught them in midair. *Okay, dice,* Butsko thought. *If you come up even, we go right, and if you come up odd, we go left.* He shook the dice in his big fist. Everybody watched him, wondering what he was up to. Drawing back his arm, Butsko threw the dice onto the jungle floor, and they rolled over the rotting leaves and sprouts of grass, finally coming to a stop. Butsko leaned over them and took a look.

They were snake eyes, and snake eyes meant you crapped out. Snake eyes also added up to two, an even number, and according to the deal he'd made with the dice, that meant he had to go to the right. Butsko was a tough guy, but he was also superstitious. He didn't like the idea of the snake eyes, but he'd made a deal, and a deal was a deal. He dropped Frankie's dice into his own shirt pocket.

"We're going that way," he said, pointing to the right.

"But Sarge," protested Bannon, pointing straight ahead, "our lines are that way."

"I know where our lines are, and so do the Japs. I figger the Japs'll try to get between us and our lines, so we'll fake them out. Any objections?"

"How do you know that's not the way the Japs are coming from?"

"I don't know, but we've gotta go somewhere. You got a better idea?"

Bannon thought for a few moments. "No."

"I didn't think so. Let's saddle up and move out."

Captain Shimoyama led his company through the jungle, holding his samurai sword in his hands, swishing it menacingly through the air whenever he had room, to show his men that he was an aggressive combat commander. His company moved quickly, because he thought speed was more important than silence. He had to cut the Americans off and annihilate them so that he would have credibility with his men and win the attention of his superiors.

"Forward!" he said. "Hurry! Don't let the American swine get away!"

Behind Captain Shimoyama, Sergeant Kikusaki trudged through the jungle. He wanted to whip out his Nambu pistol and shoot Captain Shimoyama in the back, but he couldn't be that blatant about it. Maybe later, when no one was looking, he could do it and blame it on an American sniper.

Captain Shimoyama's company crashed through the jungle in a long column. His intention was to form his men into a vast circle and then tighten it like a noose around the Americans.

He wondered how many Americans were out there, and he hoped he had enough men to do the job easily. If not, he'd call for help. The main thing was to find out where the Americans were and stop them.

Longtree stopped suddenly and listened to the jungle. He'd heard something like the sound of wind rustling leaves and branches, but no wind was blowing. Concentrating on his ears, wrinkling his brow, he realized that the sound was far away. A substantial number of Japs were moving through the jungle. Listening a few moments more, he perceived that the Japs were headed toward his patrol.

Longtree turned around and ran back to Butsko, who saw him coming and could read trouble all over Longtree's face.

"Whatsa matter?" Butsko asked, Homer Gladley's body sprawled over his back and shoulders.

"Japs headed this way!"

"From where?"

"From there!" Longtree pointed.

Butsko realized that the dice had led him in the wrong direction. *Snake eyes,* he thought. *I crapped out.*

Longtree looked toward the Japs. "They're getting closer."

Butsko heard them faintly and tried to determine their exact location. "Shit!" he said. "Fuck! Piss!"

A new, difficult decision had to be made, and Butsko was tired of carrying Homer Gladley. The thought crossed his mind that maybe he wouldn't be in the mess he was in if he'd left that Japanese gas dump alone last night, but he'd been full of piss and vinegar, and blowing it up had seemed like the right thing to do. Now it didn't seem so right.

38

He decided to attempt to outflank the Japs once more. "We'll try to ease around them in the direction we're going," he said. "Keep it quiet, because if we can hear them, they can hear us. Longtree, take the point."

Longtree ran forward and then stopped when he was fifteen yards in front of the rest of the patrol. Then he bent into his old Apache crouch and slunk forward, holding his Thompson submachine gun in both hands. His captured Arisaka rifle was slung across his back.

His mind was concentrated on his eyes and ears. Relentlessly he searched the leaves and branches for the movement of Japs, and he listened to the sounds of the jungle, trying to differentiate natural sounds from the sounds of Japs on the march.

He couldn't hear much, because the patrol of his fellow GIs behind him overpowered the other sounds. Five minutes passed, and Longtree decided to stop them so he could hear clearly again. He raised his hand, and the patrol shuffled to a halt. Furrowing his brow, he turned his head from left to right, listening for the Japs, and he heard them.

He ran back to Butsko. "They're headed this way, and it sounds like they're spread out all over the jungle from there to there."

Longtree pointed, and Butsko realized that the Japs were circling around his patrol. They hadn't closed the ring yet, but they would in another several minutes. He could get out the back way, but that led deeper into Japanese territory. The only thing to do was take cover and hope the Japs didn't see them.

"Longtree," he said, "find a good place around here for us to hide, and don't take too long. I don't think we have much time."

"They're within two hundred yards of us," Longtree replied. Then he turned and disappeared into the thickest part of the jungle.

Butsko looked at his men, and they looked back at him. The situation was grim, but they'd been in grimmer ones and come out okay. Butsko didn't tell them anything, because there was nothing to say. Bannon and Shaw were haggard from carrying Frankie La Barbara around, and Butsko figured he didn't make such a pretty picture himself. Nutsy Gafooley lit a cigarette. Butsko could hear the Japs in the distance. They weren't even attempting to be quiet, and they were drawing

39

closer. In another five or ten minutes they'd be swarming all over the place.

Branches and leaves trembled, and Longtree stepped into sight, beckoning.

Butsko shifted the weight of Homer Gladley on his back. "Let's go," he said softly.

They followed Longtree into the thick jungle. Long vines hung from the trees and the air was fetid. The GIs had to drop low to avoid the foliage, and it was dark because the clutter of treetops blocked the sun. If a Jap was ten feet away, he couldn't be seen.

They came to a boulder eight feet high, covered with moss. A green lizard six inches long jumped off it and ran away as the GIs approached. Beside the boulder was a depression in the ground, and Longtree pointed to it. Butsko stepped into the depression and sank into muck halfway to his knees.

"Fuck!" he whispered.

"Hey, Sarge," said Bannon, looking at the hole, "do you think maybe we should spread out? If we all get into that hole, one grenade'll finish us off."

"Who said anything about all of us getting into this hole? Don't anticipate orders. Just do as you're told. The rest of you guys dig in around here, and hurry. Longtree you camouflage the area after we're all set."

"What about the wounded men?" Bannon asked.

"Throw 'em in here with me."

"If I throw Frankie in there with you, you're liable to kill him."

"Then keep him with you. I don't give a fuck. Get moving. The Japs are almost on top of us, for Chrissakes, and you're worried about Frankie La Barbara?"

Bannon and Shaw got on their hands and knees and crawled underneath a thick bush, dragging Frankie La Barbara behind them. Nutsy Gafooley squeezed himself between a tree and a bush covered with red berries. Longtree roved over the ground on his hands and knees, covering everybody's tracks. He backed into the space occupied by Nutsy and pulled the branches closer. Nutsy snuffed out his cigarette and field stripped it. He and Longtree peered through the foliage and listened to the sounds of the Japanese soldiers maneuvering closer. They gripped their submachine guns and hoped the Japs would pass through without noticing them.

Beneath their bush, ten feet away, Bannon and Shaw lay on either side of Frankie La Barbara, their fingers on the triggers of their submachine guns. Bannon had laid his three hand grenades in front of him and loosened the pins in case he had to throw them quickly. They heard Japanese soldiers cursing and shouting orders as they cut their way through the thick jungle. Bannon felt strangely calm. He'd been in many horrible situations during his combat career, and it was difficult for him to become as afraid as he had at the beginning. *Let the bastards come,* he thought. *Nobody lives forever.*

Butsko tried to make himself comfortable in his muddy hole, but nothing worked. The filthy water had seeped through his pants and was aggravating the case of crotch itch that he already had. To distract himself, he threw a handful of dead leaves over Homer Gladley. He checked his weapons and ammunition, then laid his grenades in front of him and loosened the pins.

The Japanese weren't more than thirty or forty yards away. The GIs were tense, hoping the Japs would pass them by. They didn't want to think too much of what might happen if the Japs didn't pass them by, but they couldn't help themselves. They all knew that Japs were vicious and sadistic with their prisoners, and none of the GIs wanted to be captured alive. Each swore to himself that he'd die fighting, if it came to that. Better to die a quick, clean death than have your fingernails torn out or a live rat stuffed down your throat.

Adrenaline pumped through the GIs' arteries, and their hearts pounded in their chests. Their mouths were dry as they searched the jungle, hearing the Japanese soldiers crashing through the foliage. So intent were they on the advancing Japanese that they didn't pay any attention to Frankie La Barbara, who lay stretched out on his back and unconscious between Bannon and Shaw.

A deadly blue spider, large as a man's fist, walked silently over the leaves and grass, unmindful of the drama going on around him, headed toward Frankie La Barbara's face. Nothing was moving nearby, so the spider felt he had nothing to worry about. Frankie La Barbara exuded an odor that the spider thought interesting, and the spider thought Frankie La Barbara's face might be something good to eat.

The spider placed one of his long, crooked legs against Frankie La Barbara's cheek, and nothing happened, so he put another of his legs into Frankie La Barbara's ear. Again nothing happened, so the spider proceeded to crawl on top of Frankie La Barbara's face and find a soft spot to bite.

Frankie La Barbara was in the depths of a malaria coma, but the movement of the spider stimulated nerve endings on Frankie La Barbara's face, and the nerve endings transmitted the messages through Frankie's nervous system. Frankie La Barbara had always hated bugs, and although he was unconscious, a peculiar uneasiness ruffled his mind as the spider came to a stop atop his nose. In the depths of his coma, Frankie felt that something was amiss. It was a vague, indefinite disquiet in a remote convolution of his brain, but it was enough to rouse him slightly, and from that new level he became even more aware that something was wrong.

The spider moved around, prodding for a soft spot, and he placed one of his toothpick legs atop Frankie La Barbara's eyeball. An eyeball is one of the most sensitive parts of a person's body, and Frankie La Barbara stirred.

Meanwhile, next to Frankie La Barbara, Bannon saw the metallic flash of a Japanese machete as it slashed through the thick green wall of jungle. The machete sliced again, and Bannon saw the arm of the Japanese soldier appear. The Japanese soldier pushed forward, and now Bannon could see his whole body. The Japanese soldier was five feet six inches tall, built on the lean side, and had bow legs. He looked around and stepped forward. Behind him, through the newly hacked opening, sidled another Japanese soldier. Bannon looked at Shaw, and Shaw looked at Bannon. Their mouths were set in grim lines. They turned away from each other and watched the Japanese soldiers move past them, headed toward the hole where Butsko was. They walked by the hole and didn't even look into the bush where Longtree and Nutsy Gafooley were hiding.

The spider on Frankie La Barbara's face changed his position, prodding a leg into Frankie's other eye. Frankie opened his eyes and saw the big, hairy spider on his face. The movement of eyelids caused the spider to lose his balance, and he dug legs into each of Frankie La Barbara's eyes.

"Yyaaaaahhhhhhhhhhhhhh!" screamed Frankie La Barbara.

Bannon's blood froze. The Japanese soldiers stopped suddenly and looked in the direction of the screaming.

"Yyyaaaaaahhhhhhhhhhhhhh!"

The chatter of a submachine gun drowned out Frankie's voice, and the two Japanese soldiers were riddled with bullets. Blood spurted out of their wounds as the Japanese soldier's pirouetted and collapsed onto the ground.

Bannon turned around and saw Frankie sitting up as the gigantic spider leaped off his face.

"Yaaaaaaahhhhhhhhhhhh!"

Bannon drew back his submachine gun and slammed Frankie upside his head. Frankie's lights went out and he fell backward.

Butsko jumped out of his hole. "I'm gonna kill that son of a bitch!" He shook his submachine gun menacingly and advanced toward the bush where Shaw and Bannon were hiding.

Bannon stood up, holding his own submachine gun at the ready. "Calm down, you crazy fucking madman!"

Nutsy Gafooley swooped out of his hiding place and stripped the Japanese soldiers of their guns and ammunition. Longtree rushed forward and got in Butsko's way.

"Sssssshhhh," Longtree said. "There's Japs all around here."

Butsko opened his mouth to scream bloody blue murder, then shut his mouth because he knew Longtree was right. He could hear Japanese soldiers babbling all around him, and the sounds of foliage being cut with machetes. "We're in a real pickle now," he said in a low voice. "Everybody into the hole with me!"

"But, Sarge," Bannon protested, "one grenade will wipe us all out."

Butsko looked up to the heavens and held out his arms in supplication. "Why do these morons argue with everything I say? Why can't they do as they're told?" He leveled his gaze at Bannon. "I don't have time to play games. Move your ass."

"Hup, Sarge."

Bannon and Shaw carried Frankie to Butsko's hole and laid him down beside Homer Gladley. Nutsy Gafooley jumped into the trench with his collection of weapons and ammunition.

43

Longtree was the last one in; he turned around and looked at the bodies of the dead Japanese soldiers.

"Maybe I should go out and hide them."

"It's too late for that," Butsko replied. "Now we're *really* fucked."

"But, Sarge," Bannon said, "what if a hand grenade—"

Butsko interrupted him. "Shaddup." He turned to Nutsy. "You're job is to throw back any Jap hand grenades that land in this hole, got it?"

"I got it, Sarge."

"That's all you have to do. You don't have to fire any weapons or shoot off your mouth. Just throw back the hand grenades. You think you can handle it?"

"Sure thing, Sarge."

"Good." Butsko glanced at his other men. "Maybe we can hold 'em off and maybe we can't. I doubt that we will but we've got to try. It'll take them awhile to figure out how many of us are here and where we are, and by then it might be dark, if we're lucky."

Butsko wanted to say more, but he heard Japanese soldiers approaching. He placed his finger in front of his lips, signaling for his men to be quiet, and then motioned for them to get ready. They laid their submachine guns on the rim of the wet, smelly hole and aimed at the sounds of the Japanese soldiers.

Two Japanese soldiers, side by side, pushed through the thick foliage and discovered their two dead comrades. They stared, not believing their eyes, and then babbled to each other. One turned and headed back in the direction from thich they'd come.

"Get them!" Butsko shouted.

All the GIs except Nutsy opened fire at the same time, and the two Japanese soldiers were dead before they knew what hit them. They toppled to the ground and lay still.

"Somebody get their weapons," Butsko said.

Nutsy leaped out of the hole, but Butsko grabbed him by the leg and dragged him back. "Didn't I just tell you what your job was? Didn't I say that was *all* I wanted you to do?"

"I forgot, Sarge."

"Try to remember, okay?"

"Okay, Sarge."

"Bunch of birdbrains I got here," Butsko muttered.

Bannon sprang out of the hole and collected the Japanese rifles and ammunition. He searched through the dead men's knapsacks and found cans used for the storage of cooked rice. He carried everything back to the hole.

"I think I got some chow," he said.

"Quiet."

Butsko wrinkled his nose and listened to the jungle. It sounded as if the Japs were straight ahead and not to his back or sides. Japs jabbered excitedly, and Butsko knew they were trying to figure out where he and his men were. Butsko knew what was on their minds, because often he'd had to search for well-camouflaged Japanese bunkers.

"They're gonna start combing this area any minute now," Butsko said. "Keep your eyes open and your mouths shut."

Bannon shook one of the cans he'd taken from the dead Japanese soldiers. "Can I eat some of this?"

"I thought I just told you to keep quiet."

Bannon shrugged and unscrewed the top of the can. Inside was white rice, cooked and sticky. He scooped some out with his finger and put it into his mouth. Butsko looked at Frankie La Barbara to make sure he was still unconscious. Butsko wanted to slit Frankie's throat to make sure he wouldn't wake up screaming again, but the others wouldn't let him get away with it.

I wonder how long it'll take for the Japs to find us, Butsko thought.

FIVE . . .

Meanwhile, back at Twenty-third Infantry Regiment Headquarters, Colonel Bob Hutchins sat behind his desk, glancing through reports, communiqués, orders from higher headquarters, messages from subordinate commanders, and supply requisitions. Sitting on the desk next to the stack of documents was his canteen, full of white lightning manufactured by his mess sergeant, who had operated an illegal moonshine distillery in Alabama before the war. Occasionally Colonel Hutchins took a sip from the canteen, gritted his teeth, and sucked in air to cool the flames in his mouth. He was five feet nine inches tall and had skinny legs, a flat ass, and a big paunch. His face was puffy and florid, a characteristic common to people who consume large amounts of alcoholic beverages. The white lightning in his canteen was 150 proof.

A voice came to him from the other side of the tent flap. "Sir?"

"Whataya want?" asked Colonel Hutchins.

Major Cobb, the operations officer of the Twenty-third Infantry Regiment, pushed aside the tent flaps and entered Colonel Hutchins's office. "We've received reports of automatic-weapons fire and explosions about a mile in front of our lines, sir."

"Got any idea what it's all about?"

"Well, Butsko's patrol from the recon platoon is still out there."

"It must be them."

"Unless it's a patrol from another outfit that got lost."

"Either way, it's our responsibility." Colonel Hutchins scratched his vein-lined nose and tried to think. "Send the rest of the recon platoon out there right now, and follow up with J Company."

"It might be a trap, sir."

"I'm sure the rest of the recon platoon and all of J Company can handle whatever's there. Tell them to come right back if it gets too hot. Hurry up. If Butsko and his boys are in trouble, we don't want to leave them hanging."

"Yes, sir."

Major Cobb saluted, did an about-face, and marched out of Colonel Hutchins's office. Colonel Hutchins reached for his canteen and took another swig of white lightning.

Captain Shimoyama stormed through the jungle, slicing vines and branches with swipes of his gleaming samurai sword. *"What's going on here?"* he demanded.

He entered a clearing in which a group of his soldiers were gathered and talking excitedly. They snapped to attention at the sound of his voice. Corporal Goto stepped forward.

"I believe we've found the Americans," he said.

"Excellent," replied Captain Shimoyama. "Where are they?"

Corporal Goto pointed toward the darkest part of the jungle. "In there."

"Whereabouts in there?"

"We don't know, sir. We've sent men in to find the Americans, but they haven't come back."

"Sounds like sloppy soldiering to me." Captain Shimoyama turned around and faced Sergeant Kikusaki. "The Americans are right in there." Captain Shimoyama pointed his samurai sword toward the area Corporal Goto had indicated. "Gather

47

the company here, line them up, and have them sweep through."

"What about our men on our flanks, sir? The ones who're trying to encircle the Americans."

"I just told you I want the entire company to converge on this point! Can't you understand plain Japanese?"

"Yes, sir."

Sergeant Kikusaki's face was flushed with anger as he turned around and reached for the headset of the radio, carried by Corporal Teramoto. Captain Shimoyama raised his samurai sword and touched his thumb to the blade. It was razor sharp, and Captain Shimoyama reflected that he hadn't killed anyone with it yet. He'd only worn it as an ornament at staff meetings and on furloughs, but now at last it would drink American blood.

"About four more hours till the sun goes down," Butsko said, looking at his watch. "That's not so long."

Bannon puffed a cigarette. "Depends on what you call *long*, Sarge."

"Fuck you, Bannon. You used to be a nice, quiet kid, but now you can't keep your mouth shut. I think you been hanging around with this stupid fuck too long." Butsko glanced at the reclining Frankie La Barbara.

Bannon didn't feel like arguing with Butsko. He gazed at the bodies of the dead Japanese soldiers that Longtree and Shaw had piled in front of the hole during the lull. Flies swarmed around the bullet holes in the Japanese soldiers' bodies and flew in and out of their mouths. The sun was hot and the bodies would stink in a little while. Bannon wondered if he was going to see the sun go down that night or whether it would set on his corpse.

Longtree was eating rice out of a tin container, when suddenly he stopped. "I hear somebody coming," he said.

Butsko perked up his ears. He heard the sound too. Numerous Japs were headed in their direction. "Well, boys, I guess this is it," he said. "Get ready. You remember what I told you, Nutsy?"

"Yo."

"What did I told you?"

"To throw away any hand grenades that landed in this hole."

"You remembered something. I'm proud of you."

48

"Sssshhhhh," said Longtree.

They rested the barrels of their submachine guns on the bodies of the dead Japanese soldiers, except for Nutsy, who kept his hands empty and ready to throw hand grenades. They heard Japanese soldiers scrambling through the jungle, looking for them.

"Don't fire until they see us," Butsko said.

Flies buzzed around the dead Japanese soldiers, and mosquitoes swarmed over the GIs as they lay in the muck at the bottom of the hole. The Japanese soldiers came closer. The GIs saw pale green Japanese uniforms moving behind the leaves and branches of the jungle. The Japanese soldiers pressed forward and burst through the dense foliage. Three of them looked around and spotted their dead comrades. They babbled excitedly to each other and pointed to the corpses.

"Get them!" Butsko yelled.

The GIs opened fire with their submachine guns and the three Japanese soldiers were flung backward by the fusillade of bullets. Other Japanese soldiers babbled in the nearby jungle. Then the jungle fell silent.

Longtree turned to Butsko. "They're trying to creep up on us."

"That's because they're a bunch of slant-eyed, yellow-bellied creeps. Shoot them as soon as they get close. You ready, Nutsy?"

"Hup, Sarge."

The GIs waited, their submachine guns ready. They knew the Japs were drawing closer with every passing second. They also knew they were outnumbered astronomically. They expected to become casualties within the next half hour.

Longtree's eyes and ears were a shade sharper than everybody else's and he spotted the first Jap, ten yards away to his left, crawling through the underbrush. The Jap wore a soft cap with flaps down to his shoulders, to protect him from the sun, and Longtree thought the top of the cap would make a dandy target. He aimed his submachine gun, took a deep breath, and squeezed the trigger.

The submachine gun bucked and stuttered in his hands, and the head of the Japanese soldier blew. apart, blood and brains splattering everywhere. Longtree let go of the trigger and smiled with satisfaction. Maybe he was going to die, but he'd take a lot of enemy soldiers with him.

"What you fire at?" asked Butsko.

"A Jap."

"You hit him?"

"Yep."

"Good man."

They heard Japanese soldiers calling out to each other, and then there was silence again. The GIs knew that the Japs were trying to zero in on the sound of the submachine-gun fire that they'd heard. Longtree saw movement near the Japanese soldier he'd just shot. Another Japanese soldier had seen the body and was crawling forward to find out what had happened. Evidently he couldn't see that the soldier in front of him was dead and that his head was blown off. The live Japanese soldier crawled closer, pausing every few seconds to listen and look around, but the GIs were still and the Jap saw nothing. The Jap continued his snakelike progression and drew close to the dead soldier. Now he could see the blood and brains everywhere, and the neck without much of a head left.

The Japanese soldier opened his mouth to speak, and Longtree pulled the trigger of his Thompson submachine gun. One bullet clipped the Jap on the shoulder, the second flew into his open mouth, and the third blew off the top of his head. The Jap collapsed onto his back, never to move again.

"Got another one," Longtree said.

Butsko grunted. The others continued to search the jungle. They didn't have to worry about their rear, because they had the huge boulder there, but they were vulnerable from every other direction. Their faces were covered with perspiration and their uniforms were plastered to their bodies. They caressed the triggers of their submachine guns and waited for the next Jap to show his face.

The jungle became quiet, and the GIs knew that Japs were trying to find them. Longtree heard the crackle of a twig and turned to the right. He saw something move in the bushes on Bannon's side. Longtree pointed in that direction, and Bannon focused his eyes on the spot. He saw the leaves shake, although there was no wind. The leaves shook again, and Bannon realized they were festooned on the helmet of a Japanese soldier. Then Bannon saw movement to the left of the Japanese soldier. Two of them were crawling forward. Bannon held up two

50

fingers in front of Butsko's face.

"Wait till they get closer," Butsko whispered.

Bannon nodded and turned to face the two Japanese soldiers. He leveled his submachine gun at them and paused. The one on the right wore the helmet with leaves stuck into it, and the other wore a soft cap with flaps down to his shoulders. The two Japanese soldiers stopped and the one on the right raised his head to take a look around him. His face moved from side to side, and then it stopped suddenly as he distinguished the pile of his dead comrades and something that resembled the barrel of a gun.

Bannon pulled the trigger, and the Jap's face disintegrated into a bloody gruesome mess. The bullets sent the Jap's helmet flying into the air, and the suddenness of the shots made the other Japanese soldier flinch and hug the ground.

The Japanese soldier shouted something. Another Japanese soldier replied. Bannon fired a burst at the Japanese soldier next to the one he'd just killed, but the live one was too close to the ground.

Butsko knew that the live Jap was shouting the position of him and the other GIs, and he had to be shut up. Since bullets couldn't do it, Butsko reached for one of his hand grenades, pulled the pin, let the lever go, and hurled it at the Jap, who was in the middle of a sentence when the grenade plopped down beside him. The Jap stopped talking abruptly and looked at the grenade for a split second, and then it exploded in a fiery flash. The Japanese soldier was blown to bits, along with the foliage around him. Trees crashed against other trees and a cloud of smoke rose into the air.

One less Jap, Butsko thought. *I wonder how long it'll take for the rest of the cocksuckers to find out where we are.*

SIX . . .

Sergeant Larry Cameron from Brummit, Arkansas, heard the explosion in the distance and held up his hand. He was leading the rest of the recon platoon in the search for Butsko and his patrol, and he and the recon platoon were in no-man's-land, about a half-mile from the Twenty-third Infantry Regiment's front line.

"You guys, take a break," Sergeant Cameron said. "I'm gonna try to see what's going on."

The men dropped to the ground and took out their packs of cigarettes. Cameron looked around for a low-hanging branch, found one, and jumped up, grasping it with both his hands. He pulled himself up to the branch, placed his knee on it, stood, and reached for the next branch over his head.

Cameron was six feet one inch tall, lean and rangy, with red hair and bulging green eyes. He was only twenty-five years old but looked forty because he'd seen too much war. He'd been a nice young man when he enlisted, but now was a rotten son of a bitch, like most of the men in the recon platoon.

He climbed higher up in the tree, biting his lower lip, hoping he wouldn't fall out of the tree. He wished Jimmy O'Rourke were there, because O'Rourke had been a movie stuntman in Hollywood before the war, and he usually did all the fancy tree climbing for the recon platoon. But O'Rourke had been shot in the guts on Hill 700 during the big Jap offensive and was recuperating in a hospital someplace far behind the lines.

Cameron ascended to the higher branches of the tree; before him stretched a sea of green treetops. He raised his binoculars and scanned the jungle from right to left, looking for something that might indicate the presence of Butsko's patrol.

Then he saw it: a faint cloud of blue-black smoke to the northwest of where he was. Could that be the smoke from the explosion he'd just heard? It was in the direction of the automatic-weapons fire reported by front-line observers and relayed to Major Cobb. Cameron took out his map and estimated the coordinates of the smoke. It might be some natives roasting a pig, but he didn't think so. Most natives had fled that part of the jungle long ago.

A burst of automatic-weapons fire echoed over the treetops. Cameron wished he had Longtree along, because Longtree was good at locating the sources of sounds, but Longtree was with Butsko. Cameron cocked his head, and it appeared to him that the automatic-weapons fire was coming from the direction of the smoke.

He might be wrong, but it seemed like a reasonable course of action to head in the direction of the smoke. He had no alternatives, anyway. Scrambling down the tree, he saw the men below him, sprawled on grass and leaves, smoking cigarettes. He dropped to the ground in their midst.

"Let's go," he said. "I think I know where they are."

Another Japanese soldier lay dead in the area of the hole where Butsko and his men were lurking. They'd let the Jap get real close before ripping him apart with submachine-gun fire, and now the Jap lay still, blood oozing from holes in his face.

The jungle was alive with the sounds of Japanese soldiers drawing their noose tighter. Every time the GIs killed a Jap, it permitted the other Japs to home in on the GIs' position a little more. Japs shouted to each other in the jungle, and their voices sounded as if they weren't more than five or ten yards away.

"Don't fire until they're right on top of us," Butsko said softly. "Otherwise we'll just show them where we are."

Longtree pointed to a bush. Butsko followed his finger and saw two slanted eyes peering out from underneath it. Butsko shook his head, indicating that all should hold their fire. He wondered what the Jap was thinking, because all the Jap could see were heaps of his buddies lying around the jungle. The Jap took off his hat, raised it on a stick, and waved it around, trying to be cute, hoping he'd draw some fire. Butsko grinned. The Jap put his hat back on and crawled out from underneath the bush, keeping his ass and nose close to the ground. He crept close to his buddy, who lay bleeding nearby, shook him, and said something, but his buddy didn't reply. The Jap crawled closer to his buddy's head and saw there wasn't much of it left. Grimacing, the Jap got low to the ground again and looked around. He saw two of his other buddies lying near the hole, but he couldn't see much of the hole. He hesitated and pursed his lips in thought, then shouted something in Japanese.

A voice answered from several yards away. Another Jap crawled into view. The first Jap pointed to the dead bodies in front of the hole. The second Jap nodded, and both of them crawled toward the hole. They wanted to see what had happened to their friends.

In the hole Butsko winked at Bannon and pulled out his bayonet. Bannon withdrew his bayonet, too, and so did Longtree. Shaw held his submachine gun ready, and Nutsy was poised to throw hand grenades.

The Japs crawled closer, inch by inch, glancing in all directions, being extremely cautious. They reached the bodies of their friends and prodded them, trying to figure out why they were laid end to end the way they were.

Suddenly four hands reached over the dead Japs and grabbed the two live ones, who shouted in alarm. The Japs had been taken by surprise, and before they knew what was happening they were dragged into the hole. Butsko held one Jap with his left hand and drew back his right, slashing forward with his Ka-bar knife and cutting the scream out of the Jap's throat.

Bannon held the other Jap while Longtree ripped his guts out. A foul odor from the Jap's guts filled the ditch, and Butsko wrinkled his nose.

The two Japs were stripped of weapons and ammunition, then thrown out of the hole and piled in front of it to furnish more protection. They heard someone yelling in Japanese not more than twenty or thirty yards away.

"What is the delay?" said Captain Shimoyama. "Where are the Americans?"

The soldiers near him kept their mouths shut, because none of them knew. Sergeant Kikusaki didn't say anything either, because every time he opened his mouth, Captain Shimoyama insulted him.

Captain Shimoyama turned to Sergeant Kikusaki. "I just asked you a question!"

"I thought you were talking to everybody."

"I was talking to you!"

Sergeant Kikusaki pointed to the jungle. "The Americans are in there."

"Where in there?"

"I don't know exactly."

"Why not?"

"Because the Americans are well concealed. Evidently there aren't many of them. They're killing our men without us finding out where their position is."

"I see," said Captain Shimoyama, scowling. "So what are we supposed to do, have the entire company killed piecemeal?" He glanced around. "How many men are here?" he asked, then counted them and answered his own question. "Eleven. Good." He pointed in the direction Sergeant Kikusaki had indicated. "You men, form a tight skirmish line and comb that area. The first man who locates the American position will receive a promotion."

Sergeant Kikusaki raised his hand. "May I go with them, sir?"

"It would be wonderful if you'd do something useful around here for a change."

Sergeant Kikusaki pulled his sword out of its scabbard. "Follow me," he said to the men.

Holding his sword straight up and down in front of him, he marched into the jungle, and the men filed in behind him. The thick foliage enclosed them and bugs attacked from all directions. Everything became silent, and Sergeant Kikusaki was happy to be away from Captain Shimoyama.

Sergeant Kikusaki motioned to his men, and they got down onto their stomachs. He signaled again, and they formed a tight skirmish line. Crawling to their center, he waved them forward and led the way, heading toward the sounds of the submachine-gun fire he'd heard.

"A lot of them are headed this way," Longtree whispered.

"Get ready," Butsko said.

They crouched in the hole and heard rustling in the jungle ahead of them. Longtree determined that it was a skirmish line and drew it in the muck. Butsko looked at it and nodded.

"Don't fire until they get on top of us," he said quietly.

The GIs waited, holding their weapons tightly. Nutsy squatted on the balls of his feet, ready to catch and throw hand grenades. Longtree peeked over the bodies in front of him and saw the skirmish line of Japs crawling through the underbrush with another Jap in front of them, carrying a samurai sword in his right hand. Longtree nodded to Butsko. Butsko winked at the other men, trying to instill confidence in them.

Sergeant Kikusaki saw the dead bodies of Japanese soldiers ahead of him and held up his hand. The skirmish line stopped. He narrowed his eyes and examined the area in front of him, counting bodies. It appeared that all the men who'd been reported missing were ahead. That meant the Americans were in the immediate area. Sergeant Kikusaki decided that the best thing to do was report what he'd seen to Captain Shimoyama, who could concentrate all the energies of the company on this small area. "Stay here," he whispered to his men. "Keep an eye on things. I must confer with the captain."

Sergeant Kikusaki turned to crawl back to Captain Shimoyama.

"One of them's trying to get away," Longtree said.

"Stop him," Butsko replied.

The Jap was crawling low to the ground and moving quickly. Longtree wasn't sure he could stop him with bullets, so he yanked a hand grenade from his lapel, pulled the pin, and let it fly.

The gray metal ball crashed through the leaves and bounced on the ground, stopping beside one of the Japanese soldiers. *"Grenade!"* he screamed, staring at it, frozen with fear.

Sergeant Kikusaki crawled away feverishly. The Japanese soldier overcame his fear and rolled to the side in an effort to get away from the grenade. He stood to run away, and Longtree raised himself a few inches, shooting him in the back. The Japanese soldier reached behind him to plug up the holes in his back, then passed out and collapsed.

The grenade exploded, causing the ground to shake, filling the jungle with thunder. Japanese soldiers nearby were blown to bits, and Sergeant Kikusaki felt a sharp pain in his left foot. The pain traveled up his leg to his hip, and he shouted involuntarily, then bit his lip. He crawled as quickly as he could away from the scene, and when he felt safe, he stood up and walked, but his left foot wouldn't support him and he fell down.

Tumbling over, he perched on his knees and looked at his foot. The top of his foot was all right, but blood oozed out of a ragged hole in the sole. *Those damned Americans,* he thought. *They got me.* He spotted a thick stick and used it as a cane, to help himself rise. Limping and leaning on the stick, he made his way back to Captain Shimoyama.

"What happened to you?" asked Captain Shimoyama, an incredulous expression on his haughty face. Near him, sprinkled through the jungle, were twenty-five more men than were there before.

"The Americans threw a grenade, and shrapnel hit my foot."

"A curious place to be hit by shrapnel. Were you holding your foot up in the air?"

"I was crawling back to notify you, sir, of the location of the Americans, when the grenade was thrown."

Captain Shimoyama chortled. "A bizarre wound for my bizarre sergeant. Where are the Americans?"

Sergeant Kikusaki pointed. "Back in there."

"Did you see their position exactly?"

"Not exactly, but we can assume it was within grenade-throwing distance from where I was wounded." Sergeant Kiku-saki gritted his teeth in pain. "By the way, is the medical corporal in the vicinity?"

"You need him?"

Sergeant Kikusaki looked down at the pool of blood forming around his boot. "I believe I do."

"It doesn't look like such a serious wound to me, Sergeant. I'm sure a strong, brave noncommissioned officer such as yourself can keep going without immediate medical attention. Show us where the Americans are and then the medical corporal can attend to your little wound."

Sergeant Kikusaki's leg was numb with pain, and his lips quivered as he replied: "I don't think the wound's so little."

"Who told you that you know how to think, Sergeant? Come, now, and show us where the Americans are. Don't be a cry-baby. We expect more from you than that."

Sergeant Kikusaki glanced around and saw all the men looking at him. It would be humiliating if he refused to do as Captain Shimoyama requested. Japanese sergeants were supposed to be tough guys.

"As you wish, sir," Sergeant Kikusaki said elegantly, with a slight bow. "This way, please."

"I can see them," Longtree said, "and they can see us."

Butsko took a cigarette out of his pack and noticed that he only had three left. Now the situation was really getting desperate. Not only did the Japs know where they were, but he was running out of cigarettes.

"Fill your clips," Butsko said. "If we can stop their first charge, it might take them awhile to regroup."

Shaw spit over the top of the hole. "They're gonna get us anyway."

"Whataya wanna do, Shaw? Surrender?"

"No."

"You wanna commit chop suey–cide, like the Japs do?"

"No."

"Then whataya wanna do?"

"I dunno."

"If you don't know, keep your fucking mouth shut."

Butsko lit the cigarette and inhaled deeply. He believed it wasn't over until it was over. When he'd been buried alive in the Jap tunnels underneath Kokengolo Hill on the island of New Georgia, he'd never thought he'd get out, but the Corps of Engineers found him and Sergeant Cameron and dug them up. Since then he believed there was always hope no matter how bad things got.

Longtree raised his nose in the air and sniffed. "I smell more Japs coming."

"Get ready," Butsko muttered.

Sergeant Kikusaki and Captain Shimoyama crawled forward, with twenty-five men to their sides and rear. Sergeant Kikusaki saw the boot soles of the men he'd left behind to keep watch on the Americans. He also saw blood dripping from leaves and branches, the blood of the Japanese soldier who'd been too close to the last hand grenade.

"This is the place," Sergeant Kikusaki said to Captain Shimoyama. "We're within grenade distance of the Americans."

Captain Shimoyama was horrified. "Right now?"

"Yes, sir."

"They could throw a hand grenade in our midst at this very second?"

"That's right, sir."

"I didn't want to get *this* close! I just wanted to get close enough to see!"

"You have to get this close to see."

"All right, I've seen. Spread the men out and sweep them through this area. I'll go back and send for the others."

"But my foot, sir—"

"Stop worrying about your foot. Carry out your orders. You can worry about your foot later."

Captain Shimoyama turned around and crawled away. Sergeant Kikusaki examined the jungle around him and concluded that the Americans had to be in front of him or slightly to his left and right. He had enough men to cover the whole area if they spread out a little.

"Skirmish line!" he shouted. "Move forward on my signal!"

The new soldiers lined up with the ones already there. Sergeant Kikusaki was impatient, because the pain was becoming worse.

"Hurry!"

• • •

59

"Do you see which one is hollering his ass off?" Butsko asked.

Longtree nodded. "I can see approximately where he is."

"Throw a hand grenade at him."

"Hup, sarge."

Longtree pulled the next to last hand grenade from his lapel and plucked out the pin. He looked in the direction of the Japanese voice, extended his arm behind him, and hurled the grenade. It sailed lazily through the air and disappeared behind the leaves in the trees.

The grenade bounced off a branch, rolled across a thick profusion of leaves, and fell to the ground directly in front of Sergeant Kikusaki's face.

Sergeant Kikusaki blinked his eyes. One moment the space was brown crusty leaves, and the next moment an armed American hand grenade was lying there. His eyes bulging out of his head, Sergeant Kikusaki scooped up the grenade and threw it forward, then pressed his fingers into his ears and lowered his head.

Just before he closed his eyes, he saw something move in the jungle ahead.

It was the butt of Longtree's submachine gun. Longtree saw Sergeant Kikusaki throw the grenade back, and Longtree turned his submachine run around, holding it like a baseball bat, while Nutsy Gafooley crouched behind him, ready to catch and throw it if Longtree swung and missed.

But Longtree didn't miss. The butt of his submachine gun connected solidly with the hand grenade, and it went flying straightaway like a line drive from the bat of Jolting Joe DiMaggio. The grenade shot through the jungle, swished through the leaves, and wasn't deflected by any branches. It landed fifteen yards behind Captain Shimoyama, who was returning to Corporal Teramoto and his radio.

Captain Shimoyama heard the grenade plop onto the ground, but his ears weren't attuned to the sound of the front lines, and he didn't think twice about it. It was just another jungle sound to him—nothing to worry about.

Barrrrooooooommmmmm! The grenade detonated with such ferocious intensity that Captain Shimoyama jumped into the air. He was a fair distance 'from the explosion, but a piece of shrapnel the size of a quarter hit him on the left shoulder and spun him around.

"*I'm hit!*" he screamed as he toppled to the ground. "*Save me, somebody!*"

Corporal Teramoto and several other men were nearby, and they ran to him. "Are you all right, sir?" Corporal Teramoto asked, kneeling down.

Captain Shimoyama was assailed by horrible waves of pain, and the jungle spun around him. "*Get me the medical corporal at once!*"

"Yes, sir!"

Captain Shimoyama heard the sound of people running. He wondered if he was seriously wounded. The pain was all over his upper body. Perhaps he was going to die. He saw his life flash before his eyes: his childhood in Kobe, the military academy, his work on General Hyakutake's staff. *What an end to a brilliant military career*, he thought.

He closed his eyes and fainted from the pain.

The jungle was crawling with Japs. Butsko looked at his watch: It was five o'clock in the afternoon. The sun wouldn't go down for another two hours. It was going to be a tough two hours.

He and his men gripped their submachine guns tightly and were ready for the next onslaught of the Japs, who crawled closer with every passing moment. They were converging on the hole and Butsko realized that he and his men had been spotted. Now it would be bloody and gruesome until the last shot was fired.

Butsko picked up a grenade from the stack that lay beside him. Next to his American grenades were Japanese ones taken from the bodies of deed Japanese soldiers.

"First we'll grenade them," Butsko said, "and then open fire. That ought to make them stop and think for a while. Ready?"

Everyone except Nutsy took out a hand grenade each and pulled the pin. They looked at Butsko, who nodded. He let go the lever of the hand grenade, arming it before he threw it, so that the Japs wouldn't have time to throw it back. Bannon, Longtree, and Shaw did the same. They drew their arms back

61

and tossed the grenades at the Japanese soldiers, who saw the gray orbs of death flying toward them. They scrambled to catch the grenades and throw them back, and the grenades exploded in their faces, blowing off their arms and heads, driving chunks of metal into their chests. Horribly mutilated, they collapsed onto the ground, and the soldiers from the recon platoon rose up and opened fire with their submachine guns.

Like cobras the GIs swung back and forth, spraying the Japs with hot lead. The attack was so sudden that the Japs were taken by surprise. They were peppered with bullets, but some had the presence of mind to fire back. The jungle was filled with flying lead. One Japanese soldier threw a hand grenade, but Nutsy Gafooley was crouching in the back of the hole, waiting for it. He caught it and threw it back, and the grenade exploded in the air over the Japanese soldiers, shrapnel raining down on them.

"Get back!" Sergeant Kikusaki hollered. "Take cover!"

The Japanese soldiers crawled backward trying to get away from the fearsome hail. Although they outnumbered Butsko and his men, the GIs had more firepower because they all had automatic weapons. The Japanese soldiers retreated into the jungle, leaving their casualties behind.

"Hold your fire!" Butsko said.

The GIs ducked and brought their smoking submachine guns into the hole with them.

"Conserve your ammo," Butsko told them. "How much we got left?"

"Two clips," said Longtree.

"One clip," said Bannon.

"About a clip and a half," said Shaw.

Butsko looked at Nutsy. "What about you?"

"I thought you told me just to throw back hand grenades."

"That *is* what I told you. Now I'm asking you how many clips you got left."

Nutsy looked in his ammo pouch. "Five, and about a half of one in my gun."

"Give 'em here."

Nutsy handed over the clips and Butsko passed them out. Now everybody had at least three clips, which wasn't much, because a clip could be fired off in less than a minute.

The jungle was quiet. Butsko wondered what the Japs would do next. He knew what he'd do if he were they. He'd try to blow his enemy out of their hole. He hoped the Japs didn't have any artillery with them, but he knew they had hand grenades. They'd probably try to lob some hand grenades pretty soon.

"Watch out for hand grenades," he told his men. "I think that's what the little slanty-eyed buggers'll try next."

Sergeant Kikusaki was thinking along the same lines as Butsko. The Americans had good cover and could not be struck by bullets, and the thick foliage would not permit the use of mortars. That left hand grenades. His body throbbed with pain as he pulled a hand grenade out of the pouch that hung from his belt. He raised the grenade in the air so his men could see it. They got the message, taking out their own hand grenades. They pulled the rings at the bottoms of the grenades, pulled back their arms, and threw them toward the hole where the Americans were.

Sergeant Kikusaki squealed in pain as he tossed his hand grenade, because the motion aggravated the pain in his leg. The hand grenades floated through the air and dropped into the hole where the Americans were hiding.

"Get rid of them!" Butsko yelled, diving toward one of the grenades.

He picked it up and threw it away in one swift move. The other men did the same, chucking grenades as quickly as they could, sometimes two at a time. The hole was showered with grenades, and the men scrambled to get rid of them, hurling them in all directions; the grenades exploded powerfully, lifting dirt and trees into the air, devastating the jungle and making the ground shake as if an earthquake were taking place. Shaw picked up the last grenade and threw it with all his strength, then dived into the bottom of the hole, banging heads with Longtree on the way down. The collision opened a cut on Shaw's forehead.

Sergeant Kikusaki pressed his face to the ground and tried to make himself as flat as a pancake so that no shrapnel would hit him. Shrapnel, chunks of trees, and entire bushes flew over

63

his head, and clods of earth dropped down on him. He cursed the Americans in the ditch up ahead, because they were being very difficult. They couldn't be hit with bullets, and they threw back hand grenades. More sophisticated tactics would be called for. Sergeant Kikusaki's leg hurt fiercely, but he didn't want to go back for medical attention yet. The Americans in the ditch had become a personal challenge to him. He had to wipe them out, and he would if it was the last thing he did.

"Withdraw!" he shouted.

The jungle was full of smoke, and a few fallen logs were on fire. Sergeant Kikusaki turned around and crawled away from the scene of devastation. His soldiers followed him, leaving behind those blown apart by hand grenades manufactured in their own country.

"They're leaving," said Longtree, peering over the dead bodies in front of him.

"They'll be back," Butsko muttered. He knew the Japs would continue attacking, in increasing numbers, until they won. "Maybe it's time we got out of here. Pick up your ammo and let's hit the fucking road."

"Where to?" Bannon asked.

"Anywhere but here."

"But, Sarge, don't you think we'll be safer here than out on open ground?"

"No, because they know where we are here, and will keep attacking until they wipe us out. If we go someplace else, they'll have to find us again, and maybe we can squeeze out enough time so that it'll get dark before they figure out where we are."

Bannon nodded his head slowly. "Makes sense."

"There's just one little problem," Butsko said, glancing at Homer Gladley and Frankie La Barbara, lying unconscious on the ground. "We're gonna have to leave them behind."

"Leave them behind?" Bannon asked.

Butsko stuck his little finger into his right ear and twisted it. "I think there's an echo in this fucking hole."

"We can't leave 'em behind," Bannon said.

"Who says we can't?"

"I say we can't."

"Who the fuck are you?"

64

Bannon didn't flinch or back down. "Who the fuck are *you?*"

"There goes that fucking echo again."

Shaw wiped blood off his forehead. "I don't think we should leave Frankie and Homer behind."

"Neither do I," added Nutsy Gafooley.

"Me neither," said Longtree.

They all looked at Butsko as if he were utterly loathsome, but Butsko was used to that. "You guys are sick in your heads," he told them. "We're in this fix because we been lugging them two nitwits all over the jungle, and we won't get out of here unless we leave them behind. They'll probably die anyway, so what does it matter?"

Nutsy Gafooley jutted his stubbled chin forward. "They're not gonna die anyway. If they see a doctor within the next twenty-four hours, they'll be just fine."

Butsko looked around. "Where's the fucking doctor? I don't see no fucking doctor. You guys are like a bunch of sentimental old ladies. You'd rather see all of us die than just those two, who'll probably die anyway."

"They're not gonna die anyway!" Nutsy said emphatically.

Butsko looked at him and grimaced. "Who are you, God? How do you know who's gonna live and who's gonna die?"

"I'm not the one playing God. You're the one playing God. You're the one who wants to decide who's gonna live and who's gonna die."

Butsko closed his eyes and shook his head. "I'm so fucking sick of you guys, I can't believe it."

"Let's take a vote," Bannon said.

Butsko took off his soft cap and hurled it with all his strength at the ground. "A vote! What in the hell do you think this is, the Boy Scouts?" He pointed both of his thumbs at his chest. "I'm in charge here! What I say goes! Saddle up and move the fuck out!"

They all shook their heads and made no effort to get up.

"I said *move!*"

"We're not moving unless we take Frankie and Homer with us," Bannon said.

"This is insubordination in the face of the enemy!" Butsko screamed.

65

Nutsy wrinkled his nose at Butsko. "So go ahead and court-martial us, you big gorilla."

"What!"

Butsko dived on top of Nutsy Gafooley with the intention of beating him to death. The others jumped Butsko and tried to pin back his arms, but Butsko was a mighty and powerful man. The GIs struggled with each other, rolling around in the bottom of the watery hole, cursing and sweating, and somebody stepped on Frankie La Barbara's stomach by mistake, bringing that stalwart fighter out of his coma.

Frankie opened his eyes and saw fighting all around him. Shaw stepped on his leg. The GIs pushed Butsko backward, and Butsko fell on top of Frankie.

"Halp!" Frankie yelled. "Yaaaahhhhhhhhhh!"

Sergeant Kikusaki and his men had retreated from the scene of the fighting, and now were gathered around in a small clearing. Sergeant Kikusaki took a hand grenade out of his pouch and stopped when he heard loud American voices coming from the direction from which they'd just come. *Sounds like they're fighting among themselves*, he said to himself. *How very odd*. It would be an ideal time to attack. But he couldn't attack because he'd called all his men back so he could talk with them.

He raised the grenade up to the level of his chest and perched it on his fingertips so that his men could see it. "We must employ a new tactic against the Americans," he said. "We have observed how they threw our own grenades back at us. They were able to do this because we threw our grenades immediately after arming them. We must arm our grenades, hold them for three seconds, and then throw them. In that manner the grenades will explode before the Americans can throw them back. Does everyone understand that? Is that clear?"

A young private with a pimply face raised his hand timorously.

"Yes?" asked Sergeant Kikusaki.

"What if the grenade explodes before we are able to throw it?" the young private asked.

Sergeant Kikusaki turned down the corners of his mouth. "That question is not worthy of a Japanese soldier," he replied.

• • •

Bannon, Longtree, Shaw, and Nutsy Gafooley finally succeeded in pinning down Butsko, who bucked and twisted but couldn't get loose. "If we ever get out of this mess," Butsko said, "I'll kill you all!"

Bannon was sitting on Butsko's chest. "Calm down, Sarge," he said.

"I am calmed down! You calm down yourself! This is *gross* insubordination in the face of the enemy! Your asses are gonna be in slings if we ever get out of here."

"First let's get out of here," Bannon said. "The way I see it, if you don't wanna take Frankie and Homer with us, then you can go alone, and the rest of us'll take Frankie and Homer."

"You mean we'll split up?" Butsko asked.

"You got it, Sarge."

Butsko laughed. "Are you kidding me? You guys couldn't survive five minutes on your own!"

"That's the way we want it, and there ain't much time, so let's go. We're gonna let you up now, Sarge. If you give us any more shit, we're just gonna haveta shoot you."

"Shoot me! Why you stinking son of a—"

Longtree cocked an ear. "They're coming back."

Nutsy, who was holding down one of Butsko's legs, jerked his head around. "They're coming back?"

"There goes that echo again," Butsko said.

"We don't have much time," Bannon said. "Let's go!"

"It's too late now," Longtree said. "They'll see us."

Butsko snorted angrily. "You see what happens when you guys do what you wanna do? Everything gets fucked up. Are you gonna hold me down all day? Don't we have Japs to fight, fellers?"

They loosed their grips on Butsko and pulled away. Butsko sat up and rubbed circulation back into his wrists. He was bleeding from a cut lip where somebody had punched him in the melee, and licked away the blood with the tip of his tongue.

"Okay," he said, "we'll split up. I'm sick of you guys and you're sick of me. When we get back to our lines I'll tell everybody that you all died like heroes, because you guys'll never get out of here without me. They'll send medals to your mothers and everybody'll be sad, except me."

Longtree peered over the tops of the dead Japanese soldiers. "They're getting into position for something out there."

Butsko chortled. "You guys don't know what to do, right? You're totally fucking confused, aren't you? You think it's too late to get out of here, right? Well, it's never too late when you're with Master Sergeant Butsko. I'll tell you what we're gonna do. We're all gonna throw our hand grenades out there to make the Japs take cover, and then, while they're taking cover, we hightail it out of here, got it?"

"Got it," said Nutsy Gafooley.

"Don't talk to me, you fucking traitor."

"But you just asked if I got it!"

"I said don't talk to me. I'll do the talking. You traitors just do as you're told, got it?"

"Got it," said Nutsy.

Butsko stared at Nutsy and felt overwhelmed by the urge to kill.

Longtree lowered his head. "The Japs are getting closer."

This distracted Butsko from Nutsy Gafooley.

"Good," Butsko said. "We'll kill more of them that way. Get your grenades ready. We'll throw them on the count of three."

The GIs grabbed hand grenades and pulled the pins, poising themselves and waiting for Butsko's count.

Butsko looked around and saw that the men were ready. "One," he said, *"Two ... three!"*

They threw their grenades as far as they could, then ducked down in the ditch. Japs shouted warnings in the distance, and then the grenades detonated, causing even greater devastation in that part of the jungle. The few trees still standing were torn apart, and huge craters were blown out of the earth. One Jap was killed two were wounded, and the rest hugged the ground, shaken but not harmed.

In the ditch Butsko picked up his submachine gun. "So long, fuckheads. It's been nice knowing you."

He bounded out of the ditch, sheathed with smoke from the grenade blasts, and ran into the jungle to the right of the big rock. Shaw lifted Homer Gladley and positioned him across his shoulders, and Bannon did the same with Frankie La Barbara. Nutsy gathered up extra weapons and ammunition, and Longtree gazed over the bodies of the dead Japanese soldiers.

"We ready?" Longtree asked.

"I'm ready," Bannon said.

"Me too," said Shaw.

"I got everything," said Nutsy, glancing around the ditch to make sure he wasn't telling a lie.

Longtree climbed out of the ditch and moved into the jungle to the left of the big rock. The others followed him, and in seconds the jungle and smoke had enveloped them.

Sergeant Kikusaki waited impatiently for the smoke to go away. He wished the wind was blowing, but it was one of those still, hot days that followed each other in relentless succession on Bougainville. He looked down at his foot: It wasn't bleeding anymore, but it still hurt considerably. It was probably infected, but he couldn't worry about that right now.

Gradually the smoke cleared and Sergeant Kikusaki could see the big rock in back of the hole where the Americans were. The time had come to kill those Americans. They'd made enough trouble. Sergeant Kikusaki held up his hand grenade so all their men could see it. He pulled the ring on the bottom and began counting. His men imitated him. On the count of three, Sergeant Kikusaki hurled his grenade and watched it arc through the jungle, landing on one of the bodies in front of the American position and then bouncing into the hole where the Americans were. The air filled with dark streaks as the grenades thrown by his men flew through the air. They landed in or around the hole where the Americans were, and Sergeant Kikusaki lowered his head, a smile on his face.

The grenades exploded with such power that they cracked the gigantic boulder behind the hole. The dead Japanese soldiers who'd been stacked in front of the hole were blown all over the jungle, and the hole was deepened and widened until it was four times its former size.

Sergeant Kikusaki picked up his samurai sword and waved it through the air. "Forward!" he screamed. "Attack! *Banzai!*"

"*Banzai!*" shrieked his men as they jumped up and lunged forward, carrying their long Arisaka rifles with bayonets affixed to the ends. They charged through the jungle, and Sergeant Kikusaki limped after them, slashing branches out of his way with his sharp samurai sword.

"*Banzai!*" shouted his men as they closed with the hole. They jumped over craters blown out of the ground by grenades, and over trees that had been knocked down. Their dead comrades who'd been lying in front of the hole were obliterated, their bones and chunks of flesh lying everywhere, and the Japanese soldiers charged through them, only a few feet now from the edge of the hole, and they angled their rifles and bayonets downward to stab the American soldiers inside, expecting the Americans to rise up and meet the attack at any moment.

But no Americans rose to meet the attack. The Japanese soldiers in the front rank stopped at the edge of the hole and looked inside, seeing nothing except dirt. The Japanese soldiers in the second rank crashed into the Japanese soldiers at the edge of the hole, and they all toppled into it, fighting and clawing at each other.

"Kill them all!" shouted Sergeant Kikusaki, hopping forward on one leg, swinging his samurai sword through the air.

He approached the edge of the hole, looked down, and saw the squirming bodies of his men. It looked as if his men were overpowering the Americans, and then he realized he was looking at pale green uniforms of the Japanese army but not the dark green of the American Army uniform or the camouflage cloth used by the American Marines.

"Stop it!" he yelled. *"Get out of that ditch!"*

The men who'd been in the second rank couldn't understand why he was telling them to stop, but his voice made them pause long enough to see that they were fighting with each other. Sheepishly they let each other go and stood, looking down into the hole for the remains of the Americans, who they presumed must have been blown to bits by the hand grenades; but they saw nothing except their feet. They climbed out of the hole and Sergeant Kikusaki leaned over the edge so that he could see inside. The hole was empty. The Americans had disappeared.

Where are they? Sergeant Kikusaki asked himself. *What happened to them?* He knit his eyebrows and realized that the Americans must have snuck away after throwing that last round of grenades.

"They're here someplace, men!" Sergeant Kikusaki said. "Fan through the jungle and track them down!"

The soldiers turned to follow their orders, and Sergeant Kikusaki grabbed the shoulders of one of them. "Go back and tell Captain Shimoyama to come here at once!"

"Yes, Sergeant!"

The soldier gripped his rifle and ran back to find Captain Shimoyama while the other soldiers spread through the jungle, searching for the American soldiers who'd flown the coop.

SEVEN . . .

Sergeant Cameron held his binoculars to his eyes and watched the cloud of smoke rise into the sky. "It's about a mile away, I reckon," he said to Corporal Gomez, the former pachuco from Los Angeles.

"We better get a move on," said Gomez, who was short and husky, with a deeply tanned meaty face.

"I'd better call Lieutenant Thurmond first. *Delane!*"

"Yo!"

"Bring that fucking radio up here!"

"Hup, Sarge!"

Delane ran toward Sergeant Cameron, the platoon walkie-talkie hanging from his neck. He was five nine and had a handsome, clean-cut look when he was shaved, but he wasn't shaved now. He was from New York City, the scion of an old, wealthy family.

Sergeant Cameron turned to him. "See if you can raise

72

Lieutenant Thurmond on that fucking thing."

Delane held the walkie-talkie against his face and pressed the button. The rest of the platoon was lying around the top of the hill, smoking cigarettes and drinking from their canteens. They were florid-faced and drenched with perspiration, because Sergeant Cameron had been setting a fast pace.

Delane made contact with Lieutenant Thurmond and handed the radio to Sergeant Cameron.

"Do you see that smoke up ahead?" Sergeant Cameron asked Lieutenant Thurmond.

"What smoke?"

"Should be northwest of where you are right now."

"I can't see anything except the jungle."

"You might have to climb a tree to see it, or go to the top of a hill."

"I'm not about to climb any trees, and I don't see any hills. You say it's northwest of where I am?"

"Yeah, if you are where I think you are."

"Don't you ever say *sir* to officers, Sergeant?"

"Yes, *sir*."

"That's better. Now, let me think. Hmmmmm. We've been following your trail, and I estimate we're about a mile to three-quarters of a mile behind you. You head for that smoke, and we'll come in right behind you. That make sense?"

"Yes, sir, but I'd just like to suggest that you hurry."

"We are hurrying."

"Well, I thought you'd be closer than you are."

There was silence on the other end for a few moments, then Lieutenant Thurmond spoke. "Let's get something straight, Sergeant: I'm the officer and you're the enlisted man, and I don't have to answer to you, got it?"

"What does that have to do with you and your men dragging your asses? For shit's sake, we've laid out the trail for you. All you have to do is follow the goddamn fucking thing."

There was a pause at the other end, and the earpiece of Sergeant Cameron's walkie-talkie crackled and fizzed. Then Captain Thurmond's voice came through.

"I don't like your attitude, Sergeant."

"I don't have all day to talk with you, sir. Just try to get a move on, sir. If I make contact with the enemy, I'll shoot up

73

a flare so you can see where we are, sir. Get the picture, sir? Over and out, sir."

Sergeant Cameron handed the walkie-talkie back to Craig Delane. "Everybody up! Let's get this show on the road!"

Butsko lay underneath a bush in the thickest part of the jungle and was happier than a pig in shit. He'd gotten away from the others and was confident that he could get back to his lines alone. Glancing at his watch, he saw that it was six o'clock. In another hour or so it would start getting dark. The Japs would never find him. All he had to do was sit tight for another hour.

Bugs flew around his face and he brushed them away. Occasionally one would get through and sting him and he would squash it against his skin. He was a restless man and never liked to stay in one position for long. He glanced at his watch, and the hands were moving too slowly. *There aren't any Japs around here,* he thought. *Maybe I can get rolling now. The sooner I get back to the regiment, the sooner I can get a good meal and bum some cigarettes off somebody.*

He inched forward, paused, and heard only the normal sounds of the jungle. Everything seemed okay. Japs weren't in his vicinity. He crawled out from underneath the bush and rose to his knees, scanning from side to side. Nothing moved. The coast was clear. He drew himself to his full height and walked forward in a crouch, holding his submachine gun in both hands with his right forefinger wrapped around the trigger, just in case, but he thought he was perfectly safe, all alone in that part of the jungle.

He moved through the jungle quickly but not too silently, because he didn't think any Japs were nearby. He wasn't making a racket—Butsko was too skilled an old soldier for that— but it wasn't as if Japs were close and he had to make no sound whatever.

This is what he thought as he slid down the side of an incline, heading toward a dark little valley. *I'm free,* he said to himself happily. *Them other fucking assholes only bog me down. They cramp my style and get in my way. I'd be back at regiment right now, eating Spam and beans, if it wasn't for them. They'll never make it back without me. They can't func-*

74

tion at all without me. They'll probably get killed, and it'll serve 'em right.

A little voice inside Butsko's head told him to get into the thick part of the jungle, where he couldn't be seen, but he was in a hurry and could make better time on the trail he was on. *There ain't no Japs around here,* he said to himself. *I've left them goddamned Japs far behind me, because I'm one smart motherfucker.*

The trail rose, and Butsko paused next to an old jungle tree whose trunk was six feet thick and covered with vines. A big jungle rat dived into a hole near the roots of the tree, then raised his head and looked up at Butsko.

Butsko reached for his package of cigarettes and saw that he had only one left. He pulled it out and lit it with his new Zippo, his old Zippo having been lost somewhere in the jungles of Guadalcanal. He inhaled the cigarette and watched the molten red sun sinking lower on the horizon. *What a beautiful sight,* Butsko thought. *It's so nice not to have them other assholes hanging around me all the time, bothering me, pissing me off. I never have any time to think when they're around. They all give me a big pain in the ass.*

Butsko was so enchanted with his view of the setting sun that he didn't notice the figure inching toward him on the other side of the tree. He didn't see the butt of the Japanese Arisaka rifle rise into the air behind him, and he didn't hear it streak through the air toward his head. He felt it connect with his skull, but only for a moment. The sun exploded and made tiny flickering stars as he crumpled to the ground.

Sergeant Kikusaki sat in the deep hole, resting his back against one of the walls, as Captain Shimoyama approached, his right shoulder bandaged underneath his torn and bloody shirt. Captain Shimoyama was followed by a pack of soldiers, among them Corporal Wachi, the company medic.

Captain Shimoyama looked around at the devastated jungle. It appeared as if a huge struggle had taken place in the area. He peered into the hole and saw only Sergeant Kikusaki.

"Where are the Americans?" Captain Shimoyama asked.

"Gone, sir,"

"Where are they?"

"I don't know, sir."

"How did they get away without you seeing where they went?"

"They threw hand grenades and fled in the ensuing confusion."

Captain Shimoyama put on a stern face. "I thought you were a seasoned combat veteran, Sergeant Kikusaki. One does not expect seasoned combat veterans to become confused just because a few hand grenades went off."

"It would have been interesting to see what you would have done," Sergeant Kikusaki said with a sour smile.

Captain Shimoyama raised his eyebrows. "Don't you stand when you speak to officers?"

"I can't stand. Shrapnel in my foot. Remember?"

Captain Shimoyama turned to Corporal Wachi. "Take care of his foot."

Corporal Wachi jumped into the hole and unlaced Sergeant Kikusaki's boot.

"Ouch!"

"That hurt?"

"Yes!"

Captain Shimoyama placed his hands on his hips and stood on the edge of the ditch. "Really, Sergeant, how can you expect the medical corporal to help you if you insist on shouting and squirming like a child?"

Corporal Kikusaki clenched his teeth as Corporal Wachi removed his boot and peeled off his stocking. A terrible odor filled the air.

Captain Shimoyama took a step backward. "You should bathe your feet more often," he said, wrinkling his nose.

Corporal Wachi adjusted his wire-rimmed spectacles and moved his face closer to the bottom of Sergeant Kikusaki's foot. "I do believe it's infected," he said. "That's where the foul odor is coming from. I'll have to cut the infected flesh away, I'm afraid."

"Oh, no," said Sergeant Kikusaki.

Captain Shimoyama smirked. "Can't tolerate a little pain?"

Sergeant Kikusaki closed his eyes and tried to calm down, because he was tempted to yank out his Nambu pistol and shoot Captain Shimoyama, and that wouldn't do in front of so many witnesses.

76

Corporal Wachi took out a match and a small tin bottle filled with alcohol. He lit the wick at the top of the bottle and held his surgical knife over the flame to sterilize it. He had no painkilling drugs or antibiotic medicines, because the Japanese high command believed that that stuff was for sissies. The Japanese had contempt for the US Army because the Americans fussed so much over their wounded.

Captain Shimoyama gazed into the jungle. His shoulder wound hurt, but it wasn't as deep a wound as Sergeant Kikusaki's, and it hadn't become infected yet. He felt tougher than Sergeant Kikusaki as he wondered where the Americans were. He figured the Americans would run into his men sooner or later, because his men had encircled that part of the jungle and were closing in on it at that very moment.

Corporal Wachi cut into Sergeant Kikusaki's skin, and Sergeant Kikusaki fainted from the sudden incredible pain.

This did not escape the eyes of Captain Shimoyama. "It appears that our brave sergeant cannot hold up under a little pain," he said, derision in his voice.

"Somebody's coming," said one of his soldiers.

Captain Shimoyama jumped into the hole and ducked his head, just in case. His men dropped to their stomachs and turned toward the direction of the sound. Four Japanese soldiers pushed their way through the jungle and became visible. In their midst was a gigantic American soldier, his hands tied behind his back and a big bloody lump on his head.

"What have we here?" asked Captain Shimoyama, climbing out of the ditch.

"We caught this American soldier, sir."

"Where?"

The Japanese soldier pointed with the barrel of his Arisaka rifle. "That way."

"He was alone?"

"Yes, sir."

"How very interesting." Captain Shimoyama approached the American soldier to get a closer look. He'd never seen a live American soldier close up before. This one had enormous proportions, and Captain Shimoyama had to look up to him. Dried blood was on the American soldier's cheek and defiance was in his eyes, but Captain Shimoyama had contempt for him, because the Japanese believed that to be captured alive was the

77

greatest dishonor that could befall any man.

Captain Shimoyama wished he could speak English so he could interrogate the American soldier. He knew the American soldier had valuable information that Captain Shimoyama could use. He'd have to radio Colonel Akai and tell him that the American soldier had been caught; then Colonel Akai could send an interpreter for the interrogation.

"Corporal Teramoto!"

"Yes, sir!"

"Radio Colonel Akai's headquarters and notify him that we have this prisoner here!"

"Yes, sir!"

Captain Shimoyama stared at the American soldier, amazed at his size. The American soldier was twice as broad as Captain Shimoyama, and his bicepses were as thick as Captain Shimoyama's thighs. The American soldier glowered at Captain Shimoyama, not attempting to hide his hatred. Captain Shimoyama thought the American was being impertinent, because he had permitted himself to become a prisoner of war, and that was something to be ashamed of. The American obviously was too stupid to feel shame. He had none of the finer sensibilities of Japanese soldiers. Captain Shimoyama didn't like the haughty expression in the American soldier's eyes. He drew back his fist and punched the American soldier in the mouth.

It was like punching a brick wall. Captain Shimoyama's knuckles crackled and the American soldier's lower lip split open, but the American soldier didn't flinch. Captain Shimoyama shrieked with pain and danced up and down, waving his damaged hand in the air. Then he became aware that all of his men were looking at him. He stopped dancing, stiffened, and placed his aching hand at his side.

"Tie the prisoner to a tree!" he shouted. "See that he's watched at all times! My temporary headquarters will be right here!" He looked into the ditch and saw that Sergeant Kikusaki was still unconscious. "Who is the next ranking enlisted man after Sergeant Kikusaki?"

"Sergeant Atsugi, sir."

"He is the new first sergeant of this company! Send for him at once!"

The soldiers were confused. They didn't know which one of them should go. Captain Shimoyama pointed to Private Sato.

78

"You, find Sergeant Atsugi!"

"Yes, sir."

Captain Shimoyama felt tired. His shoulder ached and so did his hand. He thought he might have broken a knuckle. Jumping into the big hole, he sat as far away from Sergeant Kikusaki as possible. Corporal Wachi applied a bandage to Sergeant Kikusaki's foot, and it became suffused with blood before it could be taped down.

"How is he?" asked Captain Shimoyama.

"He should be all right if the infection doesn't return."

Corporal Teramoto jumped into the ditch, carrying his field radio. "I have Colonel Akai's headquarters, sir."

"Give me the headset."

Corporal Teramoto knelt beside Captain Shimoyama and handed him the headset, which Captain Shimoyama adjusted on his head. Captain Shimoyama identified himself, and then Colonel Akai's voice crackled through the airwaves.

"What is it, Shimoyama?"

"I have taken a prisoner, sir!"

"Is he well enough to be interrogated?"

"Yes, sir. He has no serious wounds and can even walk."

"Excellent. Send him to my headquarters at once."

"Um...I don't think I can spare the men, sir. I have over thirty casualties—including myself, I might add—and there are still Americans in the vicinity."

"You've made contact with the Americans?"

"Yes, sir."

"Well, what happened?"

"We're still searching for them. They're around here someplace. But we have the prisoner, sir!"

"Do you mean to say you have over thirty casualties and all you have to show for them is one American prisoner?"

"Yes, sir."

"You evidently are not a very skilled combat commander. I ought to relieve you of command, but I have a shortage of company commanders as it is. If you've made contact with the Americans, why haven't you wiped them out?"

"They've been very elusive, sir. Evidently there aren't very many of them, and the jungle is vast. It's been difficult to locate them."

"Can't be that difficult. You merely surround them and kill

79

them. It's getting dark now. Don't let them slip through your lines tonight."

"Yes, sir."

"If you do, I shall relieve you of command. Is that clear?"

"Yes, sir."

"Over and out."

EIGHT . . .

The molten copper sun hung low on the horizon, and the trees made long shadows in the jungle. Longtree crawled forward, trying to find the path to safety for himself and the men with him. He knew the area was full of Japs, but he and the others hadn't encountered any yet.

Silently he glided over the ground, making no noise, peering through ferns and leaves, trying to see Japs. He could hear Japs in the vicinity but couldn't see them yet. Behind him were Shaw and Bannon carrying Homer and Frankie La Barbara, with Nutsy bringing up the rear.

If they didn't have Homer and Frankie, they could probably break through. They all knew that, but they couldn't bring themselves to desert their buddies, although they knew a time might come when they'd have to. That time might be approaching right now. It sounded as if a lot of Japs were headed their way.

Longtree stopped and peeked at the sun. He could see streaks of it through leaves and knew it would set soon, perhaps in another helf hour. If they could hold out that long, they'd have a chance. Otherwise all the fighting and sacrifices would have been for nothing.

He heard Japanese soldiers moving closer and then caught glimpses of their uniforms. He crawled underneath a bush and watched their progress. They advanced slowly, prodding into bushes with their bayonets, searching behind trees, examining every nook and cranny.

Uh-oh, Longtree thought. *Here they come.* He could see that they were being very thorough, making certain that no Americans would slip past them. Longtree saw a Japanese soldier headed straight for him. The Japanese soldier had round shoulders and the loose, hanging features of a bloodhound. He carried an Arisaka rifle with a bayonet attached, and he parted bushes with his bayonet, peering inside to see if Americans were lurking there. To his left and right were more soldiers, looking behind every leaf, sticking their bayonets into every possible hiding place.

Longtree knew that he and the others were in deep trouble this time. If they had a hole they could fight it out as they had before, but they were out in the open, burdened with two wounded men. He couldn't get away because the Japs would hear him. He'd let them get too close, but he hadn't known there'd be so many of them combing the jungle with such seriousness.

The Japanese soldier continued his slow progress toward Longtree, who wondered whether to shoot him or wait until he was close and knife him to death. The easiest thing would be to shoot him, but that would alert the other Japanese soldiers, who would probably gun down Longtree before he could get away.

He'd have to wait until the Japanese soldier was right on top of him and then kill him quickly so that the others wouldn't suspect anything. Then Longtree would dash back and warn the others. But could he get away? He analyzed the situation and realized he was in trouble no matter what he did. There were simply too many Japs out there.

Longtree was confused. He wished Butsko were there to take charge and tell everybody what to do. *What would Butsko do right now?* Longtree wondered. The answer came to him in a second: *Butsko would throw a hand grenade and run like hell.*

Longtree didn't have any more American hand grenades, but he had three that had been scrounged from dead Japs. He pulled one out of his pants pocket, yanked the ring on the bottom, took a deep breath, and threw it at the Jap with the face like a bloodhound's.

The Jap was bending over a bush, his face buried in its leaves as he searched for American soldiers. The grenade hit his hip and he spun around, astonishment on his face. He looked about, saw nothing, and then glanced down. Three feet in front of him was the grenade. His jaw dropped open.

"Yyyaaaaaaaaa—"

His scream was terminated by the detonation of the grenade. The Japanese soldier's legs were blown off and his torso was lifted ten feet in the air. Longtree jumped up and sped through the jungle, hearing Japanese soldiers shouting behind him. He heard rifle shots, and bullets whizzed over his head. Turning around, he dropped to one knee and fired three bursts from his Thompson submachine gun, emptying the clip.

He exchanged clips, fired two more bursts, then leaped to his feet and ran in the direction of his comrades. After a brief pause the Japanese soldiers returned the fire, their bullets spreading death throughout the jungle. Longtree kept his head down and dived to the ground, landing beside Bannon and the others.

"What happened?" Bannon said.

"Japs! We've got to get out of here!" He pointed in the direction from which they'd come. "That way! Look for some good cover! Let's go!"

They got to their feet. Shaw lifted Homer Gladley to his shoulder, and his knees nearly buckled under the weight. Bannon carried Frankie La Barbara. They made their way back toward the big hole, Longtree hanging back and firing submachine-gun bursts to slow down the Japs.

Bannon and Shaw staggered through the jungle, their progress slow because of the tremendous weight they were carrying. Bullets zinged around them, whacking into tree trunks and making leaves tremble. Nutsy lagged back with Longtree, to help slow down the Japs. Bannon and Shaw knew they could move faster if they got rid of Homer and Frankie La Barbara, but neither could bring himself to toss his burden aside.

The Japanese soldiers advanced cautiously, not knowing what was in front of them, fearful of running into a trap. Gradually the GIs put more distance between themselves and the Japanese soldiers, while the jungle resounded with gunfire and the sun sank lower on the horizon.

"Now what!" screamed Captain Shimoyama, jumping to his feet. He heard the gunfire and leaned in its direction, listening and trying to analyze what he was hearing. Suddenly it occurred to him that the gunfire was headed his way, and for all he knew there might be a hundred Americans out there.

He glanced around nervously and tried to figure out what to do. He had only ten soldiers with him, and that might not be enough to hold off the Americans.

"Retreat!" he said, pointing in the direction opposite the gunfire. "That way!"

Pulling his samurai sword out of its sheath, he ran into the jungle, and his sudden disappearance panicked the men who'd been with him. They fled into the jungle behind him, leaving Butsko tied to the tree, and Sergeant Kikusaki in the big hole.

Painfully and laboriously Sergeant Kikusaki raised himself from where he'd been lying. It didn't surprise him that he'd been left behind, because Japanese soldiers never let themselves be slowed down by their wounded. Sergeant Kikusaki climbed out of the hole and turned in the direction of the gunfire. It sounded quite close, and he spat at the ground when he thought of how Captain Shimoyama had run away like a frightened dog with his tail between his legs. He should have stood his ground and fought, but Captain Shimoyama was a rear-echelon staff officer and didn't have the courage of a front-line soldier. His poor leadership had a bad effect on the men, because they'd run away too.

Sergeant Kikusaki limped in the direction in which Captain Shimoyama and the other men had gone. He spotted a sturdy stick about four feet long lying on the ground, and he bent over to pick it up so he could use it as a cane, but he lost his balance and fell down.

Cursing, he picked up the stick and raised himself. His eyes fell on the American soldier, still tied to the tree. The American soldier looked at him with hatred in his eyes, and Sergeant Kikusaki pulled out his Nambu pistol to shoot the American.

Leaning on his makeshift cane, Sergeant Kikusaki limped toward the American soldier, whose eyes were ablaze with rage, watching his every move. Sergeant Kikusaki stopped when he was three feet in front of the American soldier, checked the clip of his Nambu pistol to make sure bullets were in it, clicked off the safety, pulled back the cocking mechanism, and aimed at the American soldier's face.

Sergeant Kikusaki was surprised, because the American showed no fear. The American knew he was going to die, but instead of shrinking back and closing his eyes, he stared defiantly at Sergeant Kikusaki as if daring him to do it. The American soldier snarled and bared his teeth, straining at the ropes that bound him to the tree, reminding Sergeant Kikusaki of a wild jungle animal.

Sergeant Kikusaki aimed down the barrel of the Nambu and squeezed the trigger.

The American opened his mouth. *"Fuck you and fuck your mother!"* he yelled, his bloodshot eyes bulging out of his head.

Sergeant Kikusaki couldn't understand what he was saying, but the American's loud voice startled him and upset his aim. Sergeant Kikusaki settled himself down and aimed again, squeezing the trigger.

"Up your ass with a ten-inch meat hook, you slant-eyed, yellow bellied Jap cocksucker!"

Sergeant Kikusaki squeezed the trigger all the way back. *Click!*

Sergeant Kikusaki wrinkled his brow. *Must be a faulty round in the chamber,* he thought. There was no time to reload, because the sound of fighting was getting closer. He rammed his Nambu into its holster and pulled his samurai sword out of its scabbard. Gripping the handle in both hands, he raised the samurai sword high in the air, aiming for the American soldier's head, getting his feet set so he'd be able to put maximum power into the blow.

"Go ahead!" shouted the American soldier. *"Fuck you where you breathe, you bastard!"*

Sergeant Kikusaki tensed himself and swung the blade down.

A submachine gun fired a burst close by. Butsko watched

in amazement as the Japanese soldier's chest was blown apart, covering Butsko with blood, guts, and bits of lung, throat, and heart. Butsko leaned to the side and the samurai sword sank into the trunk of the tree a few inches above his head. The Japanese soldier collapsed on top of Butsko.

Longtree leaped into the clearing, holding his submachine gun tight to his waist. He looked left and right and sniffed the air, holding the submachine gun ready to fire again. His eyes fell on Butsko, and he blinked to make sure Butsko wasn't a hallucination.

"Cut me the fuck loose!" Butsko said.

"I don't know if I should," Longtree replied, stalking toward him, still holding the submachine gun ready to shoot.

"What do you mean, you don't know if you should!"

Longtree bent over and picked up the samurai sword. "You deserted us when we needed you, you rotten son of a bitch."

"I just gave you an order! Cut me the fuck loose!"

Longtree grinned evilly. "You wanna get cut loose? Okay, I'll cut you loose." He laid down his submachine gun and raised the samurai sword high over his head.

"Hey," Butsko said, "take it easy, there."

"You're a prick of misery. You never think of anybody except yourself."

"Wait a minute!"

Longtree swung the sword.

Thunk!

Butsko gasped. He thought that Longtree had chopped his head off, but when he opened his eyes he realized his head was where it had always been. The ropes that bound him to the tree were loose. Butsko leaned forward and they fell to the ground.

Bannon and Shaw staggered into the clearing, their faces red from exertion, carrying Frankie La Barbara and Homer Gladley on their backs. To their rear, firing behind them into the jungle, was Nutsy Gafooley. Bannon and Shaw jumped into the big hole and collapsed. Longtree turned away from Butsko and dived into the hole. Butsko jumped to his feet, pulled the samurai sword loose from the tree, scooped up the Japanese soldier's Nambu pistol and ammunition pouch, and dashed toward the hole, diving in headfirst.

"Hiya, guys," Butsko said.

Nobody replied. Nutsy Gafooley backed toward the hole, firing his Thompson submachine gun into the jungle, moving the barrel from side to side, spraying everything in a wide arc in front of him.

"Get in here!" Bannon shouted at him.

Nutsy turned around and jumped into the hole, then kneeled and rested the barrel of the submachine gun on the edge of the hole. The others clustered near him and took aim at the jungle. Butsko picked up the submachine gun that had belonged to Frankie La Barbara and lined up with the other men.

The hole was considerably deeper and wider than before, thanks to the Japanese grenade barrage. It provided much more protection, and the big boulder was still behind them, protecting their rear.

The GIs heard thrashing and cursing in the jungle and tightened their fingers around their submachine guns. Ten Japanese soldiers burst through the foliage all at once, followed by twenty more. The GIs opened fire, raking from side to side with their submachine guns, cutting down the Japanese soldiers, who hadn't realized the GIs were in a hole, waiting for them.

The initial bursts of submachine-gun fire killed eight Japanese soldiers and wounded ten. The rest retreated quickly. The GIs stopped firing. Their ears rang for a few moments. Then they heard the moaning of the wounded Japanese soldiers.

"Bannon," Butsko said, "go get all them Jap weapons and hand grenades, and kill any Jap who ain't dead!"

Bannon turned around and looked at Butsko incredulously. "Who do you think you're talking to?"

"You!"

"Hey," Bannon said, "wait a minute. You deserted us when we needed you, so now you ain't shit around here. You even got yourself captured by the Japs, you big asshole. Frankie La Barbara was right about you all along. We ain't taking orders from you anymore. You oughtta be lucky we even let you stay in this hole with us."

Butsko stared at Bannon and turned purple. Then he quivered with rage and bared his tobacco-stained teeth. *"You can't talk to me like that!"*

"You don't like it, get lost."

"What!"

Butsko lifted his submachine off the parapet, intending to aim it at Bannon and shoot his head off, but he'd only moved it a few inches when he felt the hot mouth of a submachine gun against his temple, making him flinch.

"Hold it right there, scumbag," Nutsy Gafooley said, aiming his submachine gun at Butsko's face.

Butsko was so angry and frustrated he couldn't even speak. Opening his mouth, he sputtered and stuttered, and his face turned green.

"Listen to me," Nutsy Gafooley said. "You'd better cool your motor, because if you don't, I'm gonna turn off your ignition for good."

Butsko thought the top of his head would explode. Never had he encountered such insubordination, and not only that, Nutsy Gafooley was the littlest man in his platoon.

"Calm down, Sarge," Nutsy said. "Wouldn't wanna kill you."

Butsko calculated his chances. Could he whip his submachine gun around and kill Nutsy before Nutsy killed him? He didn't think so, and now the others were aiming their submachine guns at him too. They all looked at him with hatred, and he gave them back the same emotion.

In a sudden melodramatic move Butsko dropped his submachine gun and ripped the front of his shirt open, baring his massive hairy chest. *"Go ahead!"* he yelled. *"Shoot your old sergeant—who's been through hell with you—who's worked his ass off for you . . . go ahead, see if I care!"*

Nutsy Gafooley sneered. "Don't tempt me."

Bannon prodded Butsko's stubbled chin with the barrel of his submachine gun. "We oughtta shoot you for desertion in the face of the enemy."

Shaw jabbed his submachine gun into Butsko's gut. "You wanted to leave Frankie and Homer behind, you rotten sack of shit."

Butsko looked at each of their faces and realized they were very angry at him. It occurred to him that they might actually shoot him! And they'd probably get away with it, because who'd ever know the truth? They'd probably never escape from the Japs anyway, but if they did, they'd just say that Butsko was lost in action.

Butsko held up both his hands. "Now, wait a minute, fellers. Let's be reasonable."

"How reasonable were you when you wanted to leave Frankie and Homer behind?" Bannon asked.

"And how reasonable were you when you deserted us in our time of need?" Nutsy asked.

"And what about all the shit you been giving us lately," Shaw said.

Butsko forced himself to smile. "It's not good to hold a grudge, boys. These are hard times. There's a war on. We need each other."

Bannon shook his head. "We can't trust you, Sarge, because you bugged out on us once, and if you did it once, you'll do it again."

"Not only that," Shaw added, "you nearly shot Bannon, here, a few moments ago."

Butsko made his smile broader. "I was only kidding, fellers."

"Sure you were."

The three GIs set their mouths in grim lines and aimed their submachine guns at Butsko, whose hair nearly stood on end. He realized that they were mad enough to kill him, and he couldn't talk them out of it! He had to do something! His eyes bobbled around as he tried to figure out a way to save his worthless ass. Their fingers tightened on their triggers. Butsko looked over their heads at the jungle behind them.

"Japs!" he screamed.

They spun around and faced the jungle, ready to mow down Japs, and Nutsy Gafooley opened fire before he even saw any Japs, but no Japs charged toward them, and it took a few seconds for them to realize what Butsko had done.

"Okay," said Butsko's voice behind them. "Hold it right there, and no funny moves, please."

They froze, realizing he'd tricked them. Bannon groaned. Shaw spat at the ground. Nutsy wished he'd shot Butsko while he had the chance.

"Drop your guns, boys," Butsko said.

They dropped their submachine guns.

"Now turn around real slow."

They turned around and faced Butsko, who leaned against the dirt wall of the hole, smiling happily, aiming a submachine gun level with their waists.

"Don't ever try to fuck over your old sergeant," he said, "because you'll never do it. You're not smart enough to do it. You're just a bunch of dumb dogfaces and that's all you'll ever be. I can't believe you were actually gonna kill me, after all I've done for you, but now you've kinda put me in a bind. I can't turn you loose because you tried to kill me, so I guess I'm gonna have to kill the pack of you in self-defense."

Bannon smiled in his friendly Texas way. "Hey, Sarge," he drawled, "you didn't actually think we was gonna shoot you, do you?"

"You're damn straight I thought you were gonna shoot me, and if I hadn't outsmarted you, you would've."

"Aw, Sarge," Bannon said, "you don't believe that, do you?"

"You fucking A-well-John I believe it."

"But, Sarge," Bannon continued, "don't you remember that time I save your life on Guadalcanal? You said you owed your life to me and you'd never forget it, remember?"

"I forgot it," Butsko replied. "That was then, and this is now."

Shaw forced himself to laugh. "Hey, Sarge, that's funny, but we gotta stop playing around here. There's Japs in the vicinity."

"Who's playing?" Butsko asked. "I ain't playing. I'm dead serious, and in a few seconds you're gonna be just plain dead. May the Lord have mercy on your rotten, stinking souls."

Nutsy Gafooley shook his head. "People always told me that the son of a bitch was a psycho case, but I always stuck up for him. I always told them that he wasn't really a psycho case; he just acted that way once in a while. Now I realize they were right. The son of a bitch *is* a psycho case."

Butsko chuckled. "For that you're gonna get it first, Nutsy, my boy." Butsko aimed his submachine gun at Nutsy. "Say your prayers, if you know any."

Longtree perked up his ears. "I hear something."

Butsko laughed. "Don't think that old trick is gonna work on me."

"I really hear something," Longtree said, wrinkling his brow.

"And I suppose it's coming from right behind me."

"As a matter of fact, it is."

"And naturally you expect me to turn around, so's you can

get the drop on me, right? Isn't that the way you want it to go?"

"I'm serious, Sarge. Somebody's coming from that direction."

"Sure they are."

Bannon looked worried. "I can hear it too."

"Then how come I can't hear it?"

"Maybe your ears are full of shit."

Butsko shrugged the insult off and aimed his submachine gun at Nutsy, squeezing the trigger, when he heard the sound of a foot on dry leaves behind him. Butsko spun around just as a rifle was fired. He saw the muzzle blast and heard the bullet pass over his head. Dropping down, he aimed his submachine gun at the horde of Japs charging out of the foliage.

Click!

His submachine gun was empty. He yanked the Nambu pistol out of his belt and fired at the lead Jap, bringing him down. The other GIs picked up submachine guns and pulled their triggers, ripping up the Japanese soldiers. The Japanese fired back as they charged the hole, their bullets ricocheting off the rim and zipping over the GIs' heads. The Japanese continued charging until they reached the edge of the hole, and the GIs chopped them down. The Japanese withered before the hail of hot lead, but one jumped into the trench in front of Butsko.

"Banzai!" screamed the Jap, thrusting his rifle and bayonet toward Butsko.

Butsko shot him in the stomach, but the Jap kept coming, his bayonet streaking toward Butsko's heart. Butsko sidestepped, batted the rifle and bayonet out of his way, and slammed the Jap in the face with the Nambu pistol. The Jap's nose split apart and his blood spurt into the air. He fell onto his back and Butsko hit him again, cracking his skull.

Meanwhile the GIs continued firing at the Japanese soldiers, who withdrew into the jungle. One of the Japanese threw a hand grenade, and it landed near the rim of the hole.

"Get down!" Butsko yelled.

The GIs dived to the bottom of the hole, bumping against the unconscious Homer Gladley and Frankie La Barbara. The grenade exploded and its concussion caved in one of the dirt walls, burying Nutsy Gafooley, who coughed and spit and clawed his way to the fresh air while Bannon, Longtree, and Shaw fired their submachine guns and Butsko shot Japs with his Nambu pistol.

Click! Longtree's submachine gun ran out of ammo. He ejected the clip and reached into his bandolier for a fresh one, but the bandolier was empty. Dropping the submachine gun, he picked up one of the Japanese Arisaka rifles lying in the bottom of the hole, pulled back the bolt, and rammed a round into the chamber. He rested the front of the rifle on the edge of the hole, aimed at a Japanese soldier in the jungle, and pulled the trigger. The Japanese soldier flew backward, blood squirting from his throat.

The GIs maintained their steady base of fire as the Japanese soldiers retreated farther into the jungle. The evening twilight made visibility difficult, and the muzzle blasts of weapons were like lightning and thunder.

"Hold your fire!" Butsko said.

The GIs loosened the triggers of their submachine guns and rifles.

Japanese soldiers continued to fire their rifles sporadically. It sounded as though they were retreating.

"They'll be back," Butsko said. "What's the ammunition situation?"

The men counted their remaining clips of ammunition, hand grenades, captured weapons, etc. Butsko remembered the showdown he'd been having with his men when the Japanese attacked. He realized they might try to shoot him and reached for the nearest Arisaka rifle, working the bolt and turning around to face his men.

They saw him make his move and grabbed their own weapons. When the dust settled down, Butsko was aiming his Arisaka rifle at Bannon, while Bannon, Shaw, and Nutsy Gafooley held their submachine guns pointed at Butsko, and Longtree sighted down the barrel of an Arisaka rifle.

There were a few moments of silence in which everybody was ready to open fire, but nobody wanted to fire the first shot. The tension was so intense that it became ridiculous, and Butsko's ugly face creased into a smile.

"I think all of us have been on this stinking island too long," he said, a conciliatory tone in his voice. "We're surrounded by Japs, but it looks like we're fixing to do their job for them. I think we'd better calm down and fight the Japs instead of each other. We can settle our differences when we get out of this mess—*if* we get out of this mess."

Bannon, Longtree, Shaw, and Nutsy Gafooley looked at each other as the jungle grew darker and their faces became swathed in shadows. Nutsy shrugged. Longtree spat over the rim of the hole. Shaw glanced toward the jungle where the Japs had retreated, because he expected them to return at any moment. Bannon looked Butsko in the eye.

"There's just one thing we gotta settle now."

"What's that?"

"We don't wanna hear no more talk about leaving our wounded behind."

"That's okay by me, but I ain't carrying none of the motherfuckers. I got better things to do."

"What if *you* get wounded, big Sergeant?"

"Me get wounded? I ain't gonna get wounded."

"You been wounded before. What if you get wounded again? Who's gonna carry your stinking ass?"

"You just leave me right where I fall, with my bayonet, a rifle, and a clip of ammunition. I'll be just fine."

"What if you're unconscious, big Sergeant?"

"Then it won't make a fuck either way, will it, young Corporal?" Butsko sniffed and wiped his nose with the back of his hand. "I'm getting tired of this conversation. Let's get ready for the Japs. What's the ammo situation?"

NINE . . .

Captain Shimoyama paced back and forth in the jungle twilight. His shoulder ached and he could barely move his left arm, so he clasped his hands behind his back in order to maintain the semblance of military posture.

It had been a catastrophic day for him, and he was so mad he could spit. Like a rooster who'd had his tail feathers plucked out, he stormed across the clearing, then did an about-face and stormed back. His men sat around and watched him solemnly. They thought he was losing his mind.

Captain Shimoyama wanted to drink some sake, but he couldn't afford to get tipsy. He had to keep his mind clear, because he had major decisions to make.

He'd had an American prisoner but lost him. An envoy was on his way from Colonel Akai's headquarters to interrogate the American prisoner, and what would Captain Shimoyama say? That the American had been shot while trying to escape? Yes, that seemed like a reasonable lie. No one would contradict him,

94

because Japanese soldiers would never dare to call their commanding officer a liar. But the truth might get out someday: that he'd turned tail and run away from an American counterattack, leaving his prisoner behind him. Captain Shimoyama knew that the incident would haunt him for the rest of his military career.

On top of all that, he'd lost more than one-third of his company in his day-long efforts to wipe out a handful of Americans. That was the greatest disgrace of all. Now it was night and he could do nothing. If his men couldn't eliminate the Americans during the day, they certainly couldn't eliminate them at night, when it was difficult to see.

Captain Shimoyama glanced around and realized that it wasn't that difficult to see. The full moon shone overhead and he could perceive objects nearly as clearly as during the day. He wondered if he could overrun the Americans now and finish them off once and for all. If he were really clever, he might be able to take one of them prisoner and solve all his problems at once!

His mind became electrified by the prospect of turning his misfortunes around through a series of bold moves in the middle of the night. His brow wrinkled in thought, he sat down at the base of a tree and leaned his back against the trunk. *How should I proceed?* he asked himself. Tactics of various kinds hadn't worked that day. The Americans had been very clever so far. But one fact was clear: He outnumbered the Americans by a factor of five to one, perhaps even ten to one. That meant that he should be able to overwhelm the Americans with the sheer weight of his superior numbers.

Perhaps that's what I should do, he thought. *I'll just concentrate the remainder of my men in front of them and charge. The battle shouldn't last long. Then at last I'll be able to report that I have accomplished my mission, and I might even capture another prisoner.*

Captain Shimoyama stood. "Sergeant Atsugi!"

"Yes, sir!"

"Report to me at once!"

"Yes, sir!"

Captain Shimoyama saw a stout figure arise from the group of men lying around the jungle. The figure walked toward him, and as he drew closer Captain Shimoyama could see the unshaven, surly features of his new first sergeant.

"Sergeant Atsugi reporting, sir!"

"I want you to assemble my entire company right here in this clearing, except for the men standing watch around the American position. We are going to attack the Americans tonight and finish them off for once and for all. Is that clear?"

"Yes, sir."

"Carry out your orders."

Sergeant Atsugi walked away, to get on the radio and call in all the rifle squads still working their way through the jungle. Captain Shimoyama clasped his hands behind his back and paced back and forth, his head inclined toward the ground, feeling confident and happy again, because he was certain that he would soon destroy the Americans in his area and be able to report that fact to Colonel Akai.

Perhaps I shall even lead the attack personally, Captain Shimoyama thought. *Perhaps then I can show my men that I'm not the coward they evidently think I am.*

It was night in the jungle, which glowed spectrally in the light of the full moon. Sergeant Cameron slept at the edge of a clearing a half-mile from where Captain Shimoyama was pacing back and forth. Nearby, other men from the recon platoon also lay in slumber. Surrounding the clearing were six guards, ensuring that no Japs would sneak up on them.

Private Craig Delane, the former rich playboy from New York City, was guarding the trail that led back to the American lines, and he was struggling to keep himself awake and alert. He was tired and the jungle was quiet. It was awfully easy to drift away into dreamland.

He rubbed his eyes and chewed his lips in an effort to hold off sleep. He tried to think interesting thoughts, such as the beautiful debutantes he used to date when he was back in New York. He never screwed any of them, because he'd always been trained to respect women, but now, after nearly three years in the Army, he regretted never trying harder, because he'd always wanted to screw those sweet, giggly girls in their pretty dresses, flowers in their hair. Now he knew what to do. He'd learned that women like to fuck, too, and you just had to be a little persistent, kissing their ears, tickling their boobs, getting them worked up.

If only I knew then what I know now, he thought, and then he froze, because he heard a footstep on the trail in front of him. The jungle became silent again. He wondered if he'd really heard that footstep, or imagined it. Then he heard it again. He aimed his M 1 rifle down the trail.

"Halt—who goes there!" he shouted.

There was a pause, and then someone replied: *"Sergeant Puccio, L Company!"*

"Advance to be recognized!"

The footsteps came closer, and Craig Delane held his M 1 ready to fire, because it might be a sneaky Jap trick. Delane had never met Sergeant Puccio and never heard of him.

A short, stocky figure appeared on the trail, wearing the uniform of the US Army. Delane waited until he was ten feet away and it was clear that the soldier was an American, but Delane had to follow through with the challenging procedure.

"Halt!" said Delane.

The soldier stopped.

"Snow," Delane said softly.

"White," replied the soldier.

"Pass on," Delane said.

The soldier approached, carrying a light field pack and a carbine. "You from the recon platoon?" he asked.

"Yes."

"Where's Sergeant Cameron?"

Delane pointed his thumb over his shoulder. "Back there around twenty feet."

"The rest of J Company's coming through right behind me. Don't shoot anybody by mistake."

Sergeant Puccio walked passed Craig Delane and entered the recon platoon bivouac, looking for Sergeant Cameron, who was a light sleeper and had been awakened by Delane's challenge.

"I'm over here," Cameron said.

Sergeant Puccio angled in his direction, and men from the recon platoon looked up at him, because they'd been awakened also. Sergeant Puccio saw Cameron sitting against a tree, taking out his canteen.

"We're here," Sergeant Puccio said, kneeling beside Sergeant Cameron. "What's going on?"

"Just what you see." Sergeant Cameron took a swig from

97

his canteen. "Where's the rest of your company?"

"They'll be here any minute now," Sergeant Puccio replied.

"Make contact with the enemy?"

"Nope."

"We heard some shooting and explosions. Guess it didn't come from you."

"No, it didn't come from us. It probably came from Butsko and his patrol. Sounds like they're in a jam back in there someplace."

The rest of J Company trudged into the clearing, led by First Lieutenant Ed Thurmond from Denver, Colorado, a ninety-day wonder and former real-estate salesman. Thurmond was a small, wiry man with fierce eyes, and his helmet looked three sizes too big for his head. His eyes fell on Sergeant Cameron and he hustled over to find out what was going on.

"That's okay, you don't have to stand up," Lieutenant Thurmond said to Sergeant Cameron. He knelt between Sergeant Cameron and Sergeant Puccio, sniffed the air, licked his teeth, and gazed into Sergeant Cameron's eyes. "Where's the Japs?"

Sergeant Cameron pointed. "Somewheres over there, I think."

"No contact yet?"

"Not yet."

"Who's been doing all the shooting around here—you know?"

"I reckon it's Butsko and his patrol, fighting Japs."

Lieutenant Thurmond looked around nervously, and Sergeant Cameron thought he resembled a rat about to jump on a piece of cheese.

"Well," said Lieutenant Thurmond, "why don't we go in there and see what's going on?"

"I don't think that's a very good idea, sir," Sergeant Cameron said. "I don't know where the Japs are or where Butsko is, and the visibility is none too good this time of night. We're liable to go off on a wild goose chase."

"I don't think the visibility's so bad. I can see all right. Sergeant Puccio, tell your men to take a ten-minute break; then we'll move out. Sergeant Cameron, you get your men ready to move out."

"But, sir," Sergeant Puccio said. "The men are tired. They need more than a ten-minute break."

"They can't be any more tired than I am, and I don't need

more than a ten-minute break."

Sergeant Cameron took a deep breath and wheezed. He got easily tired of arguing with officers, but sometimes it had to be done. "Sir, we're here to find Butsko, not get in a scrap with the Japs. We're liable to get into a fight that we can't get out of. Butsko and his men might need us someplace else, and we won't be able to help him."

Lieutenant Thurmond sucked one of his teeth. "You got a point there, Sergeant. But how in hell are we gonna find Butsko if we don't go looking for him?"

"We'll just head for the sound of fighting, sir. That's where he'll be."

"I don't hear any sound of fighting."

"You will before long, if Butsko's still alive. And if he's not, it won't make a fuck anyways. For all we know, he might be close to our lines right now. We don't want to get into a war out here for nothing, do we? I mean, there's Japs all in this area, right?"

Lieutenant Thurmond thought it over. He was anxious to save Butsko, because he knew Butsko was Colonel Hutchins's drinking buddy. If he saved Butsko, it would make him look good at Colonel Hutchins's headquarters.

"You're right, Sergeant," Lieutenant Thurmond said. "It takes a real man to admit it when the other feller is right, and that's what I'm doing. We'll rest up here and wait until we hear some fighting before we go farther. If we don't hear anything by dawn, we'll go looking for Butsko. How does that sound, Sergeant Cameron?"

"Makes sense, sir, but I don't think it'll be quiet here all night. I got a hunch that old Sergeant Butsko will get himself into some shit before long, provided he's still alive, of course."

Lieutenant Thurmond turned to Sergeant Puccio. "Post guards. Tell the men they can sack out."

"Yes, sir."

Sergeant Puccio backed off and walked away. Lieutenant Thurmond looked at Sergeant Cameron.

"What was that you just said—that Butsko might not be alive? You think the Japs got him?"

Sergeant Cameron shrugged his wide bony shoulders. "I don't know, sir. There's been a lot of fighting back there in the jungle today. Butsko's only got five men with him, and

99

we know these jungles are crawling with Japs. They mighta got him."

Butsko sat low in the big hole, eating cold cooked rice from a tin container taken from a dead Japanese soldier. Near him, Bannon, Shaw, and Nutsy Gafooley were sleeping. Frankie La Barbara and Homer Gladley still were in comas, the surfaces of their skin cold and clammy. Butsko wished they'd die so that he and the others would have a better chance of getting away.

Longtree's face appeared suddenly over the rim of the hole, and Butsko dropped his rice and fork.

"It's only me," Longtree said. "Relax."

Butsko picked up the fork and wiped it off on his pant leg, which was stained with dried blood and gore. Longtree slithered into the hole, awakening Bannon, Shaw, and Nutsy Gafooley.

"Well?" Butsko asked.

"There's no way out of here," Longtree replied, sitting upright in the bottom of the hole. "The Japs have got us surrounded."

"You think you coulda got through them alone?"

"I dunno. Maybe."

"Maybe you should go for help."

"It's up to you."

Butsko turned to Bannon. "Whataya think?"

"What do you care what I think? You're gonna do what you wanna do anyway."

"Just tell me what you think and cut the bullshit."

"I don't think he can make it back to our lines and return with help in time to make any difference."

Butsko looked at Longtree. "You agree?"

"I think so."

"That's that," Butsko said, placing another forkful of rice into his mouth. "This rice tastes like shit," he said as he chewed, bits of rice sticking to his lips. "Fucking Japs can't do anything right."

Nutsy Gafooley looked off into the jungle. "I bet they attack tonight."

"I bet you're right," Butsko said. "Well, I guess there's only one more thing to talk about."

Bannon snorted. "I got a funny feeling I know what it is."

"Yeah?" Butsko asked, cocking an eye. "What is it?"

"You're gonna say we all don't have to die here and some of us can get away."

Butsko sighed. "Cowboy, you're really getting smart. You actually read my mind. It's true—some of us could get away and live to fight another day, as that old saying goes."

"Hey, Sarge," Shaw said, "how about that old saying that says only cowards run away."

"That's the kind of old saying that fills graveyards."

Bannon looked at the others, then turned to Butsko again. "Well, Sarge, if you wanna go, then go. You been wanting to bug out all day, so go ahead and bug out. One bullshit sergeant won't make much difference either way."

Butsko winked and grinned like an old pirate. "Hey, kid, you got me wrong. I wasn't talking about me. I could never break out of here, because I'm too big and noisy. Too many Japs around, remember? But Longtree could probably get away, and Nutsy might make it, because he's such a little pipsqueak, and—"

Butsko was interrupted by a flying leap from Nutsy Gafooley, who grabbed Butsko around the throat and squeezed. "I ain't no pipsqueak!" Nutsy screamed. "You can't call me no pipsqueak and get away with it!"

Butsko recovered his balance and brushed Nutsy away as if he were a mosquito. Nutsy flew across the hole and landed against one of its walls, sliding down, dazed.

"Everybody's so touchy around here," Butsko said, wiping spilled rice off his filthy pants. "A man can't open his mouth without somebody jumping all over his ass."

Longtree leaned toward Butsko. "I ain't bugging out," he said emphatically.

"You don't have to die in this hole if you don't wanna, Longtree. Don't be a dumb Indian all your life."

"Everybody dies sooner or later," Longtree said, "but the main thing is to die with honor!"

"Honor?" Butsko asked, looking around. "I don't see nobody named Honor in this hole. I see Shaw, Bannon, Nutsy, Homer, and Frankie, but I don't see nobody named Honor. You sure you're in the right hole?"

"You know what I mean," Longtree said disgustedly.

"Yeah, I know what you mean," Butsko replied, mimicking

him. "I always heard that Indians get crazy when they drink, but you get crazy even when you don't drink." Butsko turned to Bannon. "I guess you're gonna stick around too."

"Fucking A."

"Spoken like the true asshole that you are." Butsko sighed and placed the can of rice on the bottom of the hole. "Well, I already know what the pipsqueak's gonna do, so that—"

"Don't call me pipsqueak!"

Nutsy Gafooley leaped at Butsko from across the hole, and Butsko casually raised his size twelve combat boot into the air. Nutsy's face crashed into it, and Nutsy collapsed, out cold, at the bottom of the hole.

Butsko chuckled. "Feisty little bugger, ain't he? Little guys are the most ornery people in the world. Take the Japs, for instance. They're little guys, and who's more ornery than they are?" Butsko pressed his forefinger to his cheek. "Now, where was I? Oh, yeah." He looked at Shaw. "I was gonna ask you whether or not you wanted to be smart, unlike your buddies here, and try to make a break for it."

Shaw shook his head. "No dice. I'm a big buy like you and I'd make too much noise. I wouldn't get very far. And besides, I couldn't run out on my buddies, like some people I know. I been with them for a long time, and as far as I'm concerned, I'm ready to die with them."

"I think I'm gonna throw up," Butsko said.

"You look like somebody threw you up," Shaw replied.

Butsko laughed. "Yeah, I guess I do, don't I? But I'd hate to say what you look like, Terrible Tommy Shaw. That's what they used to call you when you fought in the Garden, right? Well, the boxing world's gonna miss you, my friend. You're gonna fight your last fight here tonight in this smelly ditch."

Butsko shook his head and laughed again, holding his big hands on his stomach as if to hold it in. The others looked at him in amazement. Nutsy Gafooley regained consciousness at the bottom of the hole and turned his eyes upward to see Butsko laughing above him like a jovial, blood-spattered Buddha.

Bannon frowned. "What's so funny?"

Butsko's mighty shoulders heaved and he rocked from side to side. He was unable to control himself. Tears rolled down his cheeks, streaking the dried blood on his face. He slapped his leg and laughed louder, then clasped his gut and bent over, his face red and snot dripping from his nose.

Bannon shook his head. "I don't believe I've ever seen an uglier sight in my life."

"The son of a bitch has gone totally psycho on us," Shaw said.

"What's he laughing at?" Longtree asked. "There ain't nothing funny going on here."

"I think his mind just snapped," Nutsy said.

Butsko struggled to catch his breath, his mouth open wide. "You guys ain't got no sense of humor!" he said. "Here we are together; we all hate each other's guts, and we're gonna die together! When they find us, they're gonna think we were buddies till the end, and boy, are they gonna be wrong! I can hear the colonel giving a funeral speech about how we all died trying to protect each other, when a few minutes ago we were all ready to shoot each other!"

Butsko burst into laughter again, and the others looked at him curiously. Nutsy saw his chance and dived on top of Butsko, grabbing him by the neck.

"Don't you ever call me a pipsqueak again!"

Nutsy's sudden attack made Butsko laugh even harder. He fell onto his back and didn't even have the strength to push Nutsy away, but Nutsy had tiny hands and couldn't wrap them around Butsko's thick neck.

"Oh, God!" Butsko shrieked, his chest heaving with mirth. *"I can't take it anymore!"*

Bannon grabbed Nutsy by the collar and pulled him off Butsko. "Leave him alone! Can't you see he's gone off his rocker?"

Longtree nodded sagely. "Must be combat fatigue."

"I seen it coming on for a long time," Shaw said.

"Let me at him!" Nutsy screamed, dangling in the air, moving his feet and punching the night with his fists.

"C'mon," Bannon said, "settle the fuck down. We got things to do. The Japs are liable to attack at any moment."

Bannon turned Nutsy loose, and Nutsy dropped to the bottom of the hole, landing on top of Frankie La Barbara's stomach, and Frankie La Barbara sat up suddenly, looked around, and said calmly, an expression of bewilderment on his face: "What the hell's going on?"

Butsko exploded into a convulsion of uncontrollable insane

gurgling and cackling, rolling around the bottom of the hole. Bannon kicked him in the ass.

"Snap out of it!" Bannon said. "You're gonna lead the Japs right onto us!"

But Butsko couldn't stop, the peals of his laughter echoing over the treetops and slicing through the mangled, tangled, endless wall of jungle.

TEN . . .

In another part of the jungle, Sergeant Cameron woke up. He blinked his eyes and listened to the jungle. Amid the chirping of insects and calls of night birds, he thought he heard somebody laughing far off in the distance. It was an inhuman, insane, hysterical laugh, and it sounded almost as if it had come from the throat of Sergeant Butsko.

Sergeant Cameron shook his head. *I must be dreaming,* he said to himself. *It must be some jungle animal, or one of them parrots that live in the trees.*

Sergeant Cameron closed his eyes and rested his cheek on the back of his hand. The sound of the laughter echoed around in his mind as he dropped off to sleep again.

The laughter made Captain Shimoyama's blood turn to ice as he led the remnants of his company toward the part of the jungle where the Americans were. The sound came from the jungle straight ahead. It wasn't the laughter of a Japanese man; Captain Shimoyama knew that. It was an American who was laughing out there.

What is that crazy American laughing about? he asked himself. The sound was horrible and made shivers run up and down his spine. Why was the American laughing? Didn't he know he was surrounded and about to be slaughtered? What could he be happy about, or was he just mad?

He must have gone insane. The pressure of being in continual danger must have destroyed his mind, and everyone knows that Americans don't have very strong minds to begin with. They are a weak, cowardly people, accustomed to comfort and afraid of fighting at night. We will kill them all soon.

Bushes rustled in front of Captain Shimoyama. He stopped, his heart beating wildly, and raised his samurai sword in the air, expecting a crazy American to rush out at him, but instead the leaves parted and he saw a Japanese soldier stand at attention in the moonlight and salute him.

"Sir," said Pfc. Chiba, "the Americans are just ahead."

"They are? You're quite sure of that?"

"Yes, sir. We have them under observation."

"What is that American laughing about?"

"He's evidently gone insane, sir."

"That's what I thought." Captain Shimoyama turned to Sergeant Atsugi. "The Americans are straight ahead. Tell the men to form four skirmish lines. When I give the order, everyone will attack at once, in waves, behind me. Is that clear?"

"Yes, sir."

Sergeant Atsugi turned around and marched back to the men, telling them what to do. They lined up in the jungle, tripping over branches, pushing each other, and cursing, but Captain Shimoyama didn't mind. The Americans were trapped and couldn't go anywhere. He didn't care what they knew in advance. He looked at Pfc. Chiba.

"You say you have the Americans under observation?"

"Yes, sir."

"That means you can lead me directly to them?"

"Yes, sir."

"Do you know how many of them they are?"

"Approximately six, sir."

106

"Good. When I give the order, you will lead me to them, understand?"

"Yes, sir."

Captain Shimoyama drew his samurai sword, and its blade gleamed in the bright moonlight. He felt confident because he and his men should be able to overwhelm the Americans easily. A few of his men would get killed, and even he might die, but he thought the odds were against him being killed. It was necessary for him to prove to his men that he was an authentic combat commander; and besides, if he died while fighting for his Emperor, he'd be guaranteed a place in Japanese heaven alongside his illustrious ancestors.

He waited impatiently for his men to get into position so that his attack could begin.

Butsko apportioned hand grenades and ammunition while Bannon, Shaw, and Nutsy Gafooley removed their Japanese uniforms. The full moon was overhead, and Frankie La Barbara gazed up at it, his jaw hanging open. He was on his knees in the hole, groggy and feverish, and he could see the man in the moon smiling down at him as though everything was all right.

"Yeah," Frankie said softly, "everything's okay."

"What you say?" Bannon asked.

"I said everything's gonna be okay. You know how I know everything's gonna be okay?"

"No, Frankie, how do you know everything's gonna be okay?"

"The man in the moon just told me."

Bannon turned to Butsko. "You're not gonna give him live ammunition, are you?"

"Sure am."

"But he's out of his mind."

"He's always been out of his mind." Butsko placed six clips of Japanese ammunition in front of Frankie. "This is for you, fuck-up. You remember how to fire a Jap rifle."

"Uh-huh."

"Lock and load and get ready."

"Yo."

Frankie bent over and looked at the clips of ammunition gleaming in the light of the moon. Somehow they reminded him of the jewelry his wife, Francesca, used to wear back in

New York City. Blinking, he bent over for a closer look. The ammunition blurred and he felt as though he'd been dropped into a sea of ink. The ink rose up to his eyes and he leaned to the side, falling over, landing with a thud.

"There goes Frankie," Nutsy said.

Butsko took back the ammunition he'd given Frankie. "I didn't think he'd last long." He divided it up among the other men.

Leaves rustled outside the trench. Butsko looked up and saw the face of Longtree, who was returning from a reconnaissance of the area. Longtree slid into the hole, sat, and crossed his legs.

"We're trapped," he said. "The Japs've got us surrounded, and there's no openings to sneak out. We're fucked."

Butsko tossed him some clips of ammunition for an Arisaka rifle. "This is what happens to sentimental assholes who don't listen to their old sergeant. You guys don't have the guts to make tough decisions. You're like a bunch of dumb cunts."

Nobody argued with him, because his logic was irrefutable. If they'd left Frankie and Homer behind, only those two would have been lost to the Japanese. Instead, all of them were going to die.

Butsko continued to pass out ammunition. There were only six clips of .45-caliber ammunition left, and he divided them equally between Bannon and himself. Everyone else got a Japanese Arisaka rifle and eight clips of ammunition. Bannon also would carry an Arisaka rifle to use when he ran out of ammo for his submachine gun. Butsko would fight on with the combination of his captured samurai sword and his Nambu pistol.

Each man prepared himself for the final round of the fight, and each was sure he was going to die. Bannon thought of his girl friend, Ginger, back in Pecos, Texas, and the native girl he'd married on Guadalcanal, and the whore named Nettie with whom he'd fallen in love in Honolulu. He always remembered women whenever he was in dangerous situations.

Longtree's mind drifted back to the reservation where he'd lived in Arizona, the endless desert covered with saguaro cacti, the hunting and fishing, the beautiful squaws with their smoky skin and sultry eyes. It seemed odd to him that he was going to die with the kind of men who'd reviled him when he'd lived in Arizona, but these men were his warrior comrades now, and together they'd fight until they could fight no more.

Nutsy Gafooley thought of hobo jungles and pots full of Mulligan stew, of riding the rails across the country, his life of freedom. Never again would he know the thrill of jumping on a train as it highballed over the trestles. The former hobo knew he was going to die, and there was no one to weep for him.

Terrible Tommy Shaw had been a professional boxer before the war, and he'd always thought he had what it took to become heavyweight champion of the world. He'd won twenty-six out of thirty professional fights, eighteen by knockout, and would have been ranked in the top twenty by *Ring* magazine if he could have won another fight or two, but now his dream would never come true, and he would go down for the count on a stupid little island no one ever heard of before, far from the cheering crowds at Madison Square Garden. "Shit!" he said, spitting into the muck at the bottom of the hole.

Butsko was all business as he checked out his weapons and ammunition. He was a professional soldier and he'd been living with death so long he'd become numb to it. He never thought he'd survive the war, and it looked like his number was coming up that night on Bougainville.

"We all set?" he asked.

The men nodded.

"Okay," he said, "the Japs'll attack any moment now, or maybe they'll wait until it's light. I personally think they'll attack tonight, because it sounds to me like they're getting ready for something right now. All we can do now is fight it out and take as many Japs with us as we can. If anybody wants to surrender, that's okay with me, although I don't recommend it, because you know what the Japs do to their prisoners. If anybody wants to try to escape, that's okay with me, too, although there ain't no way out of here. We may not have another chance to talk, so I might as well say now good luck to all of you. It's been nice knowing you, although you're a bunch of stupid assholes. It looks like we're gonna get wiped out pretty soon, but at least it'll be quick and clean. Any questions?"

There was silence for a few moments; then Bannon smiled grimly and held out his hand. "You're a rotten fucking bastard, Sarge, but it's been nice knowing you, too. Good luck."

109

Shaw placed his calloused hand on the hands of Butsko and Bannon. "Good luck, guys."

Longtree put his hand on Shaw's. "It is a good day to die," he said.

"But it's nighttime," Butsko protested.

"Doesn't matter," Longtree replied.

Nutsy placed both his hands on the hands of the other men. "Sarge," he said, "I hate your fucking guts, but you're the best soldier in the whole goddamned United States Army, and as for you other guys, you been like brudders to me, and in fact, you been like more than brudders to me. In fact—"

Butsko yanked his hand away from the others. "The bullshit's getting pretty deep in this hole," he snarled.

"Lemme finish!" Nutsy said. "I ain't finished yet!"

"Fuck you," Butsko replied. "Who wants to hear that crap?"

"C'mon, Sarge," Bannon said. "Let him finish."

"Okay, go ahead and finish, fuck-up."

Nutsy opened his mouth, then frowned. "I forgot what I was gonna say."

"Good," Butsko said. "Well, the rest of you guys can try to get some sleep. I'll take the first shift of guard. Keep your weapons close by, because the Japs might attack at any moment."

They lay down in the hole, placing their weapons next to them and closing their eyes, but no one could sleep. They listened to the sounds of the jungle, birds calling to each other, and wild dogs barking. Japs moved through the foliage all around them; the GIs knew that the Japs were getting into position for their attack. The only question remaining was what time the attack would come. Each GI figured he had come to the end of his road, and he hoped for a quick, painless death.

Butsko knelt in the hole and looked over the edge at the moonlit jungle. His eyes were adjusted to the moonlight, and he could see nearly as clearly as during the day. The leaves and trunks of the trees were tinged with silver and looked ghostly in the light of the moon. Butsko thought of God. He recalled someone saying that there were no atheists in foxholes, but Butsko didn't feel especially religious, now that he was about to die. He hadn't believed in God since he found out, at the age of fourteen, that Father Kowalski, the pastor of Saint Stanislas Parish in McKeesport, Pennsylvania, was fucking the widow Hopp, a busty blonde whose husband had died in an accident at the local steel-rolling mill.

Butsko hoped there wasn't a hell, because if there was, he knew he would go there. They'd put him right into the broiler for eternity for all the things he'd done, but that was all fairy-tale Catholicism, he hoped. *Fuck God*, he said to himself. *Who needs him? I don't need him. All I need is about two hundred hard-charging GIs to show up and save my ass right now.*

Not far away, Captain Shimoyama stood at attention in front of his men. There were sixty of them gathered in four ranks, rifles and bayonets in their hands, ready to attack. Another thirty-two men couldn't attend the formation because they had circled around the American position so that the Americans couldn't get away. They had been told to attack on the command to be given by Captain Shimoyama.

Captain Shimoyama looked from left to right at the faces of his men. His veins and arteries surged with excitement, because this was the first time he would lead an all-out banzai attack, and he had worked himself into a frenzy. His skin was blotched with emotion and his eyes glittered. He ground his teeth together and felt as though his chest would explode. He wanted to radio Colonel Akai in an hour and tell him that the American patrol had been demolished totally.

Sergeant Atsugi marched toward Captain Shimoyama and saluted. "The men are in position, sir."

"Stand at my side."

"Yes, sir."

Sergeant Atsugi performed a left-face and moved to the spot that Captain Shimoyama had indicated, doing an about-face and standing at attention, his arms stiff at his sides.

Captain Shimoyama remained at attention also. He narrowed his eyes and a cruel expression came over his face. "The time has come to attack!" he shouted. "When I give the command, we move forward and we will not stop until all the Americans are dead! I estimate that there are twenty or thirty of them— much less than us! We have wasted enough time with these filthy Americans, but of course that was the fault of Sergeant Kikusaki! Take prisoners if possible, but if you can't, I want you to kill and kill and kill again! Those are your orders! Your ancestors are watching you! Do not fail them! Remember your

Emperor! Do not stop your attack until no more Americans are standing! Is that clear!"

Nobody said anything. It was a rhetorical question and they all knew they weren't supposed to reply.

"Very well," Captain Shimoyama said. He executed an about-face, turning toward the place where the Americans were. Pulling his samurai sword out of its scabbard, he held it tightly in his right fist. The time had come to attack. He took a deep breath and uttered a final prayer to his ancestors.

Captain Shimoyama's voice traveled through the jungle, and the GIs in the big blown-out hole heard him.

"Sounds like the Japs are getting a pep talk," Butsko said.

The GIs roused themselves and took positions along the edge of the hole. Captain Shimoyama's voice sounded weird and inhuman to their American ears.

"That guy's got a voice like a raving lunatic," Shaw said, holding his Arisaka rifle and fixed boyonet tightly in his big hands.

"They're all raving fucking lunatics," Butsko replied. "They started this fucking war and we're gonna finish it." Then he remembered that he and the others would be dead within the next few hours. "I mean our side will end it. America."

They knew what he meant as they peered into the jungle, waiting for the Japs to attack.

"When they come," Butsko said, "shoot as many of them as you can. You don't have to worry about your aim, because they'll be so close it won't matter much. Just keep pulling your triggers and load up fast when you empty a clip. If we can kill enough of them before they get on top of us, we'll have a better chance; but when they get on top of us, we'll charge right back at them instead of waiting for them to jump into this hole, here. Maybe we can rock 'em back, but if we can't, all we can hope for is to go down like soldiers. Everybody set?"

They all nodded or grunted.

"Good," Butsko said. "If we ever get out of this alive, I'll buy you all a drink in the first bar we see. And if we don't get out alive, I'll see you all in hell."

Captain Shimoyama looked at the blade of his samurai sword, and it gleamed in the moonlight. He touched his thumb to the edge; it was like a razor. He'd never killed anybody with it before. The sword had always hung from his waist as an ornament during staff meetings, but now it would drink American blood.

His men were behind him, their eyes on his back. The time had come to attack. There was nothing else to do except give the order and move out. He raised the samurai sword high in the air.

"*Forward!*" he shrieked. "*Banzai!*"

He pushed his right leg and leaped forward with his left leg. Then he whipped his right leg forward and was running. Wind whistled past his ears and dried the lips and tongue of his open mouth as branches and leaves scraped his arms and legs. He crashed through the jungle and heard the tumult of his men behind him.

"*Banzai!*" he screamed.

"*Banzai!*" they replied.

The horde of Japanese soldiers charged forward, running through bushes and dodging around trees. Their hearts chugged in their chests and their minds were wild with visions of glorious battle waged on behalf of their Emperor. Their boots tore up the jungle floor as they pressed forward, hollering and shrieking, snorting and spitting, shaking their rifles and bayonets, anxious to close with the Americans. They came to the open area that had been devastated by grenade blasts earlier in the day, and could see the big boulder behind the hole where the Americans were hiding.

"*Banzai!*" screamed Captain Shimoyama, swinging his samurai sword in circles over his head, where it flashed in the moonlight. "*Attack!*"

The Japanese soldiers burst into view, and Butsko yelled: "*Open fire!*"

His submachine gun rested on the top of the hole and he pulled the trigger. The submachine gun erupted and sparks shot out of the barrel along with hot .45-caliber bullets. He raked from side to side behind the submachine gun, spraying the Japs from left to right and then back again. The first wave of Japanese soldiers was sliced up by the bullets, and many of the Japanese soldiers fell to the ground, dead or wounded, but the rest continued their charge.

113

Next to Butsko, Pfc. Shaw pulled the trigger of his Arisaka rifle as fast as he could, working the bolt each time, wishing he had an M 1, which was a semiautomatic weapon that had no bolt to operate. Shaw didn't aim carefully; he just held the Arisaka rifle steady and pulled the trigger as fast as he could, because he couldn't miss. The entire jungle in front of him was filled with Japs.

Longtree and Nutsy also rapid-fired their Arisaka rifles, and on the far side the hole Bannon fired his submachine gun, mowing down Japs like wheat in a field. But live Japs jumped over dead Japs, maintaining the momentum of the charge, and in front of all the Japs was an officer wearing eyeglasses and waving his samurai sword above his head, screaming at the top of his lungs.

Captain Shimoyama's mouth was as dry as paper and his uniform was soaked with sweat as he ran forward. He couldn't believe he was alive, because he could see the Americans ahead of him, firing their weapons, and he could hear his men crying out in pain behind him. He was naked and alone in front of his men, and bullets whizzed past his head and shoulders, legs and arms, and a few even zipped between his legs. But he had only about ten more yards to go, and then he would be in the hole with the Americans, decapitating them with his samurai sword, winning glory for himself and his Emperor—if he lived that long!

"*Banzai!*" he yelled. "*Banzai!*"

Sergeant Cameron woke up upon hearing the echo of the first fusillade; it didn't sound very far away. Rolling onto his stomach, he turned in the direction of the firing. Around him, other men awakened and looked in the same direction.

"Lieutenant Thurmond?" he said.

"I'm awake," replied Lieutenant Thurmond, who had been sleeping a few feet from Sergeant Cameron. He, too, was peering into the jungle. "Sounds like trouble."

"Must be Butsko," Sergeant Cameron said. "I think we'd better go help him."

"I think you're right." Lieutenant Thurmond scrambled to his feet and put on his helmet. His mouth tasted like shit and his head was heavy with dreams. *"Everybody up, on the dou-*

114

ble!" he yelled. *"Prepare to move out! Let's go!"*

All across that part of the jungle, men got to their feet and wrapped their cartridge belts around their waists. They shoved their arms into the shoulder straps of their field packs and picked up their weapons.

"Column of ducks over here!" Sergeant Cameron ordered, slinging his carbine over his shoulder. *"Move your fucking asses! We ain't got all night!"*

ELEVEN . . .

The Japanese soldiers jumped over the bodies of their fallen comrades as they dashed over the final few yards that separated them from the hole, where the GIs fired their weapons as quickly as they could. The Japanese soldiers were so close, Butsko could see the expressions on their faces and the insignia on their collars. He knew they would be in the hole in a matter of seconds, and the time had come to get out and fight hand-to-hand.

"Up and at 'em!" he yelled. *"Follow me!"*

In one mighty leap Butsko was out of the hole, standing on the same ground as the Japanese soldiers who rampaged toward him. He gripped his submachine gun tightly, clasped the butt against the right side of his waist, and pulled the trigger. The bullets ripped into the Japanese soldiers, tearing huge holes in their bodies, but the forward momentum of the Japs carried them on, and they fell at Butsko's feet.

Butsko waded into them, sweeping the barrel of his submachine gun from left to right and right to left, mowing them down. He fired point-blank at a Japanese soldier, and the big bullets of the submachine gun blasted the Japanese soldier's head into hamburger. Butsko pivoted and fired at another Japanese soldier, ripping apart his ribs and lungs, perforating his heart, filling his esophagus with bone splinters. The Japanese soldier opened his mouth to scream in pain, but was dead before the sound could come out of his mouth.

The Japanese soldier dropped at Butsko's feet, and Butsko stepped over him, firing at swarms of other Japanese soldiers charging toward him. Butsko saw Japanese soldiers charge past him, and out of the corners of his eyes he could see the other GIs fighting them hand to hand with bayonets. The battle was hot and heavy now. It was kill or be killed, shoot or be shot, stab your opponent before he stabbed you.

"Banzai!" screamed a voice above and behind Butsko.

Butsko spun around and saw a Japanese soldier standing on top of the eight-foot boulder behind the hole. The Japanese soldier carried an Arisaka rifle with a bayonet attached to the end, and his beady eyes fell on Butsko looking up at him.

"Banzai!" said the Japanese soldier, jumping off the boulder, dropping toward Butsko.

The Japanese soldier sailed through the air, his rifle and bayonet angled down toward Butsko, who raised his submachine gun and pulled the trigger.

Click!

He was out of ammo, and the Japanese soldier plummeted toward him. Butsko didn't have time to reload his submachine gun. All he could do was wait until the Japanese soldier fell within striking range and then parry the Jap's rifle and bayonet out of the way. Butsko planted his feet firmly on the jungle floor and pushed his submachine gun forward and to the side. The submachine gun smashed into the Arisaka rifle, deflecting its aim and knocking the Japanese soldier onto his ass.

The Japanese soldier landed with a thud and was temporarily stunned. Butsko leaped forward and kicked him in the balls. The Japanese soldier shrieked and nearly fainted from the sudden horrible pain. Butsko took another step and brought his size twelve combat boot down hard on the Japanese soldier's face, mashing his nose as flat as a pancake, and the Japanese soldier howled even louder. He struggled to get up, although

117

he was blinded by pain and blood, and Butsko dropped to his knees on the Japanese soldier's chest, raised his submachine gun in the air, and rammed the butt of the submachine gun down onto the Japanese soldier's forehead, cracking it open like a walnut shell. Blood and brains splattered in all directions and Butsko arose, pulling the empty clip out of his submachine gun, then reaching into his pouch for a fresh clip.

He noticed something dark and ominous streaking toward his head, and ducked. The butt of a Japanese rifle swooshed over his head, and Butsko dropped his submachine gun, diving toward the Japanese soldier's legs, tackling him, and bringing him down.

Butsko and the Japanese soldier rolled over and around on the muck that was the jungle floor, trying to gain leverage on the other, trying to land the first deadly blow. Butsko noticed the three stars on the Japanese soldier's collar and knew he was a sergeant like himself. Then he saw the Japanese soldier's face, which was grizzled, lined, and scarred, like Butsko's.

Butsko knew he wasn't fighting a skinny kid, but an old combat veteran. The Japanese soldier, who happened to be Sergeant Atsugi, dug his elbow into the ground to stop the rolling. Sergeant Atsugi was on top of Butsko and raised his right fist to punch Butsko in the mouth. Butsko saw the punch coming and raised his arm to block it. Sergeant Atsugi swung, and Butsko stopped the punch in midair. Sergeant Atsugi punched with his left arm, and Butsko blocked that one too. Frustrated and furious, Sergeant Atsugi reached down with both thumbs to gouge out Butsko's eyes, and Butsko grabbed Sergeant Atsugi's wrists. Sergeant Atsugi pushed down and Butkso pushed up. They grappled with each other, trying to get leverage. Butsko had more strength, but Sergeant Atsugi had the better position. He leaned his weight on Butsko's arms and aimed his thumbs toward Butsko's eyes.

Butsko gritted his teeth and huge globules of sweat formed on his face as he held back Sergeant Atsugi. Butsko bucked to the left in an effort to throw Sergeant Atsugi off him, but Sergeant Atsugi rode him like a cowboy on a bronco and stayed erect. Again Butsko bucked to the left, and still Sergeant Atsugi maintained his position. It was easier for Sergeant Atsugi to lean on Butsko than for Butsko to push against Sergeant Atsugi, and Butsko realized he would be the one to weaken first. Time was on the side of Sergeant Atsugi. Butsko had to think of something fast.

In a flash it came to him. He diminished his pressure against Sergeant Atsugi, permitting Sergeant Atsugi's thumbs to inch toward his eyes. Then, in a sudden movement, Butsko released his pressure completely and aimed both of Sergeant Atsugi's thumbs toward his mouth.

Sergeant Atsugi looked down, horrified, as his thumbs dropped into Butsko's mouth to the knuckles, and Butsko clamped his jaw shut, his teeth biting through Sergeant Atsugi's skin, flesh, and muscle, grinding against Sergeant Atsugi's thumb bones.

Sergeant Atsugi screamed in pain and tried to pull his thumbs out of Butsko's mouth, but Butsko bit harder. Butsko wanted to bite Sergeant Atsugi's thumbs off completely, and blood flowed out of Sergeant Atsugi's thumbs and into Butsko's mouth. The more Butsko bit, the more Sergeant Atsugi bled. Butsko's mouth filled with blood, which tickled the back of his throat, making him cough; his mouth opened involuntarily, releasing Sergeant Atsugi's thumbs.

Sergeant Atsugi had been leaning backward, trying to pull his thumbs out of Butsko's mouth, and now that his thumbs were suddenly free, he lost his balance. Butsko heaved with his stomach, and Sergeant Atsugi fell off him.

Both men scrambled quickly to their feet and faced each other. Butsko pulled out his Ka-bar knife and held it in his fist, blade up. Sergeant Atsugi felt naked, because his only knife was his bayonet, and it was on the end of his Arisaka rifle, which was lying somewhere in the muck. He didn't dare bend over and look for it, because he knew Butsko would stab him. The two men circled each other, Butsko waving the blade of his knife from side to side, and Sergeant Atsugi crouching and holding out his hands, hoping to catch Butsko's wrist before the knife could do any damage.

Hand-to-hand fighting raged all around them as the two old sergeants performed their gruesome dance of death. Butsko wondered whether he should make the first move, or try to draw Sergeant Atsugi into making the first move, possibly leaving himself open for the fatal stab.

Sergeant Atsugi wished he had something to fight with, but he had only his bare hands. Yet, he'd killed many men with his bare hands before. He was a tough old soldier and he'd been through many battles. He watched Butsko's hands, hoping he'd make the first move. Sergeant Atsugi definitely didn't want to make the first move and leave himself open for that stab. Butsko had the knife. Let him go first.

Butsko changed direction, and the two men circled each other in the opposite direction. Each man's concentration was focused totally on the other. It was as if no one else in the world existed. Each wanted to live, and knew that in order to do that, he had to kill the man in front of him.

The air between them crackled with electricity. Butsko shifted direction again, and they circled the other way. Suddenly, Butsko shouted and lunged, the knife in his right hand aimed toward Sergeant Atsugi's gut. But Sergeant Atsugi had been waiting for just this move, and pounced with both hands on Butsko's thick, hairy wrist.

At the last moment Butsko tossed the Ka-bar knife from his right hand to his left, and Sergeant Atsugi's fingers wrapped around a wrist whose hand was empty. He stared at the empty hand, knowing full well what was going to happen, and a split second later it did happen: He felt a sharp, terrible, ripping pain in his stomach as Butsko's knife went in to the hilt. The pain was so overwhelming that Sergeant Atsugi went into shock, and he loosened his grip on Butsko's right hand, so Butsko punched him in the mouth.

The force of the blow sent Sergeant Atsugi stumbling backward, disengaging him from Butsko's knife. Sergeant Atsugi collapsed onto his back, and Butsko was so kill crazy he wanted to leap on him and stab him twenty times, but his immediate vicinity was filled with Japanese soldiers, and he had no time for personal pleasure. Butsko reached down to scoop up the nearest Japanese rifle, and *baammmm!*

A Japanese soldier hit him from behind with the butt of his Arisaka rifle. Butsko was strong and tough, and he could take a good punch, but he wasn't *that* strong and tough. Everything went black before his eyes, and he pitched forward onto his face.

The Japanese soldier who'd walloped him so sneakily positioned himself above Butsko's motionless body and raised his rifle and bayonet to harpoon him in the back. The Japanese soldier smiled victoriously, and then suddenly his smile sagged as a bayonet pierced his back and stuck out the front of his chest. The Japanese soldier went limp, hanging on the end of the bayonet. Longtree, who had been holding the Arisaka rifle and bayonet, angled it downward so that the Japanese soldier could slide off it, but the bayonet was stuck in the Japanese soldier's ribs.

Longtree let the Japanese soldier fall onto his stomach, then placed his foot on the Japanese soldier's back and tugged. The bayonet still wouldn't come out, so Longtree placed his foot more firmly on the Japanese soldier's back and pulled harder.

"Banzai!"

Longtree looked up to see a Japanese soldier rushing toward him, the Japanese soldier's rifle and bayonet pointed toward his heart. All Longtree could do was lunge forward and grab for the Japanese soldier's rifle. The Japanese soldier saw what Longtree was trying to do, but he was already in motion and it was too late to change direction. Longtree's long, bony fingers clamped around the rifle, and the Apache's momentum caused him to crash into the Japanese soldier. Their faces came within inches of each other's and Longtree couldn't help noticing how closely the Japanese soldier resembled an Indian; but he didn't have time to think about that, because the Japanese soldier lost his balance, and both men toppled to the ground.

Longtree landed on top of the Japanese soldier and kneed him in the balls, but the Japanese soldier squirmed out of the way and Longtree's knee struck the Japanese soldier's outer thigh. Each man struggled to pull the Arisaka rifle away from the other, and in addition to that, the Japanese soldier tried to get out from underneath Longtree. But Longtree was too strong for him in that department, although not strong enough to wrest the rifle away from him.

Longtree yanked the rifle, but the Japanese soldier held on tenaciously. Longtree twisted the rifle in all directions, but the Japanese soldier still wouldn't let go. Longtree couldn't waste time fighting for the rifle, because another Japanese soldier might come up behind him and stab him in the back.

Longtree had to gamble. He let the rifle go and quickly jabbed his thumbs toward the Japanese soldier's eyes. Before the Japanese soldier could react, he was blinded. Longtree's thumbs sank into the Japanese soldier's eye sockets, and blood spurted out in big gobs. The Japanese soldier screamed in horrible pain and let go of his rifle.

Longtree snatched it out of the air and jumped to his feet. He heard somebody running toward his back and spun around. It was another Japanese soldier, aiming his rifle and bayonet at Longtree's midsection. Longtree hadn't regained his balance yet, but you can't have everything when you want it. He thrust his rifle and bayonet forward at an angle and it bashed against the Japanese soldier's rifle, parrying it to the side.

The clash upset Longtree's tenuous balance, and the young Apache Indian fell to the ground, rolling even before he landed. The Japanese soldier's bayonet smacked into the ground where Longtree had been, the steel striking sparks from a stone.

Longtree rolled again and leaped to his feet, still holding the Arisaka rifle with both hands. The Japanese soldier charged him, his rifle and bayonet streaking toward Longtree's chest, and Longtree threw all of his 195 pounds into the parry, smashing the Japanese soldier's rifle and bayonet to the side; then, without breaking his motion, Longtree swung his rifle butt around and whacked the Japanese soldier in the face. The force of the blow broke the Japanese soldier's eardrum and splintered his cheekbone. His eyes rolled up into his head and he dropped to his knees on the ground. Longtree kicked him in the face, and the Japanese soldier fell onto his back. Standing over him, Longtree angled his rifle and bayonet downward, and thrust it into the Japanese soldier's chest, then pulled it out and looked around.

He saw men struggling in the moonlight. They grunted, burped, and farted as they tried to kill each other. Someone cried out as a bayonet pierced his stomach. Another man groaned as he crumpled to the ground. Longtree saw two Japanese soldiers charging toward Butsko, who bared his teeth and aimed his submachine gun at them.

Click!

Butsko didn't have time to reload, and the Japanese soldiers were only ten feet away, screaming *"Banzai!"*; their eyes glittered with excitement. With an angry snarl Butsko threw the empty submachine gun at them, and both dodged out of the way, giving him time to draw his captured samurai sword and hold it in his big, hairy fist.

"C'mon, you fucking slant-eyed yellow cocksuckers!"

They recovered their equilibrium and continued their charge.

122

Butsko planted his big feet on the ground and waited for them. The Japanese soldier on the left lunged forward, and Butsko dodged to the right, swinging down with his samurai sword at the soldier on the right, who was looking at the place where Butsko had been, not where he was now; Butsko's samurai sword busted the Japanese soldier's collarbone and sank into his rib cage.

Butsko snorted like a wild bull as he pulled the samurai sword loose. He jumped over the dead Japanese soldier and attacked the one who'd lunged at him first. That soldier turned around to face Butsko and screamed *"Banzai!"* while Butsko was already in the middle of a sideways swing. The blade of his samurai sword struck the Japanese soldier on the kidney, slicing it in half, and then cracked into his spine. The Japanese soldier shrieked so horribly that Butsko's ears rang. The Japanese soldier didn't know whether to jump, run, or fall down, but as blood poured out of his side, one choice was forced upon him: He collapsed at Butsko's feet, and Butsko kicked him out of the way as if he were a dead dog.

Three Japanese soldiers ran toward Butsko, who yanked his Nambu pistol out of his belt. He held the Nambu in his right hand and the samurai sword in his left. Raising the Nambu to eye level, he pulled the trigger, and one Japanese soldier tripped over his own feet and fell to the ground. Butsko moved the Nambu a few inches to the right and pulled the trigger again. The legs of the next Japanese soldier went wobbly and he dropped his rifle as he, too, fell to the ground.

The third Japanese soldier maintained his forward momentum and screamed *"Banzai!"* He pushed his rifle and bayonet forward, and Butsko dodged to the side, hacking downward with his samurai sword. The sharp, bloody blade cracked into the Japanese soldier's skull, splitting it in half. The blade continued downward, burrowing into the Japanese soldier's neck. The Japanese soldier slumped to the ground and Butsko looked around.

He expected to be charged by more Japanese soldiers, but none were close to him. Most of the fighting was taking place ten yards to his left. Butsko spat at the ground and ran toward the Japanese soldiers, firing his Nambu pistol. He shot one in the back and another in the side. Then he was on top of them, swinging his samurai sword.

His gory blade smacked one Japanese soldier on the shoulder and lopped off his entire arm. The soldier stared aghast at blood gushing out of the place where his arm had been, and then he passed out, falling back into the crowd of Japanese soldiers.

Butsko fired the Nambu pistol and a large red hole appeared suddenly next to the ear of a Japanese soldier, whose eyes closed as he pitched forward. Butsko fired the nambu again and shot a hole through the neck of a Japanese soldier. Swinging his samurai sword downward, he sliced a Japanese soldier's head in half diagonally. A Japanese bayonet ripped open Butsko's left biceps, and Butsko turned to see who'd done it. He saw a Japanese soldier swinging back with his rifle and bayonet, preparing to cut Butsko again, and Butsko raised the Nambu pistol and fired it at the Japanese soldier's face, which suddenly exploded, blood and brains splattering in all directions. Butsko swung sideways with the samurai sword, cracking a Japanese soldier's spine in half, and the Japanese soldier's body folded backward onto itself and fell to the ground.

Butsko stepped forward and swung the samurai sword diagonally, and its blade connecting at the juncture of a Japanese soldier's neck and body. The blade burst through the Japanese soldier's collarbone, cracked three ribs, and severed his aorta, causing blood to rush out as if from a geyser; it sprayed all over Butsko's face and hair.

Butsko was a fearsome sight, dripping with blood and gristle, as he waded into the crowd of Japanese soldiers. He shot and hacked a path through them and found Bannon and Terrible Tommy Shaw fighting back to back with rifles and bayonets, heaps of dead and wounded Japanese soldiers all around them. Bannon bled from a gash on his cheek, and Longtree's shirt was soaked with blood, although it was impossible to say whose blood it was.

Butsko swept forward like a fearsome apparition from hell, firing his Nambu pistol and slicing with his samurai sword. He shot a Japanese soldier in the back and swung his samurai sword at another Japanese soldier cutting off his head. It flew into the air like a basketball, bounced off the branch of a tree, and fell to earth a few feet from Nutsy Gafooley, who was fighting for his life with his rifle and bayonet against Captain Shimoyama himself.

They had been trying to kill each other ever since the first moments of the attack, when Captain Shimoyama somehow miraculously survived all the American submachine-gun fire. Captain Shimoyama had been a few feet from the hole where the Americans were fighting when the Americans charged out of their hole, and the American who'd charged toward the Japanese captain was none other than Nutsy Gafooley, the ex-hobo.

Ever since that moment they'd been in mortal combat, Captain Shimoyama becoming more frustrated and angry with every passing minute. Nutsy was smaller than Captain Shimoyama, and he looked like a little rat; yet, Captain Shimoyama had been unable to kill him, and now Captain Shimoyama's arms were growing weary from swinging his heavy samurai sword around.

He stopped and looked down at Nutsy Gafooley, and Nutsy Gafooley looked up at him defiantly. Captain Shimoyama wished he'd paid more attention to his teachers in his swordsmanship classes, but he'd thought he'd always be a staff officer and would never have to fight hand to hand in this manner.

It was annoying to be unable to kill a scrawny little soldier such as the one standing in front of him, holding an Arisaka rifle and bayonet, which looked ridiculously large for his diminutive proportions. Captain Shimoyama raised his sword and bit his lower lip, trying to pull together his remaining reserves of energy for a final victorious assault against Nutsy Gafooley.

At that moment Nutsy Gafooley lunged forward with his rifle and bayonet, taking Captain Shimoyama by surprise. Captain Shimoyama halted his swing in midair and darted out of the way; Nutsy's bayonet came so close, it tore Captain Shimoyama's shirt open.

Captain Shimoyama regained his balance and took a step backward for some sword-swinging room, and Nutsy lunged again, baring his teeth, aiming for Captain Shimoyama's gut. Captain Shimoyama swung his samurai sword to the side, striking Nutsy's rifle and deflecting its path. Then Captain Shimoyama raised his samurai sword and swung down at Nutsy, but the sword whistled through the air and nearly chopped off Captain Shimoyama's ankle, because Nutsy was not where he had been at the beginning of Captain Shimoyama's swing.

Nutsy had been in a many a hobo jungle fight with men bigger men than he, and he'd learned long ago that you could defeat a bigger man if you wore him down. He feinted toward Captain Shimoyama's stomach, and Captain Shimoyama raised his sword to protect himself. Nutsy lowered his bayonet a few inches and this time lunged for real toward Captain Shimoyama's groin. Captain Shimoyama had been raising his sword and now couldn't bring it down in time. All he could do was jump back, but he didn't jump quickly enough and Nutsy's bayonet cut Captain Shimoyama's upper right thigh.

Captain Shimoyama screamed, and Nutsy swung his rifle around, banging Captain Shimoyama in the face with his rifle butt; but Captain Shimoyama ducked under the blow, spun away, and turned to face Nutsy again.

Captain Shimoyama was getting sick and tired of fighting Nutsy Gafooley, but he couldn't just walk away as he wanted to, because he knew Nutsy would simply cut him down from behind. He'd been fighting Nutsy for nearly a half hour and was losing his will to fight, although he had to sustain it somehow if he wanted to live.

Captain Shimoyama circled to his left, and Nutsy turned on the balls of his feet, keeping his eyes fixed on Captain Shimoyama, looking for an opening or a sneaky blow, because he knew the Japs were famous for their sneaky shit.

But Captain Shimoyama wasn't a sneaky man. He thought of himself as an honorable noble member of the Japanese army's officer corps, although he had no noble blood whatever in his veins. He would win fair and square or he wouldn't win at all.

Captain Shimoyama looked for an opening in Nutsy's defense, but couldn't find one because Nutsy was so small and compact. Captain Shimoyama wished one of his soldiers would appear and kill Nutsy for him, but all of his soldiers were heavily engaged in hand-to-hand combat. Occasionally a shot rang out, or a man screamed, or somebody swore, but in general there was pushing and stabbing and tripping, and the ground was covered with dead and wounded soldiers, all of them Japanese.

Captain Shimoyama gazed wearily at Nutsy Gafooley. Captain Shimoyama's jaw hung open, because he was so tired he had to breathe through his mouth. His sword felt as though it were made of lead, and his left shoulder ached from his earlier wound, while his right leg hurt from his more recent one. This ratlike American soldier had drawn first blood.

"Your mother's pussy!" Nutsy Gafooley screamed, lunging forward with his rifle and bayonet.

Captain Shimoyama jumped to the left, and Nutsy's bayonet cut open the right side of Captain Shimoyama's stomach. It wasn't a deep or fatal wound, but it hurt fiercely and Captain Shimoyama bellowed in pain. His lifeblood poured down his side in a substantial quantity, and an inch-long section of his upper intestine bulged out of the hole.

Captain Shimoyama looked down at his new wound and realized he was in trouble. The wound would make him progressively weaker, and if he waited too long he'd no longer have the strength to fight his opponent. He had to make his move now or never.

Gritting his teeth, holding the hilt of his samurai sword with both hands, he shifted his weight from foot to foot, crouching low to make himself a small target, ready to jump out of the way of one of Nutsy's lunges. Slowly he lifted his samurai sword in the air.

Nutsy feinted, and Captain Shimoyama hopped to the side, swinging down his razor-sharp samurai sword. Nutsy raised his rifle and bayonet, and Captain Shimoyama's sword clashed against the iron trigger guard of the rifle, sending a spray of sparks into the air. Then Nutsy Gafooley brought up his knee in a quick, hard motion.

Captain Shimoyama didn't see Nutsy's knee, and in the next moment his balls were mashed like two small boiled potatoes into the upside-down bowl of his groin. The pain was so sudden and terrible that he screeched like a woman and nearly fainted.

Nutsy kneed him again, and Captain Shimoyama went blind with pain and rage. He and Nutsy were cheek to cheek, and Captain Shimoyama leaned forward, opened his mouth, and bit hard. He caught Nutsy's ear between his teeth and clamped down. Nutsy hollered and pulled back, and Captain Shimoyama's clenched teeth tore off half of Nutsy Gafooley's ear.

Both men separated. Captain Shimoyama was bent over, half of Nutsy Gafooley's ear in his mouth and blood soaking through his right pant leg. Captain Shimoyama held his samurai sword in his hands and pressed the heels of his hands against his shattered balls.

Blood dripped out of Nutsy Gafooley's ragged ear, down

127

his cheek, and onto his shoulder as he raised his rifle for another pass. His ear hurt, but he knew Captain Shimoyama was in worse shape than he, and the time had come to finish him off. But where could he stick his bayonet with Captain Shimoyama hunched over, covering his soft spots? Nutsy would have liked to shoot Captain Shimoyama and get the whole mess over with easily, but his ammunition clip was empty.

He decided the best thing to do was feint with the bayonet and bash the tall Japanese officer in the head with his rifle butt. Nutsy stepped forward and lunged with his rifle and bayonet, and Captain Shimoyama tried to get out of the way, but his balls were bleeding inside his stomach and he'd lost his speed. Nutsy stopped the lunge at the last moment and swung his rifle butt around at Captain Shimoyama's head, and Captain Shimoyama ducked reflexively. The rifle butt whistled over Captain Shimoyama's head, and Nutsy's forward movement caused him to collide with the Japanese captain.

Captain Shimoyama lost his balance and fell on his ass, and Nutsy fell on top of him, his torn ear bleeding into Captain Shimoyama's left eye. Captain Shimoyama's body was racked with pain, and his hands were trapped between the press of his and Nutsy's bodies. Nutsy raised himself up and punched Captain Shimoyama in the cheek, jaw, nose, mouth, chin, and temples. The cumulative effect of the blows made Captain Shimoyama groggy, and something told him he was on his way out. He made a final, desperate lurch to get Nutsy Gafooley off him, and it worked. Nutsy lost his balance and toppled onto his side. Captain Shimoyama dived on him, but his aim was off and he missed. Nutsy spun around and jumped on Captain Shimoyama's back, reaching around with his right forearm and pulling it into the Japanese officer's throat, then catching the crook of his left arm in his right hand and placing his left hand behind Captain Shimoyama's head.

Nutsy clamped down hard, pressing Captain Shimoyama's head forward with his left hand while pulling back against Captain Shimoyama's throat with his right hand. It was a deadly hold that Nutsy had learned in basic training at Fort Ord, California, and it was very difficult to break out of. Captain Shimoyama dug his fingers into Nutsy Gafooley's arm, but to no avail. Nutsy's grip tightened. Captain Shimoyama's throat was like a garden hose that somebody was stepping on. He had difficulty breathing, and then he was convulsed by coughing. He tossed from side to side, trying to get rid of Nutsy, but Nutsy hung on and squeezed. Captain Shimoyama's head jutted forward at an impossible angle as his throat was compressed and flattened. His consciousness slipped away. He knew he was going to die, and he had to do something.

Captain Shimoyama lurched backward with all his strength, and he and Nutsy went flying through the air, but still Nutsy hung on. Nutsy landed on his back and Captain Shimoyama landed on top of him, knocking the wind out of him, and finally Nutsy loosened his grip. Captain Shimoyama elbowed Nutsy in the ribs and twisted hard, breaking out of the neck hold. Captain Shimoyama rolled over, dizzy with pain, his neck sprained, bleeding profusely from the cut in his side. He drew himself to his knees and stood, leaning toward one side and then the other, watching Nutsy Gafooley climb to his feet.

They stared at each other, exhausted and in pain. They'd been fighting for a half hour, and still it wasn't over. Captain Shimoyama searched around for a weapon, and his eyes fell on his sword. Groggily he stumbled toward it, but Nutsy crouched like a mountain cat and leaped on him, clasping his arms around Captain Shimoyama's legs, pressing his cheek against Captain Shimoyama's leg wound, and wrenching to the side.

They toppled over, landing on the body of a dead Japanese soldier. A rifle and bayonet lay a few feet from the Japanese soldier, and Captain Shimoyama reached for it, but it was too far away. Nutsy clasped his hands together into one big fist, raised it into the air, and hammered it down on top of Captain Shimoyama's head. Captain Shimoyama saw stars, and Nutsy hit him again.

Captain Shimoyama was nearly unconscious, but again he realized that he had to turn the fight around. He lay on his stomach and Nutsy straddled him, bashing him in the head again with his two clasped hands. Captain Shimoyama reached deep inside himself for that last ounce of energy and rolled to the side. Nutsy couldn't maintain his balance and rolled over. Captain Shimoyama rolled over again, to get away from Nutsy, and his hand fell on something big and hard. His fingers wrapped around it; It was a rock. Nutsy pounced on Captain Shimoyama just as the Japanese officer swung with the rock. Captain Shimoyama connected with Nutsy's head as Nutsy was coming in. Nutsy's head was snapped back by the blow, and he sagged to the jungle floor, out cold.

Captain Shimoyama couldn't believe his good fortune. He'd been losing and now it appeared as though he'd suddenly won! He walked on his knees toward the prostrate body of Nutsy Gafooley, the big rock still in his right hand. He stopped beside Nutsy and raised the rock in the air, to bash him in the head and bust it apart.

Nutsy opened his eyes and saw the rock streaking toward his eyes. He spun away in the nick of time, and the rock smashed into the muck of the jungle floor. He rolled onto a dead Japanese soldier's rifle and grabbed it. He jumped to his feet, holding the rifle and bayonet in both hands, and saw Captain Shimoyama rising, the big rock in his hands. Both men were bloody and bleary-eyed. Nearby a terrific battle was taking place, a crowd of men clashing and bashing each other relentlessly.

Captain Shimoyama saw that Nutsy had the rifle and bayonet, and knew he was in trouble. All he could do was wait for Nutsy to come closer and try to hit him with the rock.

Nutsy advanced, feinting with the tip of his bayonet. Captain Shimoyama raised the rock and cocked his arm for the throw, finally realizing that war was not jut a map with pins stuck into it, but men fighting to the death with anything they could lay their hands on.

Nutsy drew close enough to stab Captain Shimoyama, and Captain Shimoyama threw the rock. Nutsy was ready and held up his rifle. The rock bounced off the rifle's stock and fell to the ground.

"Now I gotcha," Nutsy said.

He pushed the rifle and bayonet forward, and Captain Shimoyama tried to dodge out of the way, but he was weak and slow. The tip of the bayonet glanced off the front of one of his ribs and buried itself between that rib and the one underneath it. It was as if someone had squirted flaming gasoline into his lungs. He cried out and looked up toward the heavens. He saw his old grandfather—and a lot of other people, whom he assumed to be his ancestors—looking down at him, smiling. Captain Shimoyama smiled back, because he knew he'd done hs duty and fought as best he could. He was dying for his

Emperor, the highest honor that could come to any Japanese soldier. He groaned and fell to the ground, the death rattle in his throat.

Nutsy pulled out the bayonet and stabbed it in again. The death rattle stopped. Captain Shimoyama was dead, but Nutsy didn't know that. He pulled out the bayonet and stuck him once more. Turning the rifle around, he smashed Captain Shimoyama in the face with the butt plate, mashing his lips and gums, knocking six teeth loose in their sockets.

Nutsy knew Captain Shimoyama was dead now. He looked down at the Japanese officer's bloody face, bloody chest, and bloody leg. The Japanese officer had been so fierce and mean when he'd jumped into the hole, but now he was a mess, his face disfigured and his uniform torn.

Nutsy's face was bleeding too. He looked around and saw men fighting in the moonlight. Nobody seemed to notice him, and that was okay as far as he was concerned. He looked down at the dead Japanese officer and felt victorious. This was the hardest fight he'd ever been in during his may months in the recon platoon, and he felt an odd primordial warrior's urge to have a trophy. In another time and place he might have taken his adversary's head, or his scalp, or his ear and then Nutsy remembered his own ear and touched it. Only a ragged chunk of flesh was left, and it still was bleeding. Nutsy wanted a tangible trophy that could be hung on his wall, although the only walls Nutsy had ever had were the walls of barracks, tents, the orphanage, or the boxcars that sped across the American landscape.

He saw the gilded officer's insignia on Captain Shimoyama's lapels, and bent down to cut them off with his Ka-bar knife, when he noticed something gleaming in the distance. Glancing up, his eyes fell on Captain Shimoyama's samurai sword reflecting the light of the moon. Nutsy had taken samurai swords as souvenirs before, but he'd sold them because he'd had no personal connection with them.

He had a personal connection with the sword that lay in front of him. That sword had tried to kill him and nearly succeeded several times. Nutsy had won the fight just barely, and he knew it. He had defeated that sword, and now he felt he had a right to it.

The sword called out to him, and Nutsy walked toward it

131

as if in a trance. He ached all over as he looked down at the sword. It was beautiful, with its long curving blade and handle bound with leather strips. Bending over, he picked it up and held it in his hands. Its weight felt perfect, heavy enough to do terrible damage, yet light enough to maneuver around. Japanese characters were engraved on the blade, and Nutsy didn't know it, but they were the signature of a famous sword maker in Tokyo. Nutsy wrapped his fingers around the handle and raised the sword in the air, the way the Japanese officer had. It felt right.

Nutsy turned toward the fighting, hearing rifle stock smash against rifle stock and bayonet clash against bayonet. He took a deep breath and ran toward the crowd of soldiers, seeing that they all were Japanese and their backs were to him.

Nutsy charged and swung the samurai sword downward. It connected with the top of a Japanese soldier's head and sliced him to the waist as if he were a big yellow banana. He swung to the side and caved in the ribs of another Japanese soldier. He swung to the other side and lopped off the head of the next Japanese soldier, and a fountain of blood gushed into the air. Stepping forward, Nutsy swung down again and split the head of the next Japanese soldier.

Two Japanese soldiers turned around just as Nutsy was in the middle of a sideways swing. The blade of his sword hit one Japanese soldier on the biceps and hacked off his arm. The Japanese soldier raised the stump and looked at it, his eyes bulging out of his head, then collapsed as blood drained out of his brain.

The Japanese soldier who'd been beside him thrust his rifle and bayonet toward Nutsy, but faltered and closed his eyes. He collapsed onto his knees, revealing Bannon behind him. Bannon looked like a demon from hell. He'd lost his hat and he was covered with blood. His uniform was torn to shreds and he charged toward Nutsy. A wild animal glaze shone in Bannon's eyes.

"It's me!" Nutsy screamed.

Bannon stopped and stared at Nutsy, blinking. Bannon at this point had gone completely kill crazy. He didn't even know who Nutsy was anymore, but he knew he was a friend and not a foe.

Bannon spun around and saw a wall of Japs running toward

him. He snorted and screamed, jumping into the air and charging them. This took them by surprise, and before they could get set, he thrust the bayonet on the end of his rifle into the stomach of the Jap in the middle. He yanked out the bayonet and swung the rifle around, whacking a Jap upside his head. He pointed the bayonet straight ahead again and harpooned another Jap in the chest. He tugged on the rifle but couldn't pull it loose, then saw a bayonet speeding toward his heart. he leaped on the rifle that carried the bayonet, snatched it out of the Japanese soldier's hands, and smashed him in the face with the rifle stock.

Spinning around, his bayonet clashed against the bayonet on another Japanese soldier's rifle, and Bannon's bayonet broke loose from its mounting on his rifle. Bannon dropped the rifle and lunged for the Japanese soldier's throat, pressing his thumbs against the Japanese soldier's Adam's apple, when suddenly, out of nowhere, a rifle butt came crashing down on Bannon's skull.

An ordinary skull would have fractured, but Bannon had a big steel plate in his head, and it held, but the force of the blow drove Bannon to his knees. Nearly unconscious, he dived forward, tackling another Japanese soldier and bringing him down. Bannon punched the Japanese soldier in the mouth, dodged a thrust from a Japanese bayonet, rolled over, and jumped to his feet.

He had nothing in his hands to fight with, and three Japanese soldiers charged him. The nearest Japanese soldier thrust forward his rifle and bayonet, and Bannon batted the front of the rifle to the side with his forearm, kicked the Jap in the balls, and tore the rifle and bayonet out of his hands.

Another bayonet sliced toward him, and Bannon parried it to the side, delivering an uppercut with the rifle butt and connecting with the Japanese soldier's chin. The Jap's head snapped backward as he was lifted six inches into the air; then he collapsed onto his back.

Bannon wanted to run him through, but he didn't have time. He still had two Japs in his immediate vicinity, and he had to deal with them. *"Yyyaaahhhhhhh!"* he screamed, thrusting forward with his rifle and bayonet.

The Japanese soldier he was aiming at tried to parry the blow, but he didn't have the strength. Bannon's bayonet shot

133

forward and went up to its hilt in the Japanese soldier's stomach. Banon pulled out the bayonet and slashed to the side to keep the third Japanese soldier off him.

That Japanese soldier jumped backward to avoid Bannon's bayonet, and Bannon went after him like a mad dog. He pushed his rifle and bayonet forward, and the Japanese soldier managed to parry it, but that didn't stop Bannon's motion. He brought his rifle butt around and smashed it into the Japanese soldier's head.

The Japanese soldier fell onto his back, and Bannon jumped with both feet onto his head, kicking and stomping until the Japanese soldier's face resembled a plate of spaghetti and meatballs.

Bannon saw a Nambu pistol lying on the ground. He picked it up and aimed it at the first Japanese soldier who appeared in his line of vision.

Click!

It was empty. He should have known it was empty; otherwise it wouldn't have been thrown onto the ground. The Japanese soldier was on top of Bannon and harpooned his rifle and bayonet forward. Bannon timed its approach and slammed down the barrel of the rifle with his left hand while whacking the Japanese soldier in the face with the Nambu pistol.

The Japanese soldier's bayonet pierced Bannon's thigh, and Bannon went insane with pain. The Japanese soldier was dazed by the blow from the Nambu pistol in Bannon's hand, and Bannon slugged him again, knocking him cold. The Japanese soldier fell onto his back, and Bannon dropped to his knees, straddling him and pistol-whipping him in the face.

Bannon would have continued hammering the Japanese soldier in the face, but more Japanese soldiers charged toward him. Wearily he got to his feet. No matter how hard he fought, no matter how many Japanese soldiers he killed, there were always more, and now all he had in his hands was an empty, bloody Nambu pistol. He threw it at the Japanese soldiers, and it bounced off the shoulder of one of them. Looking around, he saw a Japanese Arisaka rifle lying on the ground, and he scooped it up. He limped forward to do battle with the Japanese soldiers, and parried the blow from one of them, but another slammed him in the head with his rifle butt.

Bannon fell to the ground, and Terrible Tommy Shaw saw

him go down. Screaming at the top of his lungs, Shaw kicked a Japanese soldier in the balls and ran toward Bannon in order to save his life.

The group of Japanese soldiers crowded around Bannon and prepared to stab him to death, when Shaw descended upon them. Shaw buried his bayonet to the hilt in the back of one Japanese soldier, slammed another in the head with his rifle butt, and kicked a third in the balls. At that point he had the undivided attention of the rest of them.

They forgot about Bannon and charged Shaw, who raised his rifle and bayonet to parry the first thrust, elbowed the next Jap in the eyeball, kicked a third Jap in the balls, and then *slam!*

His rifle had somehow been knocked out of his hands. Shaw reached to his belt and yanked out his Ka-bar knife. A Japanese rifle and bayonet came toward him, and he dodged out of the way just as he'd dodged punches in Madison Square Garden in New York City, punching up with his Ka-bar knife.

It was swallowed up by the soft stomach of a Japanese soldier, and Shaw pulled it out, slashing wildly. He was surrounded by so many Japs that he knew he had to hit one of them, and he was right. The tip of the Ka-bar knife slashed across a Japanese soldier's cheek and ripped off half of his nose. The Japanese soldier screeched and dropped his rifle, pressing the palms of his hands against his face, and Shaw slashed wildly again, cutting open the windpipe of another Jap.

Wham! A rifle butt hit Shaw on the side of his head, and Shaw dropped to his knees. But back in New York the sports writers had said that Shaw had a head like a block of concrete; Shaw wasn't knocked out, just a little shaken. He lurched forward, swinging up with his knife, and buried its blade in the groin of the Japanese soldier who'd slugged him. The Japanese soldier screeched and covered the hole with his hands, blood spouting around his fingers, and Shaw spun around ripping a Japanese soldier across the chest. He slashed the next Japanese soldier across the mouth, stabbed a third in the stomach, and kicked a fourth in the balls; then two hands clamped around his wrist.

Shaw didn't have freedom of movement anymore. He tried to twist loose, but the hands of the Japanese soldier were like a vise. He pulled the Japanese soldier off his feet, swung him

135

through the air, and slammed him against the trunk of a tree. The Japanese soldier was knocked senseless and released Shaw's wrist.

Shaw turned around and saw four Japanese soldiers rushing toward him. He looked up and saw no branches to jump onto. The Japanese soldiers surged closer and Shaw went in to a knife-fighter's crouch. He saw that one of the Japs was bow-legged, and he thought: *What the fuck.* Lowering his head, he dived between the Japanese soldier's bowed legs, tumbled over, landed on his feet, spun around, and jammed his Ka-bar knife into the back of the Japanese soldier's neck, cutting through the spot where the Japanese soldier's skull was attached to his spine. The Japanese soldier gurgled blood and dropped to the ground, and Shaw grabbed the rifle and bayonet out of his hands. He thrust the bayonet into the liver of the next Japanese soldier, and by that time the other two had turned around to face him.

"Yaaaahhhhh!" screamed Shaw, charging toward them.

Shaw was covered with blood, and his bare teeth glittered in the moonlight. He frightened the two Japanese soldiers, and they hesitated, always a mistake in hand-to-hand combat. He plunged the bayonet on the end of his rifle into the chest of the first soldier, but when he pulled back, the rifle wouldn't disengage.

The last Japanese soldier recovered from his fright and slammed Shaw on the jaw with his rifle butt. Shaw felt a ferocious pain all through his head, because his jaw had been broken, and this was the second time it had been broken in hand-to-hand combat; plus it was broken in the same place.

Blood poured out of his mouth, and its salty taste made him furious. Shaw had always been the kind of boxer who fought best when he was hurt, and now he was hurt. The Japanese soldier readied his rifle and bayonet for the coup de grace, and Shaw kicked him in the balls, slammed him in the face with the butt of his rifle, and stabbed him through the chest as the Japanese soldier fell to the ground.

Shaw pulled his rifle and bayonet back and spat out a gob of blood. A bunch of Japanese soldiers moved toward him, and he heard footsteps behind him. Glancing to his rear, he saw more Japanese soldiers. They were fanning out and sur-rounding him, and he thought: *I'd better get them before they*

136

get me. He picked out the smallest Japanese soldier he could see and let out a battle cry, drooling blood as he ran toward him.

Stark terror came over the Japanese soldier's face, and he raised his rifle and bayonet to defend himself. Shaw banged him in the face with his rifle butt and ran over him while other Japanese soldiers cut Shaw on his shoulders and sides as he passed by.

Some of the cuts were deep, and Shaw felt boiling pain. He couldn't move so quickly and the jungle spun around him. He turned to face the Japanese soldiers, and they ran toward him to finish him off. He lunged at one of them with his rifle and bayonet, but his timing was off and the Japanese soldier sidestepped easily, cracking Shaw over the head with his rifle butt.

This time Shaw went down for the long count, lying motionless on the ground. The Japanese soldiers crowded around him, angling their rifles and bayonets downward to stab him to death, when they heard the thunder of running feet. They looked up and saw three men running toward them, and the men were so bloody that it was difficult to see at first whose side they were on, but there was something foreign about the way they moved, and they all were much taller than average Japanese soldiers.

"Get the fuckers!" Butsko screamed.

Butsko had picked up a thick branch somewhere along the line and wielded it like a club. He slammed one Japanese soldier in the head, dodged the bayonet thrust of another, and slugged him in the gut; when that Japanese soldier keeled over, Butsko cracked his head open. He swung the club and hit a Japanese soldier's head with such force that it shattered like a rotten watermelon. He swung again and hit another Japanese soldier on the forearm, breaking his bones. Then Butsko kicked him in the balls.

A Japanese soldier snuck up behind Butsko, hoping to harpoon him in the back with his rifle and bayonet. As the Japanese soldier tensed himself to strike, Nutsy Gafooley came out of nowhere and swung downward with his captured samurai sword, chopping off both the soldier's arms, which fell to the ground along with his rifle. The soldier stared with disbelief at the bloody stumps where once his arms had been, but then Nutsy

137

cut off his head, and the Japanese soldier's worries were over.

Nutsy loved his new weapon, and found that it was easy to use. He swung to the side and cut off the leg of a Japanese soldier, causing him to fall onto his face; then Nutsy swung at his back, chopping his spine in two. Nutsy spun around and swung at a Japanese soldier's stomach, slicing up his intestines, making him keel over, and as Nutsy raised his samurai sword to whack him in the head, a blood-soaked bayonet was thrust to the hilt into Nutsy's back.

Nutsy was overcome with pain and disorientation. He didn't know where he was or what had happened to him. He dropped the samurai sword, took a step, and fell onto his face. The Japanese soldier who'd stabbed him made the mistake of looking down at his handiwork, and at that moment Longtree leaped over Nutsy's body and delivered an uppercut with the butt of his rifle to the jaw of the Japanese soldier, whose head snapped back as he fell down. Longtree stood over the Japanese soldier and prepared to stab him, when he noticed a Japanese bayonet streaking toward him. Longtree jumped back to get out of the way, but the bayonet cut open his right biceps to the bone, and Longtree's hand went numb. He lost his grip on his rifle, and the Japanese soldier clobbered him in the face with his rifle butt. Longtree's skull was fractured and he dropped to the ground.

The Japanese soldier aimed his rifle and bayonet at Longtree and pushed down, when something caught his eye. It was Bannon's bayonet, and it pierced the Japanese soldier's neck, coming out the far side. The Japanese soldier gurgled blood, and Bannon pulled out his bayonet.

It was Bannon and Butsko now, fighting back to back, and it looked like the end was in sight. They were surrounded by forty Japanese soldiers, but only a small percentage of Japanese soldiers could get within actual striking distance. Butsko slammed Japanese soldiers in the head with his club. Bannon stabbed them with his rifle and bayonet and banged them with the butt of his rifle. A Japanese soldier lunged forward with his rifle and bayonet, and Bannon parried the blow, but Bannon was tired and not as strong as he'd been before. The Japanese bayonet cut open his cheek, sliced across his scalp, and jabbed into thin air dripping blood, and Bannon hammered the Jap in the mouth with his rifle butt.

Wild with pain, Bannon stepped forward to run the Jap through, imprudently opening his back to attack, and two Japanese soldiers thrust their rifles and bayonets forward. Both of them stabbed Bannon in the back, and Bannon dropped to his knees, coughing blood. The Japanese soldiers drew back to stab him again, when Butsko spun around and with a backhand swing caught one of them on the side of his head, knocking him cold. Then, with a frontal swing, Butsko struck the next Japanese soldier square on the face, flattening his nose and busting cheekbones and jaw.

The Japanese soldiers collapsed at Butsko's feet, and he stepped over them, smashing a Japanese soldier on top of his head. Blood squirted out of the Japanese soldier's ears and nose. He slammed another Japanese soldier on the shoulder, separating bones and cartilage from the soldier's torso; whacked the next Japanese soldier on the biceps, breaking his arm; and smacked the third Japanese soldier in the neck, launching his head into air.

"You fucking bastards!" Butsko screamed as he charged forward, his big combat boots pounding on the ground. Japanese soldiers lashed out at Butsko with their bayonets, cutting his arms and legs, sticking him in the stomach, but that didn't stop him. He raised his club high in the air and brought it down with all the strength of his mighty body on a Japanese soldier, whose head was squashed flat on his shoulders, the force of the blow hurling him to his knees.

Butsko swung sideways at the other soldier's head, and his power was so great that it caused the soldier's head to cave in, separating the top of his skull from the rest of his cranium. The top of his skull went flying through the air like an inverted bowl of stew.

Butsko spun around and realized he was the last GI left. He was wounded and bleeding but more dangerous than ever. He looked for a place to make his last stand, because he knew the time had come for him to die. All he wanted was something to protect his back, so that he could kill as many Japs as he could before they got him.

He saw the big boulder behind the hole and said to himself: *That's it.* Japanese soldiers surrounded him, and Butsko beat a path through them, running toward the boulder, turning around, and pressing his back against it.

"Come on and get me, you fucking bastards!" he hollered, raising his bloody club in his bloody right hand. *"Come on!"*

The Japanese soldiers looked at him; nobody wanted to get close, but they didn't want to walk away either. They muttered to each other, and one of them worked the bolt of his Arisaka rifle, pushing a round into the chamber. Several more did the same thing, and Butsko knew they were going to gun him down.

"You fucking yellow-bellies!"

Butsko threw his club at them and dashed toward the jungle. The Japanese soldiers raised their rifles and opened fire. Bullets whistled over Butsko's head, and he turtled down into his ragged collar as he moved into the jungle like an angry wounded bear. A Japanese bullet hit the back of his leg, and Butsko spun around, falling onto his back. He rolled to his hands and knees, blood soaking his pant leg, and tried to stand, but the leg wouldn't support him and he fell down again.

"I'm finished," he muttered to himself.

The night became dark around Butsko, and he pitched forward onto his face.

TWELVE . . .

The Japanese soldiers rushed into the jungle to finish Butsko off, when they heard the sound of crashing and flailing behind them. They turned around and became aware that a substantial number of men were moving toward them through the jungle, and from that direction they could only be Americans.

"Get the cocksuckers!" Sergeant Cameron screamed, erupting out of a mass of foliage, holding his carbine with bayonet attached. He pulled the trigger of the carbine and it fired in the automatic mode, spraying bullets at the conglomeration of Japanese soldiers.

Lieutenant Thurmond emerged from the jungle ten yards away, also firing his carbine in its automatic mode. *"Follow me!"*

The rest of the recon platoon and J Company charged through the jungle, firing their M 1 rifles, and the Jap soldiers didn't know whether to shit or go blind. Their commanding officer and first sergeant had been killed, and Jap soldiers had never been taught to think for themselves and improvise on the spur of the moment. All they could do was turn tail and flee toward their lines until they could find someone who'd tell them what to do.

They ran into the part of the jungle that was closest to their lines, and the GIs fired at their backs, killing many of them. The Japanese soldiers who managed to elude bullets melted into the moonlit jungle and could be heard speeding away through the thick foliage.

"Hold your fire!" hollered Lieutenant Thurmond.

The GIs eased off on their triggers, and everyone looked around at the heaps of bodies lying everywhere.

"Sergeant Cameron!" said Lieutenant Thurmond. "Send a patrol after those Japanese soldiers!" Lieutenant Thurmond then wrinkled his brow and thought about what he'd just ordered. "No—wait a minute. They might run into a trap." He looked around at the carpet on the jungle floor. "Where's Butsko and his patrol?"

Sergeant Cameron squinted toward his left. "I do believe I see Longtree."

Sergeant Cameron moved in that direction and saw Longtree lying on his back, blood oozing from a big gash on his head and a cut on his arm. He knelt down and felt Longtree's pulse. "He's alive! *Medic!*"

Pfc. Osgood, the new recon platoon medic, came running over, carrying his haversack full of medicine. He dropped down beside Longtree and saw the wound on his forehead. "Looks like a bad one," he said. "Bet his skull is fractured."

Osgood opened his haversack and took out a packet of sulfa pounder to disinfect the wound. In another part of the clearing a soldier from J Company spotted a soldier in an American uniform lying on his stomach. "Here's another one!"

"Who is he?" asked Cameron, walking swiftly in that direction.

"I don't know."

Cameron drew closer and didn't know who it was because the soldier's features were covered with blood. Dropping to his knees, Cameron brought his eyes closer and recognized Bannon. "My God," he whispered. Bannon had so much blood on him that Cameron didn't know where it was coming from. *"Medic!"*

Private Shapiro, the J Company medic, a short, roly-poly man, ran toward Sergeant Cameron as Sergeant Cameron felt for Bannon's pulse. "I think he's still alive," Cameron said.

"Lemme see," Shapiro replied.

Sergeant Cameron removed his hand from Bannon's wrist, and Shapiro placed his sensitive fingers on the spot where Bannon's pulse should be. "He's still alive," Shapiro said.

"Fix him up!" Sergeant Cameron ordered.

"I can't even see where he's bleeding from."

Sergeant Cameron spotted the big cut on Bannon's neck. "From there!" he said, pointing.

"All the blood couldn't be coming from there."

On the other side of the clearing, Corporal Gomez came upon Nutsy Gafooley crumpled onto his side, the back of his shirt soaked with blood. "*Medic!*" Corporal Gomez called.

"Who ya got?" Sergeant Cameron asked.

"Nutsy Gafooley, and I think he's dead!"

Sergeant Cameron ran toward Gomez and saw Nutsy lying on the ground, the samurai sword still in his hand.

"Fucking sword's bigger'n he is," Sergeant Cameron said, kneeling beside Nutsy and touching his pulse. "I don't feel nothing."

"Lemme see," said Corporal Gomez.

Sergeant Cameron took his fingers away and Corporal Gomez felt for Nutsy Gafooley's pulse. "I think he's a goner, Sarge."

"You don't know what the fuck you're talking about." Sergeant Cameron pushed Gomez away and again tried to find Nutsy Gafooley's pulse, but he couldn't. Yet, he refused to believe that the little ex-hobo could be dead. "I need a medic over here!"

Lieutenant Thurmond walked toward him. "Both the medics are busy. Listen to me, Sergeant: We're in Jap territory, and more of them might come back at any moment. We'd better get out of here."

Sergeant Cameron rolled Nutsy onto his back, tore open the front of his shirt, and pressed his ear against his chest. He couldn't hear anything at all, but he thought maybe he wasn't listening in the right place. He refused to believe that Nutsy might be dead. *"Medic!"*

"I'm coming!" replied Osgood, who was finished with Longtree. He dropped to his knees beside Sergeant Cameron

143

and looked down at Nutsy Gafooley. Osgood had completed one year of medical school at Georgetown University in Washington, D.C., and knew more about medicine than any other medic in the regiment. He opened his haversack, pulled out the stethoscope he'd used in medical school, plugged it into his ears, and placed the black disc on Nutsy Gafooley's motionless chest. He changed the position of the disc three times, then unplugged the stethoscope from his ears and turned to Sergeant Cameron. "I can't do anything for this man," he said.

Sergeant Cameron looked at him in disbelief. "You can't?"

"No, I can't."

"You're sure?"

"He's dead, Sergeant."

"He don't look dead to me."

"People whose hearts aren't beating are dead, Sergeant."

A voice came to them from another part of the clearing. "Here's two more."

Pfc. Osgood stuffed his stethoscope back into his haversack. "I'd better go look at them."

Pfc. Osgood stood and walked in the direction of the voice. Corporal Gomez and Craig Delane, along with the rest of the recon platoon, followed him to see which of their buddies were over there. They came to the big hole with dead Japanese soldiers piled up all around it.

Gomez looked at the dead Japanese soldiers. "Looks like some bad shit happened over here."

Craig Delane glanced around and could see that a major struggle had taken place around the hole. He was amazed at the vast number of dead Japanese soldiers he saw. How did Butsko and his tiny patrol kill all those Japs?

Osgood jumped into the hole and knelt beside Frankie La Barbara, noticing Frankie's bloodied mouth, bruised face, and bandaged leg, but those wounds didn't appear very serious. He didn't seem to have any other wounds. Osgood felt Frankie's pulse and perceived immediately that his skin was hot. He touched Frankie's forehead; it was clear that Frankie had a fever. Then Frankie went into a spasm of shaking.

"I think this man's got malaria," Osgood said.

"He's had it before," Corporal Gomez replied.

"You're sure?"

"Yeah, I'm sure. He got it on Guadalcanal and had to go

144

to the hospital for a long time."

"I'd better give him a shot of quinine."

Osgood reached into his haversack and took out a quinine ampule. He broke the seal and jabbed the needle into Frankie's arm, while a few feet away Craig Delane felt for Homer Gladley's pulse but couldn't detect anything. He figured he must be doing something wrong.

Gomez noticed him. "Feel anything?"

"I don't know how to do this," Delane said.

"Lemme see."

Gomez reached for Homer's pulse. "Jesus, Mary, and Joseph," he said. "I think Homer's dead."

"You must be feeling in the wrong place."

Osgood pulled the ampule out of Frankie's arm and threw the ampule over his shoulder. He looked at Homer, who lay completely still. It didn't appear that Homer was breathing, but sometimes a man's breath was so shallow that you couldn't detect it with the naked eye, especially at night. Osgood pulled the stethoscope out of his haversack. "Unbutton his shirt."

Osgood plugged the stethoscope into his ears as Gomez tore open Homer's shirt, revealing his gigantic pectoral muscles. Osgood pressed the metal disc against Homer's heart. He listened for a few moments, frowned, and shook his head. "He's dead."

Craig Delane blinked, because he and Homer had been in the original platoon that had formed the nucleus of the recon platoon. "You're sure?"

"Yeah."

Craig reached for the stethoscope. "Lemme listen."

Osgood pushed the stethoscope into his haversack. "I just told you, he's dead, Delane. Do I have to draw a picture?"

A group of men from the recon platoon and J Company stood at the edge of the hole, and Sergeant Cameron pushed through them. "What's going on here?"

Delane looked up at him. "Frankie's sick with malaria again, and Homer is dead."

"Homer is dead?"

"That's what Osgood said."

Sergeant Cameron looked at Osgood. "Homer is dead?"

"Afraid so."

"Jesus Christ."

145

Corporal Gomez crossed himself. Everybody looked at Homer Gladley, the mountain of a man whom everybody had thought was invincible, but a person can bleed internally for only so long, and then major organs start to fail.

"I found Shaw!" shouted Private Rutledge from another part of the clearing.

Private Shapiro, the medic from J Company, was fairly close by, and he waddled toward Rutledge, who was pulling the bodies of dead Japs off Terrible Tommy Shaw. The rest of J Company and some men from the recon platoon gathered around as Shapiro dropped down next to Shaw and felt for his pulse.

"He's alive," Shapiro said.

"Praise God," replied Rutledge.

As with all the others except Frankie La Barbara, it was difficult to see where Shaw was wounded, because he was spattered with so much blood and guts. Then Shapiro noticed that Shaw's face looked out of line. He touched Shaw's jaw, and it dangled as if held by a few threads, which in fact was the case.

"He's got a broken jaw," Shapiro said, "but that might be the least of his problems."

Shapiro unbuttoned Shaw's shirt, looking for serious wounds, and saw a few nicks and cuts but nothing major. He rolled Shaw onto his side and pulled up his shirt in back, again seeing nothing life-threatening.

Just then a sound was heard in the jungle, and everyone dropped down to his stomach, poising weapons, preparing for a counterattack. They heard movement in the thick vegetation, headed in their direction. They aimed at the sound and looked toward Lieutenant Thurmond, waiting for him to order them to fire.

Lieutenant Thurmond sighted down his barrel at the part of the jungle where the sounds were coming from and was about to order his men to open fire, when he realized that the sound indicated the presence of few people, perhaps even one. Glancing around, he saw that all of his men had taken cover. It might only be a monkey or a wild pig out there; what was the point of wasting all the ammunition?

"Hold your fire!" he shouted.

Leaves shook in front of them, and a figure appeared that was too big to be a monkey or wild pig. The figure staggered forward and looked like a monster from a nightmare. It was covered from head to foot with blood and gore, and its eyes glowed red like burning coals.

"You fucking bastards," the figure said, "it's about time you got here!"

"Butsko!" shouted Corporal Gomez.

Butsko groaned and tripped over a rock, falling onto his face and rolling over. The men jumped up and ran toward him, crowding around and watching him struggling to get up.

"Somebody gimme a hand," Butsko croaked.

"Stay where you are," Osgood said, placing his hands on Butsko's shoulders, trying to ease him back down.

"Get your fucking dick-skinners off me," Butsko replied, trying to push Osgood away; but Butsko didn't have the strength, and he collapsed onto his left biceps, the one that had been sliced open. Butsko moaned in pain, and Osgood rolled him over onto his back.

"Take it easy, Sarge," Osgood said.

"Up your ass with a ten-inch meat hook," Butsko replied.

"Where does it hurt, Sarge?"

"Everywhere."

Lieutenant Thurmond crouched on the other side of Butsko. "What happened here, Sergeant?"

"You got eyes, ain'tcha?"

Lieutenant Thurmond looked at Pfc. Osgood. "Patch him up fast, because we've got to get out of here. The Japs might return in force at any moment." Lieutenant Thurmond stood and approached Sergeant Cameron. "Tell the men to get ready to move out."

"We're gonna take our dead with us, ain't we?"

"Of course."

Butsko stirred on the ground. *"Dead! Who in the fuck is dead? I ain't dead! None of us are dead!"*

"You just take it easy, Sarge," Osgood said, cutting open Butsko's pant leg, looking for the source of all the blood on that part of his body.

"You take it easy, young soldier," Butsko wheezed. *"None of us are dead!"* he screamed, because he didn't want to believe it.

Osgood saw that Butsko wasn't going to remain still, so there was only one thing to do. He removed a morphine Syrette

147

from his haversack, pulled off the cap, and stuck the needle into Butsko's leg.

Butsko saw pinwheels of color before his eyes and felt warm all over. None of his wounds hurt him anymore, and he didn't care who was alive and who was dead. He closed his eyes and thought everything was going to be okay, although he and the others were still a long way from their own lines.

Colonel Toshio Akai slept soundly in his command tent several miles from where Pfc. Osgood was bandaging Butsko's leg. He wore only his underwear, which looked like a jockstrap, and his mattress lay on a bamboo tatami mat that had been placed on the bare jungle ground.

The tent flap opened and Lieutenant Oyagi entered, wearing his clean pale-green uniform. General Hyakutake had finally got sick of Lieutenant Oyagi and transferred him to Colonel Akai's headquarters, swapping aides with Colonel Akai.

Lieutenant Oyagi had been glad for the transfer, because he disliked General Hyakutake about as much as General Hytaku-take disliked him. General Hyakutake had been a cranky old son of a bitch, but Colonel Akai seemed to be okay. Colonel Akai was very even-tempered, as a rule, but he'd never had to wake up Colonel Akai in the middle of the night with bad news before.

"Who's there?" asked Colonel Akai, reaching for the Nambu pistol lying beside his pillow.

"Me," said Lieutenant Oyagi.

"What do you want?"

"I have bad news, I'm afraid."

"Bad news!" Colonel Akai sat upright and looked at Lieutenant Oyagi. For all he knew, the entire US Army could be a mile away. That's what bad news meant to him. "Well, out with it!"

"A radio transmission has come in from Captain Shimoyama's company. Captain Shimoyama has been killed in action, and so has most of his company. Only approximately twenty of his men are left."

"Out of how many?"

"Approximately one hundred and sixty, sir."

"Light the lamp on my desk, will you?"

"Yes, sir."

Lieutenant Oyagi struck a match and touched it to the wick of the kerosene lamp on Colonel Akai's desk, while Colonel Akai pulled on his pants and pushed his arms through the sleeves of his shirt. He walked barefooted to the desk. His head was shaved and shaped like an artillery shell with big ears. On the desk was a pack of cigarettes, and he took one out, lighting it with a match. Then he looked down at the map that lay flat on his desk.

"Have you been told how many Americans were involved in the action?" he asked.

Lieutenant Oyagi read from the scrap of paper in his hand. "Approximately two companies, sir."

Colonel Akai frowned. "Last time I asked how many Americans were out there, I was told one company. Now I'm told two companies. Are the Americans reproducing in the jungle?"

"I believe that Captain Shimoyama's company was attacked by a unit of Americans different from the one he was pursuing."

Colonel Akai puffed his cigarette. He was not terribly surprised by what had happened, because he'd known that Captain Shimoyama wasn't an experienced combat officer. Colonel Akai knew that experience was the most important element in a combat officer's training, and Captain Shimoyama had only been a staff officer, a man who knew how to move pins around on maps.

— Colonel Akai also knew that defeat could be turned into victory if common sense and resolve were applied. "Where did this battle take place?"

Lieutenant Oyagi read the coordinates from the message in his hand. Colonel Akai found the spot on his map; it was a long way from the American lines. Moreover he had other troops in that general area. Perhaps they could cut off this larger American unit and destroy it. The operation would be difficult, but the Americans were isolated in the open jungle, far from their main sources of supply, and presumably carrying wounded with them, because Captain Shimoyama's men must have wounded *some* of the Americans.

Captain Shimoyama looked more closely at the map. He knew that a military commander had to consider negative sides of operations as well as positive sides. If he positioned two companies between the retreating Americans and the main American lines, it could be assumed that the main body of

149

Americans would hear the fighting when the two Japanese companies attacked the retreating Americans, and then the main body of Americans would strike. The two Japanese companies would be caught in a giant nutcracker. They would probably be wiped out, and Colonel Akai couldn't afford to lose any more men. He decided not to order the ambush operation.

If only I had more men, Colonel Akai thought, leaning back in his chair. *If only so many mistakes hadn't been made.* He looked up at Lieutenant Oyagi. "You may return to your quarters. Wake me up if anything important happens."

"Yes, sir."

Lieutenant Oyagi saluted, did an about-face, and marched out of Colonel Akai's office. Colonel Akai stubbed out his cigarette butt in his ashtray and arose, moving toward his bed.

We may lose Bougainville, he thought, *but there will be other battles. In the end, Japan will be victorious.*

He tried to believe this as he undressed and went to bed.

THIRTEEN . . .

Colonel Hutchins drank his morning cup of coffee laced with white lightning as he sat behind his desk in his headquarters tent. He ate powdered eggs, which tasted more like cardboard than eggs, and read reports of events that had occurred during the night: Jap infiltrators trying to break through several points in the line, a fight in George Company, the appearance in Baker Company of reporters from the Associated Press; also, a young private, newly assigned to the regiment, had awakened screaming in the middle of the night and had to be taken away in a straitjacket.

Colonel Hutchins drank his coffee and ate his breakfast quickly, because there was a big meeting at General Hawkins's headquarters at 0800 hours and he had to get ready. Not only would it be necessary to shave and put on a fresh uniform, but he had to come up with ideas on how to continue the campaign into Jap territory, and Colonel Hutchins didn't have any ideas. He had never been a skilled strategist or tactician. He just

151

believed in getting there first with the most and then fighting like hell.

He heard cheering and hollering in the distance. *Now what?* he asked himself. The sound became louder and he creased his brow. "Sergeant Koch!" he shouted.

"Yes, sir!" replied Master Sergeant Koch, the sergeant-major of the regiment, whose office was in the next section of the big walled tent.

"Get your ass in here!"

"Yes, sir!"

The tent flap was pushed to the side, and Sergeant Koch entered Colonel Hutchins's office. Koch was tall, stoop-shouldered, and had a big hooked nose. He resembled a buzzard and was new to his job, having replaced Sergeant Major Ramsay, who had been killed during the big Japanese offensive ten days earlier. Sergeant Koch saluted and stood at attention in front of Colonel Hutchins's desk, although Sergeant Koch never stood straight when he stood at attention because of his stooped shoulders.

"What the hell's all that ruckus out there!" Colonel Hutchins asked.

"Don't know, sir."

"Find out."

"Yes, sir."

Sergeant Koch returned to his office, and Colonel Hutchins took another sip of coffee. The shouting and cheering became louder, and it bothered him. Front-line troops were supposed to be quiet. You didn't want to let the enemy know where you were, otherwise you'd attract artillery fire, although the Japs hadn't fired much artillery since their big offensive. Colonel Hutchins didn't think the Japs had much left on Bougainville. He thought that the Twenty-third Infantry Regiment, together with other front-line units, should just sweep across the island and mop up the slant-eyed cocksuckers.

Sergeant Koch returned several minutes later. "Sir," he said, "Company J and the recon platoon are back. That's what all the racket is about."

"They're back? What happened?"

"I don't know, sir."

"Son of a bitch!" Colonel Hutchins said. "If I wanna find out anything around here, I gotta find it out myself!" He stood

152

behind his desk and put on his steel pot, then strode toward the door. "Get outta my way!"

Colonel Hutchins walked outside and could see the first glimmer of dawn on the horizon. Visibility was still poor, but he could detect the general direction of the noise and headed in that direction, the holster containing his Colt .45 slapping up and down on his hip. He passed pup tents and men sitting around, eating powdered eggs out of their mess kits and drinking coffee out of their big tin cups. They looked up at Colonel Hutchins and knew they should jump to attention, but he shouted "As you were!" in his thunderous voice, and they stayed where they were, gazing at him in awe, because colonels are like gods to ordinary enlisted soldiers.

Colonel Hutchins saw a crowd of men in the distance, and that's where the noise was coming from. He tucked in his chin and headed in that direction, grimacing, because a grimace was his normal facial expression. He saw men jumping up and down, tossing their helmets into the air.

"What the fuck is this," he hollered, *"a goddamned circus?"*

Everybody froze at the sound of his voice, and somebody shouted: *"Ten-hut!"*

The men shot to attention, facing different directions in the darkness, and the men carrying the wounded stopped in their tracks.

"What the hell's going on here?" Colonel Hutchins demanded. "Don't you men know this is a combat zone? Who's in charge of this goddamned mess?"

Lieutenant Thurmond stepped forward, saluted, and identified himself. "Company J is returning from patrol, sir."

Colonel Hutchins looked around. "Where the hell's the patrol from the recon platoon?"

"Over there, sir."

Colonel Hutchins noticed soldiers being carried in stretchers made from shirts tied together. He pushed his way toward them and looked down at Longtree, whose head was swathed in bandages.

"Who's the medic around here?"

Pfc. Osgood and Private Shapiro both shuffled toward Colonel Hutchins, saluting sloppily.

"What's the matter with this man?"

Osgood spoke first: "Skull fracture."

153

"Where's Butsko?"

Osgood pointed. Colonel Hutchins walked toward Butsko and looked down. Butsko was unconscious, his veins and arteries full of morphine.

"What's wrong with him?"

"Multiple wounds all over his body, but the worst is his leg. I believe the bone is broken."

Lieutenant Thurmond decided that the time had come for him to put in his two cents. "Of the men from the recon platoon who went out on patrol, two were killed and the rest've been wounded pretty badly. They were ambushed by one company of Japs at least. We showed up in the nick of time."

"Which ones were killed?"

"Private Gafooley and Private Gladley."

Colonel Hutchins knew who they were, because the recon platoon was the special unit he used for all his dirty work, just as Colonel Stockton had done before him.

"See that these men get the medical care they require," he said to Lieutenant Thurmond. "Then report to me and give me a full rundown of what happened."

"Yes, sir."

"As you were."

Captain Hutchins turned around and walked back to his tent, his forehead creased with worry. He took a cigarette out of his pack and lit it up while gazing at the ground ahead. He was an old war dog and he was accustomed to having casualties, but he'd been especially attached to his recon platoon, and Butsko was an old friend of his. It bothered him that Butsko had been wounded so badly and the others had been killed and wounded. *One hundred percent casualties on the patrol,* he said to himself. *My God.*

He made his way back to his headquarters tent, thinking that maybe he'd relied on the recon platoon too much, because they were such good fighters and always came through for him. *Maybe I've pushed them past their limits,* he thought. *Maybe I'd better lay off them for a while.*

Later in the morning the Reverend Billie Jones, formerly an itinerant preacher in Georgia, returned to the recon platoon, following completion of a shit detail down on the beach, unloading boats. All units had to supply men for shit details, and

154

he'd been the man designated from the recon platoon.

He reported to Sergeant Cameron, who was supervising the construction of a machine-gun bunker.

"Hiya, Sarge," Billie Jones said. "I'm back."

"Pick up a shovel and start digging."

"I finish one job and I get another. Don't I get a rest?"

"The only rest you get in this man's Army is when you're six feet under."

Billie Jones looked around. "I guess the patrol ain't back yet, huh?"

Sergeant Cameron knew that Homer Gladley had been Billie Jones's best friend, and wondered how Billie Jones would take the bad news. He looked into Billie Jones's eyes.

"The patrol's back," he said.

"I don't see none of the guys."

"Butsko, Bannon, Longtree, and Shaw were wounded, and Frankie got sick with malaria again. The rest were killed in action."

Billie Jones wore wire-rimmed spectacles that were crooked on his button nose. His head was round and he was nearly six feet tall, on the meaty side. He closed one eye as he figured out who the other two men were.

"Homer's dead?"

"Yup."

Billie Jones took a step backward, because he couldn't believe it. "That a fact?"

"Yup."

"Good God Almighty." Billie Jones's face went pale and his knees wobbled. "Where's he now?"

"You mean his body?"

"Yuh."

"I guess the Graves Registry people have got him."

"They bury him yet?"

"I don't know."

"Can I go to his funeral if they haven't?"

"You know they don't have funerals, Billie. They're just gonna bury him, that's all, with all the other casualties of the day."

"Me and Homer were good pals. Can I go find out?"

Sergeant Cameron took out a bag of Bull Durham and a sheet of cigarette paper, thinking about Billie Jones's request as he rolled himself a cigarette, wetting the seam with his wrinkled pink tongue. He decided that Billie Jones would be grief stricken and probably not good for much else for the rest of the day anyway. Besides, somebody from the recon platoon ought to pay their last respects to Homer Gladley and Nutsy Gafooley.

"Okay," he said, "you can do it, Billie. Don't forget to say a prayer for Nutsy too."

Billie Jones smiled weakly. "Thanks, Sarge. Can I go now?"

"You mean you're still here?"

Billie Jones turned around and walked away swiftly, his M 1 rifle slung over his right shoulder. Sergeant Cameron watched him go, and counted up in his mind the number of casualties the recon platoon had sustained on Bougainville. The platoon was at less than half its full strength, and if he took into consideration what had happened to the platoon since it first landed on Guadalcanal, only thirteen men out of the original forty still were alive.

If this war keeps on much longer, he said to himself, *there ain't gonna be none of us old-timers left.*

Colonel Akai sat at his desk, sipping tea from a tiny cup and looking at his map of the area. Sometimes a night of sleep can change a person's perspective, and Colonel Akai saw his front from a different point of view now. He thought that maybe he ought to attack the Americans before the Americans came down from their hill and attacked him.

He still believed the attack he'd planned the night before hadn't been a good idea, and was glad he hadn't gone ahead with it. It would have been foolhardy to position two under-strength Japanese companies between two American units, one small but the other extremely large. However, the basic idea of offensive action had been sound. The Americans mustn't be permitted to think they'd won Bougainville already. Psychological factors were very important in war. If the Americans could be delivered a heavy blow and be forced to take heavy casualties, they might hesitate to foray into the valley for a while, and that might give the Japanese time to build up their strength. Moreover, if he won a small victory, it might encourage Imperial General Headquarters to resupply Bougainville. It could raise the morale of the entire Seventeenth Army.

156

It might even win Colonel Akai a promotion.

He wondered how soon he could launch such an attack, and decided that tomorrow night would be a good time, because Japanese officers believed that Americans didn't like to fight at night. Colonel Akai totaled up the number of units that could be employed in the attack.

Sometimes a bold attack, in a remote corner of a war, can change the whole complexion of that war, he said to himself.

FOURTEEN ...

Butsko opened his eyes, blinked, and wondered where he was. He was lying on a mattress with real white sheets, and everything smelled clean. The mattress was in a bed made of lengths of metal pipe, and chains ran diagonally from the outer corners of the bed to thicker vertical pipes.

Similar beds with wounded men in them were over him and beside him. He eased onto the side and saw that the ceiling was composed of metal beams, air ducts, and pipes a foot thick. Next to him lay a man whose hands and head were swathed in bandages, and the gauze around the man's mouth was red with blood.

I'm on a hospital ship, Butsko thought, and he knew which one it was. He'd seen it from high up in the mountains, anchored in Empress Augusta Bay. On its side the ship had a big red cross painted against a white background. He'd never dreamed that someday he'd be on the ship, far from the fighting.

Butsko was full of drugs, dazed and numb. He was relieved

to be away from the war at last, and hoped he was hurt badly enough to be shipped back to the States. *Maybe I got my million-dollar wound,* he thought. *Maybe the war is over for me.*

He looked down toward his feet and saw something that he thought might be a hallucination. It appeared to be a nurse, sitting at a desk, reading a sheet of paper. She was dressed in white, wore a white hat, had a pointy nose and thin lips, and wasn't too pretty. Her legs were crossed and Butsko could look up her dress a few inches.

"Are you for real?" he asked, surprised by the deep, gravelly sound of his voice.

She looked up at him and smiled faintly. "I hope so."

"How long I been here?"

"A few hours."

"What's wrong with me?"

"You've been wounded in action."

"I know that part. I meant how bad is it?"

"I don't know. Your doctor'll tell you later on."

Butsko patted his body to discover where the bandages were; they were everywhere. A big cast was on his leg, and he remembered getting shot there. A soldier groaned somewhere. The air was filled with the odor of antiseptic and oil. He wondered what had happened to the rest of his patrol.

He lay back and recalled the events of the previous night. Again he debated with himself the reasonableness of blowing up the Japanese ammunition dump. On one hand it had been a sensible military operation, but on the other hand the results hadn't been so wonderful. As far as he knew, every man on the patrol had become a casualty. He remembered being the last man on the patrol still on his feet, fighting Japs, and he hadn't stayed on his feet long.

Fuck the war, he thought. *I done my part. Let somebody else do the fighting from now on.*

A portion of the jungle had been cleared away by bulldozers, and the white crosses were lined up in neat little rows. The Reverend Billie Jones approached a detail of men digging several graves. They were all waist deep in their holes, throwing out shovels full of dirt, and near them was a row of canvas bags containing the remains of soldiers. Beside the bags was a stack of white crosses with names stenciled on them.

"Looking for something, soldier?"

A sergeant wearing fatigues and a yardbird hat approached Billie Jones, but Billie Jones was never intimidated by sergeants or officers, because he considered himself a man of God and beholden to no one.

"Yes, Sergeant," he replied, "I am looking for some friends of mine who were killed last night."

"What were their names?"

"Private Homer Gladley and Private Nutsy—I mean, Marion Gafooley."

The sergeant looked at the roster of names on his clipboard. "Here's Gafooley . . . and here's Gladley." The sergeant pointed to the row of dead soldiers in bags. "They should be right over there."

The sergeant made no effort to help Billie Jones, so Billie walked toward the bags and knelt down, reading the name tags tied at the bottoms where the men's feet were. He had no trouble finding Homer and Nutsy.

The Reverend Billie Jones stood and took off his fatigue cap. He was the oldest man in the recon platoon except for Butsko and Sergeant Cameron, and was prematurely bald, with large, irregularly shaped freckles on top of his head. His hair was light brown and his eyes filled with tears, because he was a sentimental man. Homer had been his best friend, and he'd always liked Nutsy, because Nutsy was like an orphan.

The Reverend Billie Jones gazed at the bag containing Homer Gladley and could easily perceive Homer's wide shoulders and bulky build. Nutsy occupied little space inside his bag. How the Army ever could draft such a puny individual was beyond the Reverend Billie Jones.

"Oh, Lord," he whispered, "why have you let these poor sheep die?"

Billie Jones knew the answer to his question. The war killed his buddies, and the Bible said there'd always be war. At least his buddies didn't have to fight anymore. The Lord had given them peace.

The hot sun beat on Billie Jones's head, and he moved back into the shade, sat underneath a tree, and put his fatigue cap back on. He watched the soldiers digging graves and looked at the canvas bags. He thought that he, Homer, Nutsy, and all the rest of them should be back in America, doing whatever

160

they were doing before the war. Homer had been a farmer, Nutsy had been a bum, and he had been a preacher, bringing the Word of God to those who needed it.

His mind returned to Homer Gladley and Nutsy Gafooley. They'd all been together for nearly three years, ever since basic training at Ford Ord. Now both of them were dead, along with many others. *Oh Lord, when will you pass the cup to me?*

The soldiers from the Graves Registry detail finished digging and climbed out of their holes to throw the bodies inside. The Reverend Billie Jones arose too. "I'll take care of these two," he said, pointing to the bags containing Homer and Nutsy.

The sergeant nodded his approval. The Reverend Billie Jones picked up Nutsy Gafooley; he was as light as a feather. *You poor little feller.* The Reverend Billie Jones jumped into a grave and lay Nutsy on the bottom. He placed the palm of his hand over Nutsy's face. "May the Lord have mercy on your soul," he said.

He climbed out of the hole and picked up Homer Gladley, who weighed nearly 250 pounds, but the Reverend Billie Jones was a big, strong man who'd performed hard work with his hands ever since he was a boy. He cradled Homer Gladley in his arms and carried him to an empty grave, jumped inside, and lay Homer on the bottom. He placed his hand on Homer's face. "May the Lord have mercy on your soul."

He looked down at Homer and thought of all they'd been through together. He'd always thought that Homer was a better Christian than he was, because Homer had childlike simplicity, and Jesus had said that the kingdom of heaven belonged to such as he.

"Soldier," said the voice of the sergeant above him, "we've got to fill up these holes now."

"I'll be right out."

The Reverend Billie Jones gazed at Homer Gladley for a few more seconds, then climbed out of the hole.

"How come there ain't no chaplain here to recite a funeral service?" he asked the sergeant.

"Guess they're all busy right now."

"Mind if I say a little prayer for all these men?"

"If it ain't too long."

The Reverend Billie Jones raised his arms to the heavens and gazed upward with reverence. "Lord," he said, "please

161

receive these lambs into your care. They may not have been angels on earth, but they always done their best, so please make them angels in heaven. From ashes we come and to ashes we return. The Lord giveth and the Lord taketh away. Praise be the Lord now and forevermore. Amen."

"Amen," muttered the men in the grave-digging detail, who had removed their hats.

"I'm finished," Billie Jones said to the sergeant.

"Fill up the holes," the sergeant said to his men.

Billie Jones stepped back, holding his hat in both his hands, and watched the soldiers shovel dirt into the holes. It was difficult for Billie to believe that Homer and Nutsy were dead, lying inside those holes, dirt falling on top of them. Tears rolled down Billie's cheeks and he ground his teeth together in anger. He knew that Homer and Nutsy hadn't died of old age or in an accident. They'd been killed by the damned Japs who'd started the war by bombing Pearl Harbor, the sneaky little slant-eyed pagan bastards.

Billie Jones hated the Japs more than ever. He wanted to pay them back for what they had done to Homer and little Nutsy Gafooley. "Vengeance is mine, saith the Lord God," he muttered. "I shall smite my enemies and send them to hell."

Two medical orderlies approached the nurse sitting behind the desk, and they pushed a padded platform on wheels.

"Which one's Master Sergeant John Butsko?" one of them asked.

She pointed. "That's him."

Butsko opened his eyes and saw the two orderlies rolling their platform toward him. One of them looked at the tag tied to the bottom of his bunk.

"You Sergeant Butsko?"

"Yeah."

"You gotta come with us, Sergeant."

"What for?"

"The doctors wanna talk with you."

"That's good, because I wanna talk to them too."

The two orderlies looked at each other and one of them winked as if to say he thought Butsko was an asshole. Butsko noticed and it made him mad. The orderlies, the nurse, and the crew of the hospital ship were all in the Navy, and Butsko

162

didn't think much of the Navy. He didn't like the Marines either, or the Air Corps, but he especially disliked the Navy because he thought sailors were all sissies and fags.

The orderlies rolled him onto the platform and pushed it down the aisle between the bunks. They passed the nurse and Butsko turned his face to wink at her. She noticed him but didn't react, continuing to read the medical record in front of her. Soldiers and sailors tried to get into her pants constantly, and she'd become accustomed to all the attention. It didn't mean anything to her, because she knew that none of them were interested in her as a person.

The orderlies pushed Butsko down a long corridor. Patients in white pajamas and other orderlies passed him by, plus a few nurses, and Butsko wanted to reach out and grab them by their asses, but he thought he might be put in front of a firing squad if he tried it.

The orderlies wheeled him into a room and closed the door. The room had a porthole and a sea gull sitting on the other side of it, looking at Butsko. Tables and medicine cabinets lined the walls. The door opened and two serious-looking men entered. Butsko figured they were doctors. They wore long white smocks and both had eyeglasses perched on their noses.

One of them held a big X-ray negative up to the light, and they muttered to each other, nodding, shrugging their shoulders, twitching their noses from side to side. Butsko wished they'd talk louder so he could hear what was going on. He couldn't see the X-ray negative but assumed it was of his leg.

Finally the doctors turned around and faced him. One had dark hair and the other blond hair. The dark-haired doctor was pudgy and the other was very short. There was nothing about them that Butsko would call military. He took an instant dislike to them.

"I'm Dr. Harris," said the dark-haired doctor, "and this is Dr. Schearson. I'm afraid we have bad news, but you're an old soldier and I'm sure you can take it like a man. Your leg is very severely damaged and I'm afraid we'll have to amputate."

Butsko couldn't believe his ears. *"What!"*

"Calm down now, soldier. I'm sure you've been through much worse things than the operation."

Butsko choked, spit, and sputtered. "My leg's that bad?"

163

Dr. Harris held up the X ray. "It's shattered very badly. It'll never heal."

Dr. Schearson nodded. "It's a very bad wound. Your leg's just hanging on by a few threads. The only thing to do is cut it off clean. Shrapnel wounds are always the messiest."

"Shrapnel wounds!" Butsko said. "This ain't no shrapnel wound! It's a bullet wound!"

Dr. Harris and Dr. Schearson smiled indulgently. Dr. Harris patted Butsko's shoulder. "It's a shrapnel wound. Bullet wounds don't make a mess like this." He held up the X ray.

Butsko looked at the X ray but couldn't make sense of it. "Listen, fellers," he pleaded, "that must be the wrong X ray. When I was hit, there wasn't any shrapnel. The Japs were shooting at me at close range. There wasn't any bombs or grenades going off, understand?"

The doctors looked at each other again and smiled in that superior, infuriating way that doctors smile.

Dr. Shearson bent over Butsko. "Sergeant, in the heat of battle, I imagine it's difficult to know exactly what's going on," he said as if talking to a child.

Butsko looked up at him. "What the fuck do *you* know about the heat of battle, you son of a bitch! I know what was going on, and I tell you there weren't no shrapnel!"

Both doctors backed off. They looked at each other as if to say *Isn't it a shame that we have to deal with stupid, uneducated people all the time?* Dr. Harris turned to the orderlies. "Take him back to his bed."

"Hey, wait a fucking minute!" Butsko shouted. "Is this operation really gonna take place?"

Dr. Schearson nodded gravely. "Afraid so, soldier."

"What!"

The orderlies wheeled Butsko toward the door, and Butsko completely lost it. He rolled over, fell off the platform, and landed on the floor. *"Oh, no you don't!"* he screamed. *"You ain't cutting off my fucking leg!"*

The doctors were aghast as they watched him climb up the drawers in a cabinet, pushing with his good leg. He leaned against the cabinet and sparks flew out of his eyes. Somehow he had to get out of there. He couldn't let the bastards cut off his leg.

164

"Calm down, Sergeant," Dr. Schearson said, winking at the orderlies.

The orderlies moved toward Butsko, and Butsko wished he had a gun, but he was weak, dizzy, and one of his legs wouldn't support him. He looked around for a weapon and saw on the cabinet beside him a package of wooden tongue depressers. He picked up the package and threw it at the orderlies. Dr. Harris ran out into the hall and screamed for help. Each of the orderlies dived for one of Butsko's arms, but Butsko timed them coming in, punching one in the mouth and slugging another on his left temple.

Both orderlies went sprawling backward, and Butsko looked at Schearson, who trembled in his shoes. "Now Sergeant," Dr. Schearson said, holding up his hand, "calm down before you get yourself into some real big trouble."

Butsko took a step toward him. "You ain't cutting off my leg, you goddamn pill-roller. You cut off my leg and I'll cut off your fucking head." Butsko saw an empty piss pot sitting on top of another cabinet. He picked it up and stumbled toward Dr. Schearson, but the plaster cast wasn't meant to carry so much weight, and it cracked. Butsko collapsed onto the floor. Dr. Schearson screeched like an old woman and ran out of the room. A few seconds later Marines and more orderlies poured into the room.

"Put him in a straitjacket!" screamed Dr. Schearson from the corridor. "He's gone stark raving mad!"

The Marines and orderlies gathered around Butsko. There were twenty of them, and only one of him, but that didn't stop him. "Get away from me, you bunch of seagoing fags!" Butsko said.

One orderly held a hypodermic needle in his hand. Another carried the straitjacket. A big, burly Marine with lumpy features advanced toward Butsko on his tiptoes, holding his arms out like a gorilla, and Butsko lay on his back on the floor, trying to get up, holding the piss pot in one hand. The big Marine looked to his right and left at the men with him, and they inched closer to Butsko, who squirmed backward until his back was against the metal wall. Butsko raised the piss pot in the air.

"The first man who touches me," he said, "is gonna wear this piss pot sticking out of his head for the rest of his life."

The big Marine oozed closer and said soothingly: "Take it easy, Sarge. Everything's gonna be all right."

"You take it easy yourself, you deck ape."

"Get him!" screamed Dr. Schearson from the corridor.

The big Marine dived on Butsko, who swung hard with the piss pot, connecting with the big Marine's head. The piss pot made a loud *bang* sound, and the Marine's eyes rolled up into his head. He collapsed onto the floor, out cold, and the other Marines and orderlies jumped on top of Butsko, grabbing his arms and legs, putting him into headlocks and neck locks.

"Lemme go!" Butsko said. *"I'll kill yez all!"*

He felt a needle go into his thigh.

"You son of a bitch!"

The morphine coursed through his veins as Butsko struggled to break loose.

"You ain't cutting off my fucking leg, you bunch of dirty bastards!"

Butsko felt woozy and weak. He heard bells ringing and birds singing. All his strength left him. He went limp on the floor, and he saw them lower the straight-jacket toward him.

"You scumbags," he whispered. "I'll get yez all for this. I'll make yez wish yez was never born. I'll blow this fucking ship up. I'll . . ."

The morphine overwhelmed his mind, and he passed out cold on the steel floor.

General Hitoshi Imamura, forty-seven years old, sat behind his desk and looked up at General Hyakutake, who was saluting him. Imamura was chubby and Hyakutake skinny and bony. General Imamura returned the salute and looked at General Hyakutake coldly, because General Hyakutake had lost Guadalcanal, and now it appeared as if he'd lost Bougainville too.

"Be seated," General Imamura said.

General Hyakutake adjusted his samurai sword so he wouldn't trip himself, and sat on a chair in front of General Imamura's desk. Through the window behind General Imamura he could see the rooftops of barracks, and then Simpson Harbor, full of Japanese ships at anchorage. The sky was becoming cloudy. The weatherman had predicted rain.

"Well," said General Imamura, "we might as well come directly to the point. What is your situation on Bougainville?"

"Very bad," replied General Hyakutake. "We have had immense casualties. Our supplies are low. We need immediate reinforcements."

The room fell silent. General Hyakutake looked at the statue of the Buddha on General Imamura's desk. General Imamura sat erectly, his hands folded on his desk.

"I have no reinforcements to give you," General Imamura said.

"In that case, consider Bougainville lost," General Hyakutake said. "With my present strength I cannot defeat the Americans; neither can I prevent them from advancing."

"Do you think you should be evacuated?"

"Do you mean me personally or the entire Seventeenth Army?"

"The entire Seventeenth Army."

"I don't know, sir. On one hand, we cannot win back Bougainville without substantial reinforcements, but on the other, if I and my men stay for awhile, we can tie up a sizable number of American soldiers who otherwise would be free to fight elsewhere."

General Imamura thought about what General Hyakutake had just said. General Imamura knew that the Americans could strike next at numerous targets throughout the South Pacific, from New Guinea and the Philippines to the Marianas and the Marshalls. The fewer troops the Americans could muster for those strikes, the better. Perhaps it would be wise to tie up the American force on Bougainville until it was known where the Americans would strike next. Then the Japanese troops on Bougainville could be evacuated to wherever they were needed most.

"Your army will not be evacuated at this time," General Imamura said. "You will continue to fight on Bougainville, but I shall leave the actual pursuit of the campaign to you. I would suggest, however, that you revert to guerrilla warfare, requiring that your troops live off the land, growing their own food if possible."

General Hyakutake couldn't imagine his soldiers laying down their rifles and becoming farmers. They had no plows, no farm animals, nothing. It was obvious to him that General Imamura knew nothing about farming, but he replied, "Yes, sir." He didn't want any arguments. Guerrilla warfare was better than

167

working behind a desk in Tokyo.

"Do you have any questions?" General Imamura asked.

"No, sir."

They then embarked on a wide-ranging discussion of logistics, tactics, things that should have been done, and things that could still be done. Finally, after a half hour, General Imamura dismissed General Hyakutake, who headed straight for the airfield for his flight back to Bougainville.

FIFTEEN . . .

It was night on the hospital ship, and a light rain hissed against the steel-plated hull. Butsko lay on his bunk and opened his eyes. He tried to move his arms and realized he was in a straight-jacket. It occurred to him that somebody had spoken his name and awakened him. Butsko laboriously turned his face to the side and saw, in the dark shadows, the grinning face of Frankie La Barbara. At first Butsko thought he was having a nightmare.

Frankie clamped his hand over Butsko's mouth so that Butsko couldn't holler for help, and then Frankie pressed the blade of a tiny knife made from the handle of a spoon and sharpened to a razor edge, against Butsko's throat.

"Hiya, Sarge," Frankie said. "How're you doing, buddy?"

Butsko's eyes darted around like peas rolling on two white plates. He tried to say something, but all he could do was blow snot through his nose.

"Don't get excited, big Sergeant," Frankie La Barbara said

through his clenched teeth. "All I'm gonna do is cut your fucking throat."

Butsko struggled to get loose, but his arms were tied to his body by the straitjacket, and the rest of his body was strapped into his bed. All he could move was his head and his eyes.

"I heard all about what happened," Frankie continued. "They told me how you was gonna leave me behind when I came down with malaria. Well, big Sergeant, I got over my malaria attack, thanks to modern medicine and the tender loving care of the doctors and nurses on this barge. Now it's time to get even, big Sergeant. You fucked with the wrong guy when you fucked with Frankie La Barbara. I'm gonna stick this knife in real slow, so you'll feel it every bit of the way, and then I'm gonna pull the blade nice and easy across your throat. And while I'm doing it, I hope you think about how you shoulda been nicer to old Frankie La Barbara, back when you had the chance, you fucking cocksucker."

Frankie pressed the point of the blade against Butsko's throat, and all Butsko could do was scream through his nostrils. It wasn't a loud scream, and it was too high-pitched to be really effective, but the nurse heard it and put down the magazine she'd been reading.

"What's going on over there?"

Frankie La Barbara froze. The nurse flicked on the light switch, and Frankie La Barbara stood in the glare, removing his hand from Butsko's mouth.

"He tried to kill me!" Butsko yelled.

Frankie La Barbara cursed and spun around, heading for the door at the other end of the ward. He fled past the bunk beds, his robe flying in the air behind him, and leaped through the doorway.

The nurse stood and walked toward Butsko. "Are you all right?"

"He had a fucking knife! He was gonna cut my throat!"

"Did you see who he was?"

"His name's Frankie La Barbara, and he's dangerous! You saw what he was gonna do! I demand a twenty-four-hour guard!"

The nurse had seen the patient with a knife in his hand and knew Butsko hadn't had a morphine nightmare. "I'll call the Marines right now," she said. "Don't you worry, Sergeant Butsko. I won't let anybody harm you."

The nurse returned to her desk and picked up her phone. Butsko reflected on how much safer it was on the front line, where he could move about freely and carried a submachine gun for protection. Here on the hospital ship he couldn't even lift a finger, and they were going to cut off his leg.

"Nurse," he said, "would you do me a favor?"

"What is it, Sergeant?"

"Would you send a message to the mainland for me?"

"That's against regulations, Sergeant."

"Come here a minute, will you, Nurse?"

She walked toward him warily; she was the same one who'd been on duty last night, the one with the pointy nose and sad eyes. "Yes?"

"What's your name, Nurse?"

"Morrison."

Butsko looked up into her eyes. "Nurse Morrison, I'm in trouble. People are trying to kill me—you saw it yourself—and the pill-rollers—I mean, the doctors—are gonna cut my leg off, and I just know they've got me mixed up with somebody else. I know my leg ain't that bad. I also know everybody around here thinks I'm a psycho case. I'll bet even you think I'm a psycho case. Do you think I'm a psycho case, Nurse Morrison?"

"Yes," she replied, crossing her arms underneath her breasts, "because you *are* a psycho case. That's why you're in the psycho ward."

Butsko tried to win her over with his soulful stare. "Nurse Morrison, I ain't no psycho case. I don't expect you to believe me, but I'm telling you anyways because it's the truth. I'm just an old soldier boy and I'm in a whole world of trouble. All I want you to do is call my commanding officer back on the mainland and tell him that I'm in trouble and I need to see him. Now, that ain't no big thing for you to do, Nurse Morrison. It ain't like I was asking you to gimme a blowjob, or sit on my face, or something nasty like that. Just make one little call to my commanding officer, okay?"

A commotion broke out at the other end of the ward, as Marines carrying billy clubs poured into the psycho ward.

"What's the problem?" asked one of them, a sergeant.

"Over here," said the nurse.

The sergeant and his Marines stormed toward her, ready to

171

go to war with the psycho cases in the psycho ward. They looked around but couldn't see anything wrong.

"You the one who called?" the sergeant asked.

"Yes," replied the nurse. "Somebody tried to kill this soldier with a knife."

The sergeant glanced around. "Did you see who tried to kill him?"

"Yes, and Sergeant Butsko knows his name."

The Marine sergeant looked down at Butsko. "What's his name?"

"Frankie La Barbara, and he's a crazy, dangerous son of a bitch!"

"Where'd he go?"

"He ran out that door over there."

The Marine sergeant told one of his men to call the OD and report what had happened.

Another Marine read the tag at the end of Butsko's bunk. "Hey, Sarge," he said, "this is the guy who tried to kill them two doctors today."

The Marine sergeant looked down at Butsko. "You're a real loonie, too, ain'tcha?"

Butsko glowered at him. "If I wasn't tied up right now, I'd show you who's a loonie, you goddamn fucking seagoing bellhop!"

The nurse couldn't help smiling. "Now, now, Sergeant Butsko," she said. "That's no way to make friends."

Butsko turned to her. "Please call my commanding officer. I'll do anything if you just call my commanding officer."

"Will you stop insulting people?"

"Yes, Nurse Morrison."

"Will you behave yourself?"

"Yes, Nurse Morrison."

"Do you promise?"

"I promise with all my heart and soul, Nurse Morrison."

"Do your promises mean anything?"

"Nurse Morrison, when old Sergeant Butsko promises something, you can build a house on it."

"Okay, Sergeant, I'll see what I can do." She looked at the Marine sergeant. "I want a twenty-four-hour guard on this man, because that Frankie La Barbara definitely tried to kill him."

"Yes, ma'am."

"Effective immediately."

"Yes, ma'am."

"Carry on."

"Yes, ma'am."

She turned to Butsko. "I'll try to reach your commanding officer as soon as I go off duty. What's his name?"

"Lieutenant Colonel Bob Hutchins, Twenty-third Infantry, Eighty-first Division."

She wrote the information on her note pad, then glanced at her watch. "You're about due for your medication."

"I don't want no fucking medication!"

"Keep your voice down."

"I don't want no medication! I don't wanna be all doped up, because when a man is all doped up, bad things can happen to him!"

"You've got to have your medication!"

"Oh, no I don't!"

She groaned. "I thought you said you were going to behave yourself."

"I don't want no medication!"

"Then I'm not calling your commanding officer."

Butsko gulped. "Now wait a minute . . ."

"A deal is a deal," she said.

"But who's gonna look out for me when the medication knocks me out."

She indicated the Marines with a wave of her hand. "They'll look out for you, and so will I."

"I don't trust any of you," Butsko admitted.

"Then why should I trust you?" she asked. "If you want me to trust you, then you'll have to trust me."

"I don't trust anybody. I don't even trust my mother."

"You don't even trust your mother?"

"No."

"What did she do that you don't trust your own mother?"

"She never did nothing, but I don't trust her anyway. I don't trust anybody. It's a mistake to trust people. They always let you down."

"I won't let you down," she said.

"Yeah, sure," he replied. "That's what people always say just before they sell you out."

"I won't do that," she said.

173

"Yeah, sure."

The Marine sergeant looked at Nurse Morrison. "This guy's really a bad egg, ma'am. I think we oughtta put him in the brig."

"He's just come from the front, Sergeant. He's been wounded and he's been under a lot of strain. We'll leave him right where he is, understand?"

"Yes, ma'am."

She turned to Butsko. "Have we got a deal or don't we have a deal?"

"What can I say?" Butsko replied. "Yeah, I guess we got a deal."

She leaned over him and said quietly, "If you don't keep your side of it, I'll pour a bottle of castor oil down your throat."

"I just told you we got a deal, lady, and when Butsko says you got a deal, you got a deal."

Frankie La Barbara crouched in a broom closet and looked into a small tin mirror while shining a flashlight on his face. He was scared shitless because he was sure Butsko told the Marines who he was, and he knew the Marines were searching for him all over the ship.

Frankie cursed himself for not killing Butsko while he had the chance. He figured if anybody deserved to die, it was that goddamned Butsko, so why had Frankie made a speech instead of killing him? He didn't know. It was very perplexing. But he did know that he had to do something to change his appearance.

With his knife he cut a length of hair from his head. Then he took the wad of chewing gum from his mouth and pressed it against his upper lip. He fastened the hair to the chewing gum and looked at himself in the mirror. Grinning, he thought the disguise quite effective. He resembled the old Mustache Petes he used to see around Little Italy when he was a kid.

The door to the broom closet opened. A sailor stood there in denim pants and white T-shirt.

"What do you think you're doing?" the sailor asked, a bewildered expression on his face.

"Who, me?" Frankie asked.

"No, the other guy."

"What other guy?"

"There ain't no other guy; I'm talking to you. What you got underneath your nose?"

"My nose?"

"You paste some hair underneath your nose? I bet you're one of them nuts from the psycho ward. You just be calm. I'll get somebody to take care of you. *Guard!*"

Frankie lunged toward the sailor like a lineman for the New York Giants and hit the sailor at knee level, bowling him over. The sailor landed on his back and Frankie jumped over him, running down the corridor.

"*Guard!*" screamed the sailor. "*Guard!*"

The door opened in front of Frankie, and a Marine with a billy club appeared. Frankie lowered his head, intending to strike the Marine in the chest and go right over him, but the Marine sidestepped and held out his foot. Frankie tripped over the foot and tumbled asshole over teakettle down the corridor. The Marine followed Frankie and cracked him over the head with his billy club. Frankie collapsed on the floor, the phony mustache crooked underneath his nose, and the Marine reached for his handcuffs.

The sailor walked up to the Marine. "You got him?"

"Yeah," replied the Marine, snapping the cuffs on Frankie's wrists, "and the silly son of a bitch is going straight to the brig."

Lieutenant Pete Pollard from Bitter Creek, Wyoming, was Officer of the Day for the Twenty-third Infantry Regiment, and he approached the snoring Colonel Hutchins with trepidation. Colonel Hutchins had a rotten temper and everybody knew it. A canteen lay on the floor beside Colonel Hutchins's cot, and Lieutenant Pollard knew what was in the canteen, because he could smell its contents in the air around the cot.

Here goes, Lieutenant Pollard thought, reaching for Colonel Hutchins's shoulder to shake him awake.

Colonel Hutchins lay on his back and lowered the sheet a few inches, revealing a Colt .45 aimed directly at Lieutenant Pollard's face. "Who's there?" Colonel Hutchins asked, the alcoholic fumes nearly overcoming Lieutenant Pollard.

"The OD, sir. You got a telephone call from a nurse on that hospital ship out in the harbor, and she says it's an emergency."

"A nurse?"

"Yes, sir. She said she's calling at the request of Master Sergeant John Butsko."

"Well, I'll be a son of a bitch," Colonel Hutchins said, sitting up in bed. "You tell her I'll be right with her, hear?"

"Yes, sir."

Lieutenant Pollard walked through the opening in the tent flaps to the other section of the big walled tent, and Colonel Hutchins swung his legs around to the floor. He stood and staggered to the desk, wearing only his green Army skivvies. He had knobby, skinny legs laced with varicose veins. His arms, neck, and face were deeply tanned, but everything else was as pale as snow. He sat at his desk and put on his steel helmet, because you never knew when an artillery shell was going to fall, and then he picked up the telephone.

"Colonel Hutchins speaking," he growled.

"This is Lieutenant Morrison on the *Red Rover*, the hospital ship in the bay."

"What can I do for you, Lieutenant?"

"Master Sergeant John Butsko asked me to call you. You know who he is?"

"Of course I know who he is!"

"Well, he told me to tell you that he's in trouble and he needs to see you."

Colonel Hutchins chortled as he reached for his pack of cigarettes. "I'm not surprised to find out that he's in trouble. Butsko has been in trouble ever since I first met him. Who'd he hit this time?"

"Two doctors and two orderlies, plus a bunch of Marines."

"Shit's whiskers," Colonel Hutchins said. "The man simply cannot stop punching people."

"That's not the worst part," Nurse Morrison told him.

"No?"

"No. The worst part is that he's supposed to have his leg amputated first thing in the morning, and on top of that, somebody tried to cut his throat tonight."

"He's having his leg amputated?" Colonel Hutchins asked. "I didn't think he was hurt that badly."

"Neither does he. That's why he got into the ruckus with the doctors."

"And somebody tried to kill him, you say?"

176

"Yes, sir, but Butsko's under guard right now. Nobody'll be able to harm him."

"Except them doctors."

"They think they've got to amputate his leg before serious problems develop."

"What can be more serious than losing your leg?"

"Losing your life."

"Lissen," Colonel Hutchins said, "are you a friend of Butsko's?"

"I wouldn't exactly say that."

"He getting into your pants or something like that?"

"Sir!"

"Lemme tell you something, kid. Butsko's a real goddamned war hero. He's one of the best soldiers I ever saw in my life, and I've seen a lot of soldiers. I want you to do me and Butsko a big favor: Stall that operation as long as you can tomorrow morning."

"But I—"

"What's the problem, lady?"

"Well, I—"

"I knew you'd do it, and don't think Butsko and me don't appreciate it. I'll be out there as soon as I can, understand?"

"But I—"

"But what, goddammit! I ain't got all night to talk to you, girl! I gotta get out to that ship! Are you gonna help or ain't you gonna help!"

There was silence for a few seconds; then she said: "I'll help."

"That's better. Now, there's only one more thing. What ward is Butsko in?"

"The psycho ward."

"The psycho ward!"

"Well, what ward would you put him in?"

Colonel Hutchins thought it over. "I guess I'd put him in the psycho ward too," he had to admit.

What am I getting myself into? Lieutenant Morrison asked herself as she hung up the telephone. She wrinkled her nose and frowned. She should be in bed, resting up for her next shift, and here she was, making calls to crazy colonels in the middle of the Bougainville jungle.

She thought of Butsko lying in his straitjacket. The man was obviously a psycho case, otherwise he wouldn't have fought with two doctors and all those marines. Butsko's medical file was spread in front of her, and she held the X ray up to the light. His leg was held together by a few ligaments. The bone was shattered beyond all hope. Such a leg had to be amputated. You didn't have to be a doctor to know that. Butsko couldn't deal with losing his leg, evidently. That was a common reaction. Somebody should tell him they had wonderful mechanical devices that would permit him to walk almost as if he still had his leg. *Maybe I'll tell him myself.*

She asked herself again why she was even bothering to get involved. The ship was full of wounded soldiers who needed her, so why was she devoting so much time to Master Sergeant John Butsko? It wasn't because he was wounded so severely, because many men had wounds that were much worse. And it certainly wasn't because he was handsome, because his face looked as if it had gone through a meat grinder about three times. In fact, his whole body was covered with wounds, many of them fresh, so why weren't they listed on his medical report?

Wait a minute, she said to herself. Could they have switched Butsko's medical records with some other guy who also had a leg wound? She knew that clerical errors had occurred in the past, often with tragic results that no one talked about. It was inevitable in a situation in which some people assigned to the ship were nearly illiterate and many of the rest were too smart for their own good. So many men passed through every day. It was much busier than any city hospital.

There was only one way to be sure. They'd have to take fresh X rays of Butsko's leg, and she'd supervise to make sure nothing went wrong. She'd have to convince Dr. Harris to give her the authorization for the X rays, and that might not be easy, because he was an arrogant son of a bitch, like most doctors. First thing in the morning she'd go to his office and tell him what she thought, not that he'd give a damn. She'd have a fight on her hands, but she'd have to do it. It wouldn't be fair for a war hero like Butsko to lose his leg if he didn't have to.

That's why I'm doing it, she said to herself. *I don't want the poor son of a bitch to be made a cripple by mistake, right?*

• • •

178

Frankie La Barbara opened his eyes and saw the gray walls of a cell in the brig. *Oh, no,* he said to himself. He touched the sore spot on his head, and there was a big knot where the Marine had hit him with the billy club. *My knife!* he thought in alarm. Reaching down toward his crotch, he felt it still taped to the inside of his thigh. The Marines hadn't found it. Frankie wondered if they'd searched him and missed it or never searched him at all. Regardless of what had happened, he still had his knife. That meant he could bust out of the brig and try to kill Butsko again.

He knew he had to kill Butsko before Butsko killed him, and cursed himself for not killing Butsko when he'd had the chance. *Me and my big fucking mouth,* Frankie thought. *Instead of cutting his fucking throat, I gave him a fucking lecture.*

Frankie knew he was in deep trouble. He'd have to spend the rest of his life looking over his shoulder to see if Butsko was sneaking up on him—unless he killed Butsko first. He had to kill Butsko first. *I'm gonna bust out of this brig right now and kill the son of a bitch.*

He sat up and his head spun. He saw the commode in the corner, the bars of the cell, and the corridor on the other side of the bars, lit by a naked electric bulb in a small wire basket. Frankie felt dizzy and weak. *Maybe I'd better get some sleep first. Then I'll bust out of here and even things up with that fucking Butsko.*

Frankie closed his eyes and lay down on the cot. Five minutes later he was snoring.

SIXTEEN ...

At dawn Lieutenant Morrison stood in front of Dr. Harris's office, waiting for him to come on duty. She kept glancing at her watch, because she was due to go on duty herself in a half hour. Orderlies, doctors, and nurses walked back and forth, and she felt self-conscious standing there, doing nothing, but she had to talk with Dr. Harris before he began operating that morning.

She hadn't slept much during the night, and her eyeballs were laced with tiny red lines. Fidgeting, pacing back and forth, she wished Dr. Harris would arrive soon. Butsko's leg had become a religious crusade for her. She thought it would be a great tragedy if such a man were to lose his leg inadvertently.

Finally she saw Dr. Harris walking toward her, carrying a clipboard under his arm, his eyeglasses flashing the corridor lights.

"Dr. Harris," she said, "I've got to talk to you."

He raised his eyebrows, obviously annoyed that such a low form of life as a nurse would be presumptuous enough to talk to him directly. "I'm busy right now," he told her, taking the key to his door out of his pocket.

"It's very important."

"It'll have to wait."

He unlocked the door to his office, stepped inside, and pushed the door closed behind him, but Nurse Morrison was there and the door slammed against the palms of her hands. She entered his office and shut the door.

He moved behind his desk and noticed her. "I thought I told you I was busy."

"I'm sorry, Doctor," she said nervously, because Dr. Harris could make a lot of trouble for her, "but I must speak with you and I'm not leaving until I've had my say."

Dr. Harris sat behind his desk and realized he'd look foolish if he called the Marines to take the nurse away, so he decided to deal with her diplomatically and fast-talk her out of whatever she wanted, because evidently she wanted something, and doctors think they can fast-talk anybody out of anything.

He put on a phony doctor's smile. "What can I do for you, Nurse—ah—what's your name again?"

"Lieutenant Roberta Morrison."

"Ah, yes, of course. What was it you wanted?"

"It's about Sergeant Butsko, sir. I think we ought to take another X ray before you amputate his leg."

Dr. Harris felt his expertise being challenged, and doctors tend to get very weird when that happens. "What makes you think we should take another X ray, Lieutenant Morrison?"

"To make sure that his X ray hasn't been mixed up with somebody else's."

"What makes you think it has been mixed up with somebody else's?"

"It happens and you know it."

Dr. Harris smiled indulgently. "Yes, it happens, but very seldom. We can't take special additional X rays of everybody who's facing an operation."

"I'm not suggesting that we take additional X rays of everybody. I'd just like to have additional X rays taken of Sergeant Butsko."

"Why him and not somebody else?"

"Because he claims that he wasn't hit by shrapnel, and his leg wasn't hurt that badly."

"How would he know? You should be aware by now that soldiers are often mistaken about these things."

"Well," she said, "Butsko is no green young soldier. He's been wounded many times and he's seen a lot of war. I'm inclined to take him seriously when he says he wasn't hit by shrapnel. I think he'd know when artillery shells or hand grenades were falling and when they weren't."

Dr. Harris narrowed his eyes and leaned back in his chair. He gazed emphatically at Nurse Morrison, and she could hear the little wheels turning inside his head, but she was no shrinking violet. She held her hands behind her back and looked down at him, because he hadn't even invited her to sit down.

"You seem to be taking an inordinate interest in this Sergeant Butsko," Dr. Harris said suspiciously. "What's going on between you two?"

Nurse Morrison blushed, and because she knew she was blushing, she blushed even more. "Nothing's going on between us. What an absurd thing to say."

"Absurd? Really?" Dr. Harris smiled victoriously, because he could see that he'd hit a soft spot. "Of all the soldiers on this ship, it seems odd that you've taken such a strong interest in Sergeant Butsko. Surely there must be a reason."

"I've told you the reason. I don't believe that the man should have his leg amputated without another corroborating X ray. I think an error has been made, and it shouldn't be compounded to the point where he will lose his leg by mistake."

Dr. Harris shook his head slowly. "I don't think that's the real reason at all. I think the real reason is a peculiar affectionate feeling that you evidently have for this man Butsko. I can't understand it, because he's an ugly brute if ever there was one, but to each his own, I suppose. Regardless of that, I'm not having additional X rays taken of Sergeant Butsko's leg, and I shall amputate it this morning to prevent infection and save as much of the limb as I can." Dr. Harris looked at the papers on his desk. "I'm afraid I have work to do before I go to the operating room. You may leave now."

Nurse Morrison wanted to jump on Dr. Harris and scratch his eyes out, but she had too cool a head actually to do it. She

182

turned and walked out of the office, heading toward the psycho ward and her duty shift. *Well, I tried,* she said to herself. *I can't think of anything else to do.*

She knew it would be pointless to go over Dr. Harris's head to Captain Forbes, the chief doctor on the ship, because Captain Forbes was a doctor, too, and all the doctors stuck together. He'd just say that Dr. Harris was the doctor on the case and he had the final word. That would be the end of it, and she'd be humiliated again—not that she minded that part of it. Men always tend to humiliate women who are unattractive, and she was used to it.

I've done all I could, she said to herself with a sigh. *Somebody else will have to carry the ball now. I wonder if Colonel Hutchins has been able to do anything.*

It was dawn on the beach, and dark, oily clouds covered the sky. Crates were stacked everywhere, and work details loaded the crates onto trucks. Motor launches of various types were prow-up on the beach, and trucks drove back and forth. Antiaircraft artillery observers scanned the skies for enemy planes, ready to load up and shoot them down.

Details of soldiers marched to their places of work, and among them moved ten selected men from the recon platoon in a column of twos, led by Colonel Hutchins, with Sergeant Cameron at his side. All carried Thompson submachine guns and plenty of ammunition.

The contingent from the recon platoon headed toward the row of boats at the shoreline, and all the men were angry. Colonel Hutchins had told them what was going to happen to Butsko, and they weren't going to let it go down without a fight.

They approached a motor launch upon which wounded men were being loaded, and Colonel Hutchins shouted: *"Detail, halt!"*

The men from the recon platoon stopped and stood at attention. Colonel Hutchins waded into the water beside the motor launch. "Who's in charge here?" he bellowed.

A sailor poked his head over the gunwale. "I am." Then he noticed the eagles on Colonel Hutchins's lapels and added: "Sir."

"When are you leaving for the hospital ship?"

"About ten more minutes, sir."

"My men and I are going with you!"

The sailor looked at Colonel Hutchins and his men, wondering what was going on. This had never happened to him before. "You are?"

"We are." Colonel Hutchins turned to his men. "Load onto this boat, and make it snappy!"

The men from the recon platoon sloshed into the water and climbed up the sides of the motor launch. The sailor thought that somehow this loading was against military regulations, but he was only a boatswain's mate third class, and he wasn't about to argue with a bird colonel. He shrugged and made his way back to the stern of the boat, where the wheel was, as the men from the recon platoon knelt among the wounded soldiers stacked side by side on the deck of the motor launch. The men from the recon platoon offered cigarettes to the wounded soldiers and shot the shit with them while the motor launch got under way.

Butsko was still knocked unconscious by powerful drugs when Nurse Morrison came on duty. She relieved the nurse at the desk, read the instructions left for her, and then walked to Butsko's bunk to see how he was. He lay wrapped in his straitjacket and his eyes were closed; he slept peacefully. She looked at his form underneath his covers, saw both of his legs, and nearly burst into tears at the thought that one of them might be cut off by mistake.

Butsko was sleeping, but his combat soldier's sixth sense was still in operation, and he became aware that someone was near him. He opened his eyes and saw her standing there.

"What's going on?" he asked, his words slurred by sleep and drugs.

She didn't know what to tell him, but the expression on her face said it all.

"They're still gonna cut off my leg?" he asked.

She nodded.

"They can't do that to me," he mumbled. "Did you get through to Colonel Hutchins?"

"Yes."

"What did he say?"

"He said he'd get out here as fast as he could."

184

"What time is it now?"

"A little after six hundred hours."

"When'll they operate?"

"Pretty soon, I guess."

"Can't you do something to stop them?" Butsko asked, and his voice cracked in his throat, because he was scared. Getting wounded in battle was one thing, but having your leg cut off on an operating table was something else, especially if it was all a big fuck-up.

"I'm afraid I've done all I could. I wish I could do more, but I can't."

Butsko looked from left to right and then whispered: "Cut me loose."

"I can't."

"Sure you can."

"No I can't, and even if I did, where would you go?"

"I'll worry about that then."

"You can't even walk."

"Put me on a wheel chair and roll me out of here."

"And then what?"

"I don't know."

She was confused, torn between her desire to help and her fear of the system. "I can't."

"You're gonna let them cut off my fucking leg, right?"

Two orderlies entered the ward, pushing a cot on wheels. They looked around and saw Nurse Morrison.

"Which one's Butsko?" one of them asked.

She couldn't reply.

One of the Marines guarding Butsko said: "This is him right here."

The orderlies wheeled their cart toward Butsko and he screamed at the top of his lungs: *"You can't do this to me! There ain't nothing wrong with my leg! Somebody help me!"*

Butsko strained against his straitjacket and squirmed around in his bed. One orderly winked at the other, and the second orderly took a hypodermic needle from a tray underneath the cart.

"I don't want no needle!" Butsko said. *"Please, don't gimme a needle!"*

The orderly pulled up the bedclothes at the bottom of Butsko's bed, revealing his thick, hairy legs. The one on the right

185

was swathed in bandages. The orderly stabbed the needle into Butsko's left thigh as Butsko struggled to break loose.

"Leave me alone! You got me mixed up with some other asshole!"

The drug worked quickly, and Butsko felt himself getting woozy. The volume of his voice dropped to a whisper, and the orderlies untied the straps, rolling him onto the cart. They wheeled him out of the psycho ward, heading for the operating room.

Nurse Morrison sat at her desk and buried her face in her hands. She felt sick and wanted to cry, but she was a tough broad and the tears wouldn't come. *I've done all I can, haven't I?* she asked herself. *What more can I do?*

She didn't know what else she could do, but she felt she had to do something. She couldn't just sit there quietly, knowing they were sawing off Butsko's leg down in the operating room. She decided to go to the operating room and make one last attempt to save Butsko's leg. She didn't know exactly how she'd go about it, but she'd figure that out when she got there.

She picked up the phone and dialed the extension of one of her friends to ask her friend to take over for her so Nurse Morrison could leave her post and go to the operating room.

Frankie was awakened by clattering sounds outside his cell. He opened his eyes and saw an orderly pushing a wagon covered with trays of food. The orderly lifted a tray and shoved it under the bars of Frankie's cell.

"Chowtime," the orderly said.

"Thanks," Frankie replied.

The orderly noticed the name tag on the front of Frankie's cell, and Frankie noticed that the orderly carried a key ring on his belt.

"Hey," said the orderly, "you're Frankie La Barbara, huh?"

"So what if I am," Frankie replied, carrying the tray of food back to his bunk.

"You're the guy who tried to kill that sergeant, right?"

"Right," Frankie admitted.

"And then they found you in a broom closet, trying to paste a phony mustache underneath your nose." The orderly laughed.

Frankie sat on his cot and looked at the food on his tray. It was powdered scrambled eggs, toast, a cup of coffee, and a wooden spoon.

"Everybody's talking about you," the orderly said. "We ain't never had somebody try to kill somebody on this ship before. What've you got against that sergeant?"

"I hate his fucking guts, because he's no fucking good."

"Well," said the orderly, "he sure ain't gonna be good for much after this morning, because they're gonna cut his leg off."

Frankie opened his mouth, morsels of scrambled egg all over his tongue. "Huh?"

"I said they're gonna cut his leg off."

"No shit?"

"No shit."

"I didn't know that."

"You know it now."

The orderly pushed his wagon away, and Frankie stared at the bars of his cell, but he didn't see them. He saw Butsko hopping around on one leg; the image disturbed Frankie greatly. He wanted to cut Butsko's throat, or shoot him, or strangle him, but somehow the image of Butsko as a cripple changed the whole picture.

Frankie considered Butsko a mean, rotten son of a bitch, but he knew that Butsko was a great soldier, a real man's man, and it would be terrible if he had to become a cripple, walking around on a wooden leg. Frankie would get no pleasure out of killing a cripple. He felt that he was being cheated of his revenge against Butsko, and Frankie caught a faint glimmer of the truth: that his ongoing, longstanding hassle with Butsko was one of the factors that kept him angry, awake, and alive.

Frankie felt his crotch; his little knife still was there. He thought he should try to bust out out of the brig and do something for Butsko, although he didn't know specifically what he should do. He had to admit to himself that if Butsko or even his buddy Bannon had fallen ill with malaria in no-man's-land, Frankie would have been the first to insist that the sick man be left behind.

Frankie finished his breakfast and stood, pacing back and forth in his cell, trying to figure out what to do. He wrapped his fingers around the bars of the cell and shook them, but the bars were solid and unmovable. He tapped the walls of the cell; they were thick steel. *If only I had a hand grenade*, he thought.

He heard the chow wagon coming back down the corridor, and Frankie leaped on the bars of his cell, trying to see. The orderly was picking up the empty trays, and Frankie realized that opportunity was heading his way. Stepping backward, he huddled in a corner and removed the knife from his inner thigh. Then he sauntered casually toward the bars, just as the wagon appeared.

"Hi," Frankie said to the orderly. "Got a cigarette by any chance?"

"Sure," the orderly replied. He reached into his white jacket pocket and took out a package of Camels, the favorite cigarette with men in the Army, Navy, Marines, and Coast Guard, based on actual sales records in post exchanges, sales commissaries, ship's service stores, and canteens. The orderly held out the pack. "Here."

Frankie smiled as he reached through the bars, but his smile vanished as he lunged and grabbed the front of the orderly's jacket with his left hand, pulling the orderly against the bars and holding the knife against the orderly's throat with his right hand.

"You'd better open up this door," Frankie muttered, "or else I'll cut your fucking throat!"

The orderly's eyes bulged out of his head and his face drained of color as he reached toward his belt for the ring of keys.

SEVENTEEN . . .

The operating room, located centrally on one of the lower decks of the hospital ship, contained ten operating tables, and every one was in use when Butsko was wheeled into the area. The orderlies moved him into an adjacent cubicle where patients were lined up, waiting to go under the knife.

Orderlies, nurses, and doctors walked past Butsko, but Butsko was out like a light and didn't know anything. Occasionally someone would look at the tag on his cot. A nurse felt his pulse. An anesthesiologist checked Butsko's graph to see how much medication he'd been given, and was surprised by the large quantity.

One by one the other patients in the waiting room were wheeled into the operating room. Finally it was Butsko's turn, and the orderlies rolled him toward an empty operating table between a soldier getting a cast put on his left arm and a Marine having particles of shrapnel removed from his eye by a giant magnet.

Butsko was placed on the operating table, and nurses hooked him up to bottles of plasma and liquid food, plus a variety of machines that monitored his bodily functions. Dr. Harris and Dr. Schearson arrived, wearing long white coats, white hats, and white masks over their eyes. Dr. Harris hung Butsko's X ray on the wall at the foot of the operating table. He talked with Dr. Schearson in medical language, pointing to the X ray, planning the operation. The anesthesiologist rolled the ether machine toward Butsko and turned knobs.

Dr. Harris and Dr. Schearson turned around and approached Butsko. Their first task was to remove the cast from his leg. Dr. Schearson picked up the special hacksaw and began sawing. The anesthesiologist placed the face mask on Butsko to give him some whiffs of ether.

Nurse Morrison entered the operating room. No one recognized her with her face mask on. She walked past the tables, looking at the soldiers on them, and finally saw Butsko, the anesthesia mask on his face, and Dr. Schearson sawing off the plaster cast.

The cast fell off, bearing Butsko's mangled, bloody leg. Nurses bathed it, and Nurse Morrison looked at the stitches and torn, angry flesh. It was a mess, but Nurse Morrison didn't think it looked bad enough to be amputated. Dr. Harris and Dr. Schearson bent over Butsko's leg and examined it as Butsko's chest rose and fell with his strong, steady breathing.

Nurses, doctors, and orderlies walked back and forth in the operating room, but one of the orderlies wasn't really an orderly. He was Frankie La Barbara, wearing an orderly's white uniform and face mask, which he'd stolen from an orderly after cold-conking him in a corridor of the ship. He spotted Butsko and walked toward the table, his knife up his sleeve, ready for instant use.

Frankie felt crazy and wild. He wasn't dealing from a full deck, and never had been in his life. Shifting his weight from foot to foot, clicking his teeth, he wondered what to do next.

The doctors picked up hypodermic needles from the tray next to the operating table. Nurse Morrison knew they'd shoot up Butsko with some additional painkilling drugs and then start cutting. She decided that it was now or never, and she was a little afraid, because she knew she was putting herself into a very messy situation.

"That leg," she said, "doesn't look anything like the leg in that X ray."

Both doctors looked up at her, aghast that anyone would question their medical skill.

"What are you doing here?" Dr. Harris demanded.

"I've come to see the operation," she replied, "and it's clear to me, as it should be to you, that that leg isn't damaged nearly as badly as the X ray indicates. I still think, more than ever, that the X ray you're using belongs to somebody else who needs to have his leg amputated right now, not Sergeant Butsko."

Dr. Harris stood erect and glowered at Nurse Morrison. "I know that romance makes people do strange things, but really, Lieutenant, please restrain yourself if you can."

The insult and sarcastic tone of Dr. Harris's voice didn't escape Nurse Morrison, but she stood her ground. "You said his leg was hanging on by a few threads, but it looks much more substantial than that to me. Why not take another X ray and be sure? What are you afraid of?"

"Nurse Morrison," Dr. Harris replied, "quite often in these cases the skin outside is quite intact and most of the damage is internal. This soldier's bones, muscles, and ligaments are destroyed, and his skin is all that's holding his leg together. I don't have to explain this to you, but I am, and now I'm afraid that I just ask you to leave this operating room."

"It would be so easy to be sure, Dr. Harris," she pleaded. "Why not take a few extra minutes for another X ray so that you *can* be sure."

"My dear Nurse Morrison, I *am* sure. If you do not leave this operation room at once, I'll be forced to call the Marines."

Nurse Morrison hadn't been able to stop the operation, but she didn't want to leave.

Dr. Harris stared at her. "I'm not going to ask you again, Nurse Morrison."

"You're making a big mistake, Doctor."

"No, *you*'re the one making the big mistake, Nurse Morrison."

Dr. Harris turned to call the Marines, when suddenly a tall orderly who'd been lurking behind him leaped forward, wrapped his arm around Dr. Harris's neck, and held the blade of a knife against Dr. Harris's throat.

"Don't nobody move!" said Frankie La Barbara.

All eyes in the operating room turned to Frankie La Barbara, who felt as though someone had plugged him into the wall. He held Dr. Harris tightly. Dr. Harris didn't struggle, because he wasn't a fighter. He just went limp.

"Do whatever he wants," Dr. Harris said, terror in his voice.

"That's right," Frankie said, "you'd better fucking do whatever I want, or I'm gonna take off the head of this croaker here, and don't think I won't, because his life don't mean a fucking thing to me!"

Frankie felt intoxicated by the fear he'd inspired in the operating room. Suddenly he was in a position to give orders instead of taking them. "Okay," he said, "all you doctors can go back to work, except the ones on this here table!"

The other doctors and their aides resumed their operations. One orderly slipped out of the room to call the Marines. Frankie held the blade of his knife against Dr. Harris's throat, and the razor edge drew some blood.

"Don't kill me!" Dr. Harris begged, his insides quaking.

"This is the way it's gonna be," Frankie replied. "I just heard what that nurse said, and it makes sense to me. You're gonna give Butsko here another X ray, right now, and if you don't, I'm gonna send this croaker here to hell, where he belongs."

"Do as he says!" Dr. Harris screamed.

Dr. Schearson held up the palms of his hands. "Okay," he said. "We'll do it. We'll all just go to the X ray room right now and take the pictures, okay?"

"No, it's not okay," Frankie said. "Bring the fucking X ray machine here."

"But it's too big! We can't do that!"

"Then I guess I'm gonna haveta kill the croaker."

Footsteps resounded in the next room, and then the Marines arrived, ten of them, carrying loaded carbines.

"What's the problem?" asked the sergeant leading them. He looked around and saw Frankie holding a knife to Dr. Harris's throat. "Uh-oh."

"Well, if it ain't the fucking jar-head Marines," Frankie said. "Hiya, jar-heads. You'd better move an X ray machine down here right now, or else I'm gonna kill the croaker."

The sergeant didn't know what to do. He looked around for help, but there was no one to give it. A lunatic with a knife was loose in the operating room. The marine sergeant had never heard of such a thing in his life.

Dr. Schearson turned to Frankie. "But you don't understand. We don't have the voltage capacity here in the operating room for our large X ray machines."

"Then run a line down," Frankie La Barbara said. "I don't give a fuck how you do it, just do it, and if you don't get started by the time I count to ten, this croaker here is a dead motherfucker. One!"

Dr. Harris fainted. Dr. Schearson wished somebody would do something. The Marine sergeant wondered if he could shoot Frankie before Frankie cut Dr. Harris's throat, and decided he didn't want to take the chance. It was a classic Mexican standoff, and Frankie continued to count.

More footsteps could be heard. Then Colonel Hutchins marched into the operating room, followed by the detail from the recon platoon. Everybody was armed to the teeth. A new wave of shock and terror swept across the operating room. The doctors and nurses weren't used to such excitement. Their routine day in the operating room was becoming a nightmare that got worse with every passing minute. Frankie La Barbara was so shocked, he stopped counting.

"As you were!" Colonel Hutchins said, looking for Butsko on the operating table, and than his eyes fell on the tall orderly holding a knife to the throat of a doctor.

"Colonel Hutchins!" said Frankie La Barbara. "Am I glad to see you!"

"Who in the fuck are you?"

Frankie took a step back and ripped off his mask. "Me— Private Frankie La Barbara!"

Free, Dr. Harris ran to the far side of the operating room, pointing at Frankie La Barbara. "I want that man put in the brig *right now!*"

Frankie backed against the wall and held out his knife. "The first jar-head that touches me'll get cut high, wide, deep, and forever."

Colonel Hutchins raised the submachine gun and aimed it in the general direction of the Marines. "Settle down over there," he said.

The Marines stepped back. The operating room became silent except for the snips of scissors and the cuts of scalpels as doctors at operating tables continued their grisly work.

"I'm the nurse who called you last night," Lieutenant Morrison said. "Remember?"

"Of course I remember," Colonel Hutchins said. "You're the reason I'm here." He looked at Butsko and saw that his leg still was whole. "Nurse Morrison, could you please tell me what the hell is going on here?"

"The doctors refuse to take another X ray," she said.

"Where the hell's the doctors?"

"Here," said Dr. Harris and Dr. Schearson in unison.

"Why won't you take the goddamn X rays?"

"Because we don't think it's necessary," Dr. Harris said.

"Well, I do. Take the goddamn X rays now."

Dr. Schearson was certain that an Army colonel wouldn't dare shoot him. "I simply refuse to do something I consider medically unsound."

Colonel Hutchins pointed his submachine gun at Dr. Harris. "You do?"

Dr. Harris suddenly wasn't so sure than an Army colonel wouldn't shoot him. "If you insist, but I wish to file a formal protest."

"Shove your formal protest up your ass. Let's get a move on and have these goddamned X rays taken. I haven't got all day."

"You'll have to go to the X ray room," Dr. Harris said.

Colonel Hutchins kept his submachine gun leveled on Dr. Harris. "Lead the way, sawbones."

Just then Captain Forbes, the chief medical officer aboard the hospital ship, entered the operating room with a few of his aides. His rank of captain in the navy was equivalent to colonel in the Army.

"What's going on here?" he asked.

Everybody spoke at once, but Colonel Hutchins had the loudest voice, and he drowned out everybody else. "My man here, Master Sergeant Butsko, is about to get his leg amputated, but there's some question about whether that's necessary."

Dr. Harris decided the time had come for him to retake charge of his operation, and he pointed at Nurse Morrison. "She's the only one who doubts whether it's necessary, and that's because she's in love with Sergeant Butsko—who, by the way, tried to kill me yesterday."

Everyone looked at Nurse Morrison.

"I think Sergeant Butsko's X rays might have been switched with somebody else's," she said, "because these X rays indicate that the wound was caused by shrapnel, and Sergeant Butsko says there were no explosions taking place when he was wounded."

"Let me examine the X rays," Captain Forbes said.

He walked toward the wall and looked at the X rays. Then he bent over Butsko's leg and checked it out. "I see no reason why we shouldn't take more X rays, just to be sure," he said.

Butsko, accompanied by Colonel Hutchins and the men from the recon platoon, was wheeled to the X ray room. They positioned his leg under the X ray machine and took pictures. Then the long wait began as the pictures were developed. Colonel Hutchins paced back and forth. Dr. Harris sweat like a pig. Nurse Morrison prayed. Finally the pictures were ready and the X ray technician pinned them on the wall next to the previously taken X rays. The doctors and nurses crowded around, but you didn't have to be a doctor to see that the pictures were different.

"Well," said Captain Forbes solemnly, "it appears that Butsko and Lieutenant Morrison were right. Evidently Butsko's X rays were exchanged with somebody else's by mistake. Now all we have to do is find the man whose leg needs to be amputated this morning."

Dr. Harris nearly shriveled up and died. Dr. Schearson muttered and stuttered and just about shit his pants.

"I think I'm gonna take Sergent Butsko back to my regiment," Colonel Hutchins said.

"But he's not well yet," Captain Forbes protested.

"I'm afraid he's gonna get worse here. I got qualified doctors in my regiment. They'll be able to take care of him. Let's go, men. Find a stretcher and put Butsko on it."

"What about me?" Frankie La Barbara asked.

"You're coming too."

Dr. Harris pointed at Frankie. "But he tried to kill me!"

Colonel Hutchins turned to Dr. Harris. "And you tried to cut off Butsko's leg!"

Dr. Harris didn't know what to say. He looked at Dr. Schearson for help, but Dr. Schearson was a coward, too, and couldn't open his mouth.

"Let's get out of here," Colonel Hutchins said. "Somebody get a stretcher for Butsko. Hurry up, because I can't stand the stink of hospitals."

Captain Forbes told two orderlies to obtain a stretcher for Butsko, who still lay on the table in the operating room, oblivious to the drama going on around him. Captain Forbes was embarrassed by what had happened and apologized to Colonel Hutchins.

"I'm very sorry about this," Captain Forbes said. "You can be sure that I'll take steps to ensure that nothing like it can ever happen again."

"If I were you," Colonel Hutchins replied, "I'd shoot those two doctors, and then I'd shoot them again to make sure they were dead." Then Colonel Hutchins turned to Nurse Morrison and shook her hand. "Well," he said, "I guess we have to thank you for saving Butsko's leg."

Nurse Morrison felt awkward and self-conscious. "I was just doing my job."

"I'm sure when the sergeant gets better he'll want to show his appreciation in some way."

"That won't be necessary."

"It won't be necessary, but I'm sure Butsko will want to do something anyway."

"Yes . . . well . . . I hope he gets well soon. If you'll excuse me now, I have work to do."

Colonel Hutchins tipped his fatigue hat. "Of course."

She walked away swiftly, passing two orderlies returning with a stretcher. Sergeant Cameron and the Reverend Billie Jones rolled Butsko onto it and then looked toward Colonel Hutchins.

"Move it out," Colonel Hutchins said.

The soldiers marched in a long procession through the corridors of the ship and up the ladder wells, heading for the main deck. Butsko, still unconscious, jiggled with every step, and Frankie wondered what Butsko would do to him when Butsko got well again. Frankie's mind did a flip-flop, because he wasn't the most mentally stable person in the world. Now he thought again that maybe he should have killed Butsko while he had the chance, because Butsko sure as hell was going to try to kill him as soon as he was strong enough.

On the main deck of the hospital ship, the sun was hidden

behind clouds. Colonel Hutchins commandeered a motor launch, and they loaded Butsko onto it. The motor launch was empty except for the men from the recon platoon; it was on its way back to the beach to pick up more wounded.

Colonel Hutchins climbed down into the motor launch and sat with his back against a gunwale, taking a sip from his canteen full of white lightning. Then he lit a Camel cigarette. *Back to the war,* he thought. *I wonder what the fucking Japs have been up to while I've been away.*

The motor launch pulled away from the hospital ship and puttered over the rolling waves, making a wide circle in the water and then heading toward the mainland.

EIGHTEEN . . .

Colonel Akai sat at his desk, studying his maps and planning the offensive that he intended to launch that night. The phone on his desk rang, and he picked up the receiver.

"This is General Hyakutake," said the voice in his ear.

Colonel Akai was surprised, because he'd thought General Hyakutake was still in Rabaul, conferring with General Imamura. "Good morning, sir," Colonel Akai replied. "When did you get back?"

"A few minutes ago, and Lieutenant Oyagi told me that you're planning an attack for tonight. Is that true?"

"Yes, sir."

"Call it off."

"What!"

"I said call it off."

"But my regiment is all ready to go. Why should I call it off?"

"For two reasons. The first is that the Americans will whip

you, because they outnumber you in every way, and the second is that General Imamura has ordered us to retreat. It is felt that the battle here on Bougainville has been lost."

"But it is not lost, sir. With more men and equipment, we can win."

"Imperial General Headquarters does not have the men and equipment to give us. Prepare your regiment to pull back toward Buka Passage."

"Will we be evacuated, sir?"

"Not yet. General Imamura has ordered us to wage guerrilla warfare against the Americans and he wants us to raise our own food."

Colonel Akai couldn't believe his ears. "Raise our own food, sir? How are we supposed to do that?"

"Call together the men in your regiment who were farmers before the war and ask them."

"But we have no seeds, no farm implements . . . and how can one plant crops in the jungle?"

"As I just told you, speak with the men in your regiment who were farmers. You have your orders and I know you will obey them as meticulously as you have always obeyed orders in the past. Do you have any further questions, Colonel Akai?"

"No, sir."

The phone connection went dead in Colonel Akai's ear. He stared at the wall of his tent for a few seconds, then hung up the receiver. His eyes fell on his desk and maps, which were covered with arrows and jagged lines. Colonel Akai frowned as he placed his elbow in the middle of the maps and rested his chin in the palm of his hand. *So Bougainville is lost,* he thought. *When will we stop retreating before the Americans?*

He reflected upon the failure of General Hyakutake's big offensive and the loss of New Georgia, Guadalcanal, most of New Guinea, and numerous other islands. It was clear to Colonel Akai that the Americans were pushing the Japanese army back, but he thought that might be a good thing. The Japanese army was spread out all over the South Pacific and had too much territory to defend. Perhaps, with less territory, the Japanese army could stop the Americans and inflict terrible defeats on them.

Then the face of the war would change, and the Imperial Army would be victorious again. Colonel Akai and his regiment would do their part, tying up as many Americans on Bougainville as they could, using hit-and-run tactics, and growing their own food.

Bougainville would become a sideshow in the war. Colonel Akai tried to convince himself that he and his regiment would still be doing important work, but he had difficulty believing it.

He knew deep in his heart that he and they had been swept into oblivion by the cruel tides of war.

Butsko opened his eyes and saw the cathedrallike top of a big walled tent. He rolled his head to the side, and there was Colonel Hutchins, seated behind his desk, fanning himself.

"What's going on?" Butsko asked.

Colonel Hutchins turned to Butsko. "You're awake!"

"What day is it?"

"The twenty-eighth of March, 1944. Wanna drink?"

"Don't mind if I do," Butsko said, glancing around. "What am I doing here? Last thing I remember was that I was on the hospital ship and they were gonna cut off my leg. *Oh my God!*" He raised his head and looked down at his leg. "I still got it! They didn't cut it off!"

Colonel Hutchins stood behind his desk, picked up his canteen, and carried it to Butsko, who was now sitting on the edge of the bed. Colonel Hutchins wore baggy green skivvies, combat boots, and his steel helmet. He handed the canteen to Butsko. "Here."

Butsko took the canteen and swallowed some of the fiery liquid. "Ah," he said, smacking his lips.

"How do you feel?"

"A little fucked up. What's been going on?"

"A lot, but you were out cold while it happened. First of all, they tried to cut off your leg, but a nurse out there named Morrison tried to stop them, and when she couldn't she called me. I went out there with a few of the boys and brought you back, along with Frankie La Barbara, because they were gonna court-martial him. He attacked a surgeon with the knife in an effort to stop the operation."

"Frankie La Barbara?" Butsko asked. "Are you sure?"

"I saw him holding the knife to the surgeon's throat."

"Frankie La Barbara?" Butsko couldn't believe it. He'd

thought Frankie wanted to kill him, and wondered why Frankie had tried to save his leg. "You just can't tell about some people."

"Who're you talking about?"

"Frankie La Barbara. He hates my guts, yet he attacked the surgeon with a knife. I can't figure it out."

"Well," Colonel Hutchins said, "everything gets turned upside down in a war, and you know, we've been at the front for a long time. Our nerves are all pretty well shot, and sometimes we get a little kill crazy, I suppose. The scuttlebutt is that they're gonna pull us off the line and send us back someplace for R&R. We might even go to Hawaii."

"No shit?" Butsko said.

"No shit. Want another drink?"

"I never turned down a drink in my life."

Colonel Hutchins handed Butsko the canteen and Butsko took another swig, rinsing his teeth with the white lightning, then swallowing it down. "Goddamn, this is good stuff."

"Sure is."

The white lightning loosened up Butsko's mind, and he recalled the big fight in the jungle. He hadn't given it much thought on the hospital ship, because he'd had more serious things to worry about, like his leg; and on top of that, he'd been doped up all the time.

"Hey, Colonel," he said, "whatever happened to the other guys who were with me on that patrol?"

Colonel Hutchins was silent for a few moments, because he didn't want to be the bearer of bad news, but somebody had to tell Butsko, and Colonel Hutchins realized it had to be him. "Homer Gladley and Nutsy Gafooley were killed in action," he said. "All the rest were wounded, but I'm told that none of them was hurt that bad."

Butsko closed his eyes and blew air out the corner of his mouth. He'd figured something bad had happened to the others, because he'd been the last one on his feet, fighting the Japs. It wasn't difficult for him to accept the fact that Nutsy and Homer were dead, because Butsko had seen many men die. Butsko wasn't as thickskinned as he made himself appear, and he hurt inside now. He remembered all the times he'd punched Nutsy Gafooley, and all the times he'd called Homer Gladley a moron. He wished he'd been nicer to them, but as Colonel Hutchins said, the war turned everything upside down.

The phone on Colonel Hutchins's desk rang, and he walked to his chair, sat down and lifted the telephone to his ear. "Yeah?"

Butsko took another drink of white lightning and screwed the cap back on as Colonel Hutchins spoke on the telephone. Butsko thought he should always treat everybody as if they were going to die tomorrow, because if they did die tomorrow, he'd have nothing to regret. He wished he could change his ways, but deep in his heart he knew he couldn't. He was a rotten bastard to the core, and there didn't seem to be anything he could do about it.

Colonel Hutchins hung up the phone. "Guess what?"

"What?"

"The Japs are pulling back all across the line. Evidently they're throwing in the towel, the little fucking bastards. Lemme have that canteen, will you?"

Butsko swung back his arm and tossed the canteen to Colonel Hutchins, who caught it at chest level, like a football player. He unscrewed the top and drank down some white lightning.

"Where do you think they'll send us next, Colonel?"

"You mean after the R&R?"

"Yeah."

"I don't know, but if I had to guess, I'd say the Philippines. General MacArthur said he was gonna return there, and I think he's about ready to do it."

Butsko groaned. "Jesus, that's gonna be a big one."

"The biggest yet," Colonel Hutchins agreed. "It's gonna make Bougainville, New Georgia, Guadalcanal, and all these other little islands look like pinochle games."

"Maybe we'll get lucky and go someplace else."

"Maybe we will, but there ain't no lucky places for a line infantry regiment in this part of the world." Colonel Hutchins leaned toward Butsko. "Listen to me," he said. "We might get sent someplace else for a while, but sooner or later this war is gonna boil down to a fight for the Philippine islands, because that's the way MacArthur wants it, and old Dugout Doug always gets what he wants. You can bet your sweet ass that Dugout Doug'll have his whole Army there for the big showdown, and we'll be there, too, if we're still alive by then." Colonel Hutchins raised his forefinger and wagged it in the air. "Mark my words, Butsko," he said. "We're all gonna wind up in the Philippines."

202

68

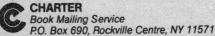